the LaGrange Legacy

Bruce I. Schindler

Copyright © 2011 Bruce I. Schindler
All rights reserved.

ISBN: 1460918983
ISBN-13: 9781460918982

Chapters

1: Personnel Action

His sword slashed through the lines holding the mainsail, which dropped on the cornered sailors of the Dutch galleon. So the pirate LaGrange ended the battle with one stroke. Chuck's imagination had merged scenes from a movie on TV the previous night with fantasies about his pirate ancestor. Unfortunately, he was far more impressive in his mind than his body. Lost in his daydreams, he stumbled on the threshold going into the office building, adding another scuff to already well-scuffed shoes.

Chuck's imaginary heroics immediately switched to how he would wreak vengeance on this insane world that actually paid for consulting about mergers and acquisitions, or M&A. They shouldn't exist at all on the one hand, but should pay him much better on the other hand.

In spite of his disconnected mental state, Chuck managed to get into the office at his usual time, which was six minutes late. Pulling his access badge out of his shirt, Chuck waved it in the direction of the guard, and ran it through the slot, which simultaneously opened the inner door and clocked him in to work. A few moments later, he arrived at the large, cube-filled area that was his professional home. He suddenly focused on the fact that someone was standing by his cube.

That was just dandy, having his team leader waiting on him. Chuck tried to remember what assignment he had due. Then he focused on the fact that the person was a security guard. With that realization, he also became aware of a number of heads peeking over and around dividers. Some were looking at him, and others looking beside him. Chuck stopped, and started to back up, only to feel a large hand on his shoulder. Turning, he saw another security guard, and in reaction tried to duck out of the guard's grasp, but couldn't.

The guard didn't say anything, but after physically turning Chuck, both pointed and pushed him toward Mr. Sherman's office, whose door was closed. Mr. Sherman always had his door open, making the situation even more terrifying. At the door, the guard knocked.

"Enter." That was a voice Chuck didn't recognize. The guard opened the door and shoved Chuck into the office. He felt the door close behind him and sensed the guard did not come in with him. Chuck stood just inside the door, bent over as though he might have to fend off physical blows. Sitting at Mr. Sherman's desk was a man Chuck had never seen before. Standing against the wall on Chuck's left was Mr. Sherman, looming over him. The physical size of his supervisor never before occurred to Chuck, but it added to his current feeling of vulnerability.

The man at the desk glared at Chuck through bloodshot eyes, and introduced himself with a gruff voice as the head of personnel. Without preface, the man launched into a detailed description of every place Chuck had not been truthful on his résumé and application. It seemed those places comprised the bulk of both documents.

The man said Mr. Sherman found some of it, and after being notified, the Personnel Division launched a full investigation. The application and résumé were both so wide of the truth, specialists tested whether his name and social security number were real, and whether they actually belonged to Charles L. LaGrange. Several people were certain the name and social security number had been stolen or fabricated somehow. He concluded, "I, for one, don't think there's anything about you that is truthful. This is why I came to conduct this session personally, and as soon as possible after confirmation of the situation. We believe every hour you are here is detrimental to the company."

He then growled, "Mr. LaGrange, or whoever you really are, you are terminated, effective immediately. As a probationary employee, you have no recourse or due process. Further, if you say or do anything that puts the company in a bad light, the company will immediately press charges of fraud. In addition, if you protest, we will send our information to the INS – that's the Immigration and Naturalization Service, just in case you aren't aware of it. I'm sure they would give you some proper treatment. We are also considering sending this to Homeland Security."

The head of personnel then slid paperwork across the desk toward Chuck, requiring him to sign several documents. After Chuck signed, the man sorted through the papers, piling Chuck's copies on the desk.

Then, the personnel guy demanded his access badge. He studied it minutely, comparing the picture with the person, and the signature with the one on the paperwork. Finally, and with a great deal of reluctance, he added a paycheck to Chuck's pile. "This pays you up to date, and through all of today, even though you haven't earned it."

After that, he seemed to soften and relax a very little bit. "Mr. Sherman has something to say to you before you leave. It isn't related to the company, and I trust he'll keep it short, considering Mr. Sherman is on company time."

The head of personnel followed that comment by glaring up at Mr. Sherman for a moment before gathering his portion of the paperwork along with the badge. He placed them carefully in a manila envelope, which went into a briefcase. The man slid off the chair, which was obviously not adjusted for his stocky, short-legged frame, and grabbing the briefcase, left the office. He seemed to make a point of forcing Chuck to move over as he brushed by him going out the door, closing it with more force than needed. Chuck was in shock. Mr. Sherman appeared to be slightly amused. Chuck could not imagine what could be funny about any of it.

Mr. Sherman reclaimed his desk, leaning back in his chair with his hands steepled under his chin. After a moment, he cocked his head and observed, "You know, Chuck, if you're going to play fast and easy with the hiring system, you'll do a lot better if you don't come across as a complete idiot." Chuck didn't know how to reply to that. Mr. Sherman sighed. "There are a couple of things I'd tell you. First, you do have some analytical ability, and that is needed anywhere you go, not just here in the Mergers & Acquisitions consulting business. Also, if you're going to be the office mouth, it will work out better if you have some idea of what you're talking about, and further if it makes some kind of sense with what you said the day before." Mr. Sherman paused and looked at Chuck like he was some kind of strange bug. "Okay, here's a quiz. Tell me your little family story of an ancestor who was a pirate."

If Chuck was in shock before, he was totally stunned now. Mr. Sherman must have been listening outside the break room yesterday. He stuttered a little, and finally got his dry mouth to function.

"My ancestor, who was also a LaGrange, was the brother of the French mathematician. He became a privateer. He took a ship that turned out to be French, and the king declared him a pirate. He saw a Dutch galleon, and got their gold ahead of two British men-of-war, who tried to chase him down. My ancestor beat them to the Oregon coast. He hauled his gold inland, and buried it. He would periodically dig some of it up, melt it down and sell it, telling everyone that he had a gold mine."

Mr. Sherman periodically glanced at a legal pad as the story was told, and finally nodded. "Okay, you've proven you can tell the same story twice," he said. "Not bad. Now, when did this happen, and to whom?"

Chuck had to mentally reconstruct some of his family tree. "It was my Dad's Grandfather's Grandfather. I've tried to track him, but he just sort of appeared about 1870."

"What makes you think this story of gold is true?"

"My Dad's Grandfather told my Dad that he spent the last of it. He had three one-thousand dollar bills."

"That's pretty specific. Okay, we'll say there really was gold, and that your ... let's see, that would be fourth great grandfather had bullion or coin from somewhere. If that's the case, and he didn't care to divulge how he got, it would make sense that he melted it down. Then he became a miner in order to sell it. How old was he at that point?"

"I've never been able to find out anything about him before he showed up in Oregon. He was young enough to get married and have two children. His wife then sued for divorce because of desertion."

"Okay. Now, by 1870, your ancestor had to have been a pirate for at least 14 years, because privateers were outlawed internationally in 1856. The French must have known about it, because the treaty was signed in Paris."

"Oh. I didn't know about that."

"There's more. Privateers were, as you probably know, privately owned and operated ships, functioning as a civilian adjunct to a country's navy. They were commerce raiders, essentially. What naval operations were the French involved in during the mid-nineteenth century? Well, quite a number, actually. Tahiti, Mexico, China, Indochina ... but none of them with enough of a merchant marine to justify privateers or commerce raiders. In any case, Napoleon III, who ruled France around that time, was far more interested in building up the French navy than in subsidizing fishermen, which was the usual trade of a privateer between wars. By the way, the French and British were more or less allies at that point."

"I didn't know that. Maybe as a pirate on the west coast, he was after ships carrying gold from the gold rush."

Mr. Sherman nodded. "Ships carrying gold would be a prime target of pirates. That's one reason why the ships they used were the biggest and best. By the time of the Civil War, they were using steamships, although there were still a few clipper ships in service. Speaking of which, there was that bit about galleons and men-of-war. That type of ship started in the 1500's and continued a long time ... until the 1700's. Good luck on a Dutch galleon full of gold wandering the Pacific Ocean in the mid-1800's. By the way, nearly every French privateer and pirate was in the Caribbean."

Chuck felt his family legacy was nearly battered beyond recognition, and had to score somewhere. "He said he was French."

It didn't help. "You also said he was the brother of the French mathematician. By the way, that mathematician's name was Joseph Louis LaGrange. Look him up. He was Italian of French descent, and only claimed to be French. I'd guess you get your Mediterranean complexion from the Italian side of your family, assuming a connection actually exists. As for your ancestor, there's no way a guy young enough to get married and have kids in the 1870's could have been the brother of a man who died in 1813 at an age of over seventy. You may be his relative, but you don't even want me to review all the things I've heard you say you are.

"But let's say I cut your ancestor some slack, and consider he had reasons for whatever tales he told. I think there might have been a connection to privateers or piracy. If that's the case, he may have had a connection with one of my ancestors. I'm a descendant of Jean Lafitte, but I haven't been able to get hard evidence of it. So, as a test of your analytical talent plus the chance that our families were connected, I'm going to offer you a deal."

The paperwork and check were still on the desk, and Mr. Sherman glanced through them, finally pointing to a square with an 'X' in it, followed by a short line of print. "That provision allows me to rehire you if I see fit, in spite of all the evidence to the contrary. The head of personnel was convinced I'd lost it when I had him include that provision after everything we've found. So I'll tell you what I told him: There is one way, and only one way I would ever see fit to rehire you. That way is by bringing me convincing evidence of your ancestor being a pirate. What is convincing evidence? It's evidence that would be acceptable to a professional genealogist – specifically this professional genealogist." With that, Mr. Sherman put a business card on top of the paperwork.

"If you're looking for an easy hit, this isn't it. After all, a pirate was a criminal, and how could we define a successful pirate or criminal of any variety? It's someone who never got caught. Since he lived long enough, not only to talk about it, but to tell it to his children, he was evidently very successful. As far as you can tell, your ancestor was never caught, brought to trial, incarcerated, or hung. The main sources of documentation would be newspaper accounts, court records, and other such things which would have detailed how he failed. Still, if you can somehow come up with the required evidence, I will hire you back because you will have proven yourself to be a truly outstanding analyst. Further, if you find convincing evidence connecting your ancestor with Lafitte, and most especially, physical evidence connecting Lafitte to me, I'll personally pay you a bonus. Just to make it more interesting, if you don't find any evidence your ancestor was a pirate, you'll owe me $100 for putting up with you. By the way, we have to specify a time constraint. We'll say two weeks, but no more than four weeks. So, do we have a deal?"

Chuck was suddenly very self-conscious, looking toward the floor, but hyper-aware of his belly hanging over his old slacks. The slacks had no crease in them anymore, the result of cheap wool having made too many trips through washing machines at the Dirty Duds Laundromat, and too few trips to the dry cleaners. Still, what could he do or say?

"Okay, I'll do it. I won't let you down, sir."

"Chuck, you've already let me down in more ways than I can count. You're smart enough, but you just aren't using it right. I hope you're able to figure it out someday. Don't forget your paperwork and check. Go clear your desk. The guards will make sure you don't get lost. Leave the door open as you go. I need to get some fresh air in the place." It wasn't clear to Chuck whether Mr. Sherman was talking about him personally, the situation in general, the head of personnel, or maybe all of it.

With that, Mr. Sherman shooed Chuck out of his office. Everyone in the area made a visible effort to act like they were working hard and not looking. Chuck was now an un-person. It only took a few minutes to clear his cube of what few personal possessions were there. The guard who had been standing by his desk even had a plastic grocery bag for his stuff. Both guards watched closely, in case Chuck might try to take a computer password, sabotage something, or swipe a paperclip.

Outside the office was a taxi, but it wasn't for him. The head of personnel was sitting in it, watching the door. When Chuck and the guards came out, he glanced at his watch, made a note and told the taxi to head for the airport. One of the guards stopped by the front door, while the other accompanied Chuck to his car. He was able to start it on only the second try. The two guards watched him as he drove down the street.

✡ ✡ ✡

In his apartment, Chuck got out his hand-me-down laptop PC, and surfed through the internet for some of his ancestors. He made some notes, and rescued a large envelope from the trash to hold whatever he found. He started with himself, following with his father, Jack Edward. His grandfather was Kenneth Otto, and his great-grandfather was Otto S. LaGrange. Beyond that, his knowledge got very hazy. Well, the family story had it that Otto's grandfather was the pirate. Information on recent generations, he found, was nearly nonexistent due to privacy issues. He did download some information on when his pirate ancestor was sued for divorce for abandonment.

The first place to go for information should have been his family. There was a problem with that. His Dad had thrown Chuck out five years ago after he showed up at home after quitting college. Well, it was a case of quit or get thrown out. Within a few minutes of his homecoming, Mom had decided she needed to go somewhere, meaning she had no stomach for the unpleasantness she knew was coming. After she left, Dad called Chuck a bum, and told him there were no bums allowed in his house. He'd worked hard to get that house and keep it, and freeloaders were not welcome. He told Chuck that when he learned how to be a man, he could come to visit. Until that time, he should stay away.

Dad had two degrees at the Masters level, but had always been defensive and apologetic about not having a PhD like his father, Grandpa Ken. Grandpa Ken had been an economics professor and department chairman at the university until his death two years ago. The point for Dad was that Chuck not even making it through two years of college was absolutely beyond the pale. Chuck recalled times when Dad would talk about Otto, though, back when Chuck was in his first couple of years in high school. That was where the pirate story came into the picture. Things had changed, however, by the time he was preparing to graduate from high school. His parents were still together, but their relations were frosty. Chuck was trying to get Dad talking, and asked about the pirate story. The response he got sent him back to his room. Dad said, "It's just a family story," and after a pause, growling, "You don't want to know."

Chuck could never imagine what Dad meant by that. Still, it was one of a number of things that made Chuck decide on a university further from home, rather than staying close, when he got several offers of minor scholarships. His grades weren't good enough to keep the scholarships past the first year. Chuck had gotten multiple part-time jobs to stay in school. It seemed, though, that no matter how much he worked, there just wasn't enough money. Beyond that, the more he worked, the less he studied, and the worse his grades got. He finally got to the point where none of it made sense anymore, and the school agreed that he should take a break from academia.

Chuck had not been in contact with his parents since then. He most especially was not going to call his father on the day he got sacked. He knew with certainty he'd not ask about a subject his Dad had already shown no interest in expanding upon. The only other thing he could think of was to call the genealogist Mr. Sherman mentioned. He left a voicemail, and tried to figure out what else he could do. He called the library, and found they had a Genealogy Department. After some conversation, it seemed like he'd need to spend some time there. The genealogist called shortly after that, and they set a time to meet the next morning.

Chuck had been hoping he'd be able to do something easy, no matter what Mr. Sherman said. He really wanted the magic bullet, so he could go collect his bonus along with reclaiming his job. He drifted along for several minutes, fantasizing about that. Then another possibility occurred: he'd just take his bonus and do this genealogy thing. If Mr. Sherman would pay for that kind of information, there must be other people who would pay as well. How hard could it be? He daydreamed along that line for quite a while, and then noticed it was getting dark. He threw a TV dinner into the microwave, and idly clicked through cable channels while he ate.

He considered some old jokes where terminated guys always seemed to end up in a bar, spilling their guts to the bartender. That didn't sound too bad, actually, but he just couldn't get up enough motivation to do such a thing. In any case, he thought he'd better not spend his money before he had something else in the bag. So he sat in his apartment watching the tube, trying not to think about the day at all. He didn't want to think about the day because it was all wrong. On the other hand, he kept hoping there'd be a news item about the personnel guy's plane crashing, preferably into the company's building.

☆ ☆ ☆

The next morning, Chuck took his paycheck to the bank, and wished he could go someplace for breakfast, but headed for the genealogist's office, which turned out to be the garage of her house. He showed her what he had. He thought Mr. Sherman had torn his story apart. He barely gave it a once-over compared to what the genealogist did. Actually, it did seem as though Mr. Sherman got his training from her, but where Mr. Sherman was finishing, she was just getting warmed up. He ended up sitting there with, he supposed, a glazed look, because she finally focused on him, and came to a total stop, considering what to do.

After a moment, she grabbed a pad of paper and a pen, and brought him up to a corner of her desk. "Do you know how to take notes?" When he nodded, she continued, "Okay, take really good, detailed notes. Let me know if I should slow down. I haven't worked with a beginner in a while." So Chuck took lots of notes, more notes than he'd taken in any class at any time. It came to him in passing that if he'd taken notes like this in college, he might still be there, getting his doctorate.

She began somewhat like Mr. Sherman had done, talking about documentation about pirates, except she tied some things in that he hadn't. She asked Chuck about the quality of analysis necessary in Mergers & Acquisitions, and he replied it had to be capable of being presented in a court of law as evidence. This was, at least in part, because if there was a dispute, it might actually be considered legal evidence. She nodded, and it was evident to Chuck she'd had this conversation before. She said genealogical evidence needed to be on that level. Unfortunately, most presumed proof didn't even come close. Further, documentation available depended on the era. For most people born in recent times, there would be a birth certificate. There would also be a death certificate. There might be a record of baptism, and a marriage license. Information could be obtained from tombstones, and some people made special studies of cemeteries.

She was careful to point out that none of these things were infallible. Information on documents might not be correct. People might change the spelling of their names, especially in times long ago. Clerks might have misspelled items. People taking the census were well known to have gotten names wrong. There were graves with no marker or tombstone. Where there was a tombstone, there was no guarantee that information was correct. It was basically a case of building an individual's lifetime using every scrap of evidence available, but even then it was almost always open to interpretation.

At this point, Chuck lay down his pen. "So what you're saying is that Mr. Sherman sent me off on a wild goose chase."

"I wouldn't say it's a wild goose chase, dear. Lee Sherman is very serious about his family. He would pay dearly for specific proof of his relationship to Lafitte. Lord knows I've tried any number of approaches to track his line back to Lafitte, including several trips to Louisiana, Mississippi, and Texas. Still, proving his link to Lafitte is ever so much easier than what you're trying to do.

"Oh, one area to be wary is information you find on the internet. There are lots of people who basically invented relationships with the famous and infamous, and published a combination of truth and fiction in books. As you know, once it's on the internet, it's there forever. I've seen published trees relating the author to all the crowned heads of Europe, together with detailed descent from Adam and Eve. In any case, keep turning over rocks. Maybe you can come up with a connection that makes everything right."

Chuck then drug himself to the library, and talked to the people in the genealogy department. It was a large department, and they were proud of their resources. When they started looking for answers to Chuck's specific questions, however, there were notable gaps. He spent several hours scanning over books and documents, and, with help, using library computer resources. Their joint conclusion was that Chuck would need to travel to Oregon, and access libraries and organizations which specialized in what he was seeking.

By the time he decided to take his burning eyes back to his apartment, Chuck was very depressed. Still, he couldn't quite figure out why his former supervisor would send him off on something he knew for a fact couldn't be found. Hell, even the genealogist, who was very well-known and respected, to judge from the comments about her at the library, couldn't find anything even when she traveled there. Maybe it was like she said, and Chuck simply represented one more chance for Mr. Sherman to obtain some piece of something no one else had noticed.

✡ ✡ ✡

Chuck worked the internet some more, but was mostly successful in finding blatant examples of what the genealogist warned against. He also found a few examples of real research, with each name having multiple references and voluminous notes. These, it would seem, showed how the job needed to be done, and considering the effort involved finding anything, made his daydreams of genealogy as an easy way of making money evaporate.

His internet access was always slow. Now, it was coming nearly to a stop. The access he had was poached from someone nearby with no security on their wireless router. Evidently, the owner of that router was so inconsiderate as to use their own equipment. Chuck scanned for any other access, but found nothing promising. He really didn't know what else he could do, anyway. Maybe he could start a job search in the morning, but in tribute to the classical laws of inertia, he pulled out some photos he'd found of his father, grandfather, and great-grandfather.

He sat there, staring at the pictures for quite a long time, wondering what the people in those photographs could tell him. He remembered some TV shows talking about primitive tribes. Some of them believed that to take a person's picture was to steal their soul. Wouldn't it be neat if a person could get the information held by the person in the picture? That could get the job done. Chuck wasn't aware of dozing off. Furthermore, he never, ever remembered any dreams he had, but there they were in a dream, or maybe it was a vision. There were those very photos he'd been staring at. The difference was that while he recognized the scene from the photo, it was all alive.

Chuck remembered the picture of his father, Jack Edward. In the summer between his sophomore and junior years in high school, tension between Jack Edward and Chuck's mother really started to escalate. They went on a picnic to have some family time. Chuck's father was about as happy as he could be, and actually relaxed. Chuck took the picture himself, having gotten some interest in photography. But this was not a picture of that memory; this was that memory itself, with a light breeze off the lake on a warm day.

Jack Edward just looked at Chuck without saying anything or reacting to him, but seemed aware of him. Chuck asked, "Are you real?" The answer came back, "Yes, of course I am real."

Chuck stammered, "Am I dreaming?" Jack Edward almost chuckled. "You have been dreaming your entire life, but you are not dreaming now."

"When I asked you about LaGrange the pirate, you told me it was just a family story, and that I didn't want to know. Why did you tell me that?"

"I have not told you that, although it sounds like something I should tell you. Your ancestors lived in reality, not dreams. Your only interest in learning about LaGrange the pirate is to add to the edifice of lies that constitute your existence. You need to wake up, and live in the real world."

It came to Chuck that the vision of Jack Edward was telling the truth. At the time of the picture, his father had not yet told him that. What was he experiencing? Chuck turned his attention to the picture of Kenneth Otto, his grandfather. At the time, Grandpa Ken had just become the head of the economics department at his university. Chuck swore he could smell the oil of cloves Grandpa Ken always wore.

"Your son, Jack Edward, always used you as an example of success. How did you get so successful?" Chuck asked Ken.

"I learned to focus. I knew who I was, and I didn't pretend to be what I was not. A large part of it was from being in World War II, learning what it took to stay alive and to keep my buddies alive."

"So, to be successful, you have to be in a war?"

"I didn't say that was the only way. Mostly, you have to learn to focus. Whatever you do, don't pretend to be what you're not."

Chuck considered Ken's advice would have him be a dishwasher. Not wanting to consider that for very long, he moved on to Otto. Chuck went directly to the question of LaGrange the pirate.

Otto chuckled, and said, "Of course there was a pirate. I spent the last three thousand dollar bills myself. That was quite an experience, having those thousand dollar bills. After getting out of the Army with asthma, and with a new bride, the doctors said I had to move to a dry climate. My father, Andrew Tyra, had died, so I emptied the cache, melted and sold the gold, and headed south."

"Can you find out what your ancestors did and knew?"

"Any direct ancestors, and sometimes not so direct ancestors, yes. I use touch stones."

"What are touch stones?"

"Touch stones are objects which have been in close proximity to a person for a long time. Knowledge about how to use them gets passed from father to son."

"Kenneth didn't pass on that information," Chuck commented, guessing.

"That figures. He was so into new ways of doing things, and his way of doing things, that he couldn't bother with what worked. It wasn't 'real' enough for him."

"Did you get a touch stone from the pirate?"

"No I didn't, but he handled the gold enough for me to know he didn't get it in any conventional way. So the pirate story was close enough."

"When you contact your ancestors, can they volunteer information?"

"No, they can't," Otto replied. "They can only answer questions."

"Can your ancestors not tell the truth, or withhold part of the truth?"

"No. They can only tell the truth as they knew it when they last handled or had connection to the touch stone."

"Can a house or other possession become a touch stone?"

"Yes, it can. I used the gold from the cache in that way, but it can take a long time to get information, and you must be in a vision state for it. I was not able to get very much, since I had to melt the gold. I wanted to spend as little time as I could in the area."

Chuck released the vision at that point, and found he'd been face-down on the photographs for quite a long time. If he'd been asleep, it had not been the restful kind, as he felt totally exhausted. He got undressed and crawled into bed without bothering to see what time it was.

When Chuck woke up, the dreams he'd had before going to sleep were still with him. In fact, he could see each part of each dream in his mind's eye, and recall every word and sight and smell – no, not recall, more like relive. Were the dreams real? He kept asking himself that, hoping to explain them away. To be rational, he'd have to accept that his subconscious was working overtime, trying to make a coherent whole out of the situation where he found himself. That sounded like something a psychologist would say. The only alternative was that he was somehow, incredibly, tuning in on his ancestors' attitudes, outlooks, and thoughts.

So, what was real? Well, the sun was coming in the window, and he didn't really feel like he had slept at all even though the clock said it was nearly noon. His eyes and his nose reported things were just as real as they could be. He was unemployed, just like he'd been before the Mergers & Acquisitions Consulting job. Unemployment was real. Further, he could see dust on the refrigerator, and there was the grimy window, smearing the sunshine outside. Yes, this had to be reality, because it was nasty, as well as being the same old stuff he'd been living with.

In addition, his stomach was crying out for food. He got up, and glancing in the mirror, thought his cheeks had become a bit sunken, but maybe it was just the angle of the light. There was a partial package of bacon in the back of the refrigerator. After checking it, he decided it probably wouldn't kill him, as long as he cut off the bad parts and fried the remainder until fairly well done. Along with the bacon, he had some eggs. To complete the meal, there was bread he'd had in the freezer quite a long time. His advanced toaster skills managed to transform it into adequate toast. He cranked up the coffeemaker, and later, with a dirty plate in front of him that he had wiped as clean as he could with the last of the toast, and sipping a second cup of coffee, Chuck considered his situation.

It seemed unlikely–make that nearly impossible, that he'd be able to get much of anything by way of professional-level work in Chicago. That personnel guy was probably busy salting the ground with their version of his story all the way between Chicago and New York, which was the company headquarters. For all he knew, the INS might show up, demanding to see his green card. What the hell did a foreigner look like, anyway? How did a natural-born citizen prove he was in the country legally? Actually, Chuck thought his life was really starting to go somewhere, up until this morning or yesterday morning, No, it was the day before yesterday when Chuck thought Chicago would be where he'd make his mark on the world. This sucky situation now had Chuck considering he didn't like Chicago all that much anyway.

So, whatever he did, he'd be doing it somewhere else. Where could he go? For starters, he could draw a circle between Chicago and New York, and exclude that from consideration. Maybe his vision of Otto, or more likely his subconscious, doing business as Otto, was telling him to try Tucson. It wasn't as big as Chicago, by any means. Still, it was a good-sized city, and he had no doubt there would be opportunities there. It would really be an easy choice if this was fall instead of getting close to summer. Tucson, from everything he'd heard, was going to be hot.

One thing Chuck really liked about going that direction was that he could stop by and see his great-aunt Millicent. She and her husband Irv constituted the only part of the family who put up with him. More than that, they actually seemed to welcome his visits. It had been a while since he'd been there, anyway. He could maybe spend a day or two there in central Missouri, and then head on to Arizona. It would be better to have interviews already scheduled, and all that happy job-hunting arranged, but now that he'd thought of it, Chuck found himself kind of cranked up by the possibilities.

He headed down to the manager's office, and told them he'd lost his job, and was going to have to move. The two people there both shrugged, and the one reminded him that he would lose his deposit. That was okay with Chuck. The place had been a dump when he'd moved in. He'd be leaving it pretty much as he found it. If he felt like it, he might give the place a quick sweep before he left.

Chuck then called Aunt Millicent, and let her know he was coming. He talked to both her and Irv, and they seemed delighted. He didn't think he'd be there before they went to bed (Irv was always eager to point out that his midnight happened at 9 p.m.), so they offered him breakfast the next morning. They were big on breakfast, having been farmers, and Chuck had no problem taking them up on their offer.

Since it was a fully furnished apartment, renting by the week, there was not much to pack. His stuff went into a few boxes, suitcases, and a duffle bag. What food was still good went into an ice chest. Packing his stuff didn't take much over an hour. He turned in his key, getting a disinterested grunt from the manager. Chuck congratulated himself on being a free man, and headed out to his car.

2: Tucson

Driving out of Chicago in the late afternoon was a challenge, and doing it in the junker-mobile upped the ante considerably. Fortunately, Chuck was starting in the suburbs, so traffic thinned sooner rather than later. Still, it was a long drive into mid-Missouri, and he didn't get there until after midnight. Fortunately, the car ran smoothly the whole way, although the torn, lumpy seats were getting pretty uncomfortable by the end of the trip. He checked into an economy motel, having to roust the manager to get a room.

The visions of the previous night kept replaying themselves in his head, like ads on late-night television. They were in full color, which Chuck understood to be unusual. There wasn't anything to prove they were real, or to disprove them, either. It was all rather spooky, actually. Further, the visions were as though someone simply recorded them. Each iteration, they were exactly the same, word for word, motion for motion. Chuck even started paying attention to peripheral things. A fly in a particular place, a leaf fluttering in a certain precise way: they all remained the same. How could that be?

The following morning, Chuck drove to the small house Millicent and Irv bought in town when they retired from the farm. He stayed with them on their farm one summer, and enjoyed both them and the life. Aunt Millicent was really his great aunt, being Grandpa Ken's sister, but he had always thought of her just as his Aunt. They were both at the door to welcome him, and to make him comfortable. Finally, Aunt Millicent asked if Chuck had visited his parents lately, and he had to tell them no. Then before he knew it, he was telling them about how his father threw him out, and how he was between jobs now, and headed for Tucson to see about work. Then he asked if they had any idea what the problem was between his parents.

Aunt Millicent said they never told her, but at least they were still together, so there was a chance they could figure things out. She also advised Chuck to have some patience, and maybe things would work out, both for him, and for his immediate family. Irv wondered if it might all go back to Ken's apparent need to show he was better than everyone, with his degrees, and positions. Millicent commented those degrees and positions must not have been such a great deal, since Ken had persisted in comparing himself to Irv, ever since they both served in WW II. The atmosphere in the room got a bit tense. Then Irv got a little spark in his eye, and asked what "PhD" stood for.

This was an ancient joke, and Chuck knew how he was supposed to play it. He replied, "No. What does it stand for?" Irv came back with "Piled higher and deeper," and all three laughed as though Irv had just come up with it that very moment. Chuck thought it had been told several thousand times, that he was aware of. At least it succeeded in getting the mood of the moment quite a bit lighter, and they chatted at length about the farm, and projects Irv was doing now.

Irv volunteered to take everyone out to a restaurant for lunch, and while they were there, Chuck asked Millicent about the pirate story. She told him substantially what he already had noted down. He then asked if she knew anything about the LaGrange line other than the pirate, but she didn't. So the conversation drifted a bit, but Chuck tried to keep the subject on LaGrange history. He got Millicent to talk a while about growing up in Tucson, and how the house had been on the prairie east of the University, and was the first house out there. She went on recalling "sock hops" at the house, where the furniture was all moved back, and they danced in their stocking feet on the hardwood floor.

It was a great day, and later, Irv volunteered to help Chuck fix a couple of things on the car while Millicent made them some supper. Not long after they ate, their favorite TV shows came on, Chuck headed back to the motel, as his relatives were getting drowsy. Later, he added up his funds, and guessed how much he'd need for gas. It didn't require advanced college degrees to see he wouldn't be staying in motels very often, not even as minimal as this one. So he made a point of taking a long hot bath that night, and another long shower in the morning before he checked out.

☆ ☆ ☆

2: Tucson

Every hour or whenever he had a rest stop, Chuck would check the oil and look over the engine as though he really knew what he was looking at. His car was new enough to need expensive diagnostics, and old enough that he knew those diagnostics would have deduced he needed a new car. Still, it kept rolling along, and finally Chuck settled into driving, lumpy seats and all. The problem was that whenever he wasn't focused on a current task, those stupid visions would start an endless replay.

Periodically, the car would start running a little rough or the steering would suddenly seem a little squirrelly or a gauge would twitch, and Chuck's attention would return to the task at hand, which consisted of trying to drive a poorly maintained vehicle fourteen hundred miles across country. At least Chuck came to take the minor glitches as a sort of blessing, and at the moment, he was glad for anything positive. Every time he filled the gas tank, it sucked his account closer to the 'dry' mark. It didn't look like he'd be able to go much further than Tucson. If, for instance, Chuck got a job offer in Phoenix, which was only another 100 miles, he wasn't sure there'd be enough money for the gas.

When he got into Tucson, Chuck found a hotspot, and scanned for jobs in the city. Nothing much appealed to him. Hell, he didn't even have an updated résumé (or one that was even vaguely accurate, for that matter). Thinking about it, he had no idea what kind of position he could qualify for. All at once, Chuck realized he no longer had much stomach for trying to misrepresent his background. Was it because of the way the company had let him go? Was it the visions? Whatever it was, he suddenly found himself willing to accept Grandpa Ken's counsel, and consider that he might have to work as a dishwasher, if such were his qualifications. He needed to think about it a while.

There was something he could do while he figured things out, and that was to go by the old family house. It was located not too many blocks east of the University of Arizona. He sat there in front of the place for a while, and pulled out a picture, dated 1938, of great grandpa Otto in front of the house. Well, the house was still there, but the entire back yard had been covered with a three-story concrete block piece of ugliness, evidently rented to students. He didn't stay very long, as the temperature was already approaching 100 degrees. He remembered family stories of going into the mountains just outside of town when it got hot.

The trouble was that access to the mountains now seemed to involve paying a fee. Finally, however, he was able to find a spot that was a little cooler, where nobody was trying to either charge him or run him off.

He was able to run his laptop and portable printer off the power in the car. He loaded the pictures of the house, and printed one that looked okay. A slight breeze came up, moderating the late afternoon sun, and Chuck realized how exhausted he was. Still, there were those pictures, and he focused on them, but especially on the one with Otto, sitting on the front step of the house.

Chuck suddenly realized he was back into a vision, and recalled what Otto had said before. "What year is this?" Chuck asked this Otto. "It's 1938," was the reply.

"Where would I find your grandfather, the pirate?"

"I was born in Blodgett, Oregon. My father was born in Philomath, Oregon. My grandfather said he was French, which would mean France. Those would be places to look."

"How can I get to those places? I'm not sure I've got enough money to get to Phoenix."

Otto just sat on the step, a slight smile on his face. Chuck suddenly knew he needed to make it a question Otto could answer. Finally, something just came to him. "Do you have any money hidden away?"

"Yes I do." Further questions established Otto had hidden several mason jars of cash at a certain spot near Gates Pass just on the west side of Tucson, where he had worked with a survey team. Chuck asked why Otto had never recovered the money, and Otto replied he'd been about to get it a number of times, but hadn't needed it that badly. The spot would be reached by going to a particular survey marker, a metal disk in concrete. Otto showed him the alignment of the surrounding peaks, and the direction and distance from the survey marker. Then he did something even stranger: he gave Chuck a vision of how he (Otto) would drive from the house, all the streets and roads, where he parked, and exactly where he walked.

Chuck knew this was a one-shot deal. After all these years, somebody may well have found the money. Even if it was still there, ground movements or municipal developments may well have made it impossible to get to the jars. When it didn't work, Chuck would be doing any kind of menial work he could find, and saving up in order to go to Oregon. He visualized having to take a bus, and discovered within himself an acceptance of the possibility.

He withdrew from the vision, and found the sun had set and the temperature was dropping rapidly. He was both exhausted and famished. He rummaged through the ice chest, a cardboard box holding what had been his pantry, and a bag of groceries, and found enough to reduce the gnawing in his gut to a tolerable level. It came to him these visions, if that's what they were, took huge amounts of energy. In fact, excessive time in visions might even kill a person. That was something to think about, since Chuck had no desire to join his ancestors just yet. Come to think of it, some LaGrange children would be a good thing prior to joining all these ancestors. It was funny. He'd never really thought about stuff like that before.

With that on his mind, Chuck grabbed a lap blanket, and made himself as comfortable as possible in the cramped quarters of the car, shivering slightly in the suddenly cool air.

Chuck spent a miserable night that would have made it almost impossible to sleep but for the fact that he was absolutely exhausted. As the sun came up, he found himself unable to sleep any more, and got out of the car. He found a place that seemed reasonably out of the public eye, and peed on a rock. This was an awfully long way from the flights of fancy with which he entertained his co-workers not that many days before. He drove on through town keeping one eye on his gas gauge, the other on the road, on which was overlaid the view Otto would have seen in 1938.

Tucson had a population of around 30,000 in 1938, compared to something over half a million now. What amazed Chuck was how the directions still worked. More of note was that as he drove into the Tucson Mountains, Gates Pass had not been developed. Evidently, it was being held as a park. So the worst case scenario of a building where the mason jars used to be evidently had not happened. Then, about where Otto would have parked, Chuck saw a tourist pull-off, with lots of parking spaces, descriptive signs, and several well-used trails. Nobody else was there this early.

He followed the trail that best matched Otto's view, and found the trail diminished rapidly going up a small ridge. While that was encouraging, the fact that several kinds of cactus were wanting to be intimate with his legs made him nervous. Otto's view of the situation included looking at his feet and seeing a pair of sturdy leather engineer boots, not the cheap jogging shoes Chuck was wearing. This was bordering on extremely interesting, as in the Chinese curse, "May you live in interesting times."

At last topping the ridge, he followed it, and suddenly came upon the survey marker, exactly as Otto visualized it to him. It came to Chuck this was the first concrete evidence these were true visions, and not just his subconscious telling him things. Chuck stopped to examine it, and Otto's vision was correct right down to the last letter. Actually, Chuck thought his vision was getting blurry, until he realized he was seeing Otto's vision on top of his current eyesight, and Otto had been a bit to the side. Once he got aligned properly, it was like focusing binoculars, and everything became perfectly sharp.

From that point, Chuck looked around, found the peak Otto showed in the vision, and started walking toward it, being careful to watch for changes in the current situation. That was, of course, a sensible precaution, and one that paid dividends rather quickly. Where the vision seemed to show a trail going downhill, Chuck now saw a cliff. A bit shaken, he followed the cliff until it merged with a lower level, and he was able to follow back until he could regain alignment with the vision. It wasn't much further when he realized he was there. He scuffed a mark, and went in search of a stick that didn't include thorns. Finally successful, he began probing the area, and after some digging, hit a likely object.

After what seemed a fair amount of effort, he began uncovering the two mason jars. It took a while, but the jars finally came out of the ground, and Chuck could see currency inside. The lids were covered with leather impregnated with what looked like engine oil. That must have been to keep the lid from rusting. It looked like there were some coins in the bottom, as well. Not knowing what, if any, value there was in the currency, it was still clear he'd be able to get gas for a while, and maybe even a room. This was a legacy from his great-grandpa Otto, and he'd use it to do something worthwhile, or so he hoped.

It dawned on him that getting this out wasn't going to be a walk in the park. He'd been using both hands for balance coming in. He'd have both hands full going out. If he'd thought about it, he could have brought a plastic bag, so he'd still have a hand free. On the other hand, he hadn't really expected to find anything. He considered stuffing the contents of the bottles in his shirt, but his shirt had next to no tail, being designed to wear outside pants, not tucked in. He could leave them there, go get bags and come back, but couldn't tolerate the possibility that someone else could haul it all off in the meantime. Also, the sun was getting higher, and the temperature hotter. Since he had no water, whatever he was going to do, he had to do now.

✡ ✡ ✡

The vision of his Grandpa Ken talking about focus, and learning to do whatever it took to stay alive came back at that moment. Chuck considered that might be it. He thought he'd focus on the car ... no, he'd focus on the road the other side of the car to keep himself going. So he held each jar tightly to him, like they talked about ball carriers in football, and he started back with his senses fully attuned to the present and his focus on the road beyond the car.

He mostly managed to keep his balance, learning how the loose rock and gravel would slip under foot. He also managed to avoid most of the cactus. There were a few times when he slipped into some cactus, and one time when, to keep from falling, he ended up bulling through a particularly nasty bit, but he kept on going. Finally, he was back on the more developed trail, and marched on. At the parking lot, he was so focused on the road, he actually had to turn around and come back to the car.

There were a number of tourists now on hand, who decided to gawk at Chuck instead of the scenery, but he ignored them other than noting their vacuous stares for future reference. The jars and himself all safely to the car, he made a new focus on getting cactus spines out of his legs and ankles. He sat sideways in the driver's seat, with the door open, pulling them out and dropping them on the pavement. Mostly, they came out cleanly, but a few had rather nasty barbs that tore his skin as he removed them. A couple of places started bleeding. There were still spines stuck in his pants legs, but the gawkers were starting to approach, and Chuck didn't feel like having a discussion just then.

He headed back toward Tucson, noting he still had a quarter of a tank of gas, and a downhill run. Remembering a convenience store along the way, Chuck wondered if it might be a hot spot. Pulling in, he found it wasn't, but saw several pay phones on the front of the store. The phone book holders were empty, but the clerks inside let him look at a phone book. He found some listings for coin dealers, and asked which might be nearby. After some head scratching, one was found near the old downtown area, they said, and gave some general directions to get there.

The shop turned out to be quite small, and in a rather run-down part of town. Chuck opened one of the jars and grabbed some bills together with a few coins from the bottom. He put the jars on the floor, and covered them with the lap blanket, and getting out, made double-sure the car was locked. Inside the shop was an older fellow behind a glass counter. The man was only vaguely interested in Chuck, and his interest didn't increase appreciably when Chuck showed him the currency and coins.

"Are these worth anything?"

The man glanced through the selection. "They're worth face value plus some premium. Why?"

"I'm looking to sell these, plus some more."

"You're selling a collection?"

"Yeah, I guess you'd call it that."

"So how did you come by this collection?"

"It was a legacy."

"Ah. It was a legacy. If I call my friends at the police department, what will they call it?"

Chuck shrugged. "Beats me. I'm sure lots of people are missing lots of things this morning. I didn't have anything to do with any of them."

"That remains to be seen. Did the originator of the legacy have a name?"

"Yessir. LaGrange."

"Kenneth?"

"No sir. His father, Otto."

"Otto. I knew him. Now there was a character. You're a relative?"

"He was my great grandpa."

The man smiled slightly. "Yes, you do have his look. Well, I'd be willing to make you an offer on this collection. Could I see it?"

When Chuck brought the two jars in, the man was looking both at the jars and at him. "How did you come by this legacy? Otto liked you a lot, did he?"

Chuck hesitated before answering. Not many days before this, that kind of invitation would have gotten him rolling on whatever story he thought he could even half-way sell. This seemed to be a new day. Now the question was how he could be truthful without sounding like a complete idiot. Getting information from pictures? No way.

"I never knew him, actually. He died before I was born. I was going over some of his stuff when I discovered it."

"Ah. There was a hidden map. How clever you were to find it."

"No, it was out there for everyone to see all along. It was a case of figuring out how to look at it."

The old guy's eyes suddenly gained a twinkle. "All about focus, isn't it? Did you walk a mile in his shoes?"

Chuck realized the old guy knew exactly what had happened. He looked at the cactus and blood stains on his pants legs, and replied "That mile in his engineer boots would have been a good deal easier."

"What year did you see?"

"It was 1938, more or less."

"Well, let's see what we can do about your legacy." With that, he went through the collection, piece at a time, looking up references on much of it. As lunch time came, he took Chuck to a diner down the block and got him some lunch, which he devoured. While they were eating, the man offered his hand, which Chuck shook. "I was so busy seeing if you were anyone I wanted to deal with, that I never introduced myself. I am Jacob Laubscher. My father, Oliver Laubscher, was Otto's lawyer for years, so I did know Otto and Kenneth. Kenneth moved away before he married, so I never knew your father."

"I'm pleased to meet you, sir. It's amazing that we'd meet like this."

"Such things happen more often than you'd imagine, actually. I've come to think we come from the same vine of life, growing up some massive tree. We think we meet people for the first time, but we're only encountering each other again further up the tree."

Things became quiet for a time, then Jacob asked, "May I tell you something?"

Chuck nodded, and Jacob leaned closer. "As you have already realized, these visions come at a high cost. I can see from your sunken cheeks and appetite that you have been paying a lot. If you allow these visions to take over, they will kill you. You must never allow the past to control your future, and I can see something of Otto looking out through your eyes. You must always see with your own eyes."

They went back to the shop, and Jacob finished his evaluation. It was now mid-afternoon. The face value of the currency was $27,000, and he was willing to pay $54,000. Chuck recalled his Aunt Millicent talking about being sent to the store to get a loaf of bread, and of how she dropped the dime she'd been given into the storm drain. She still talked of how she had cried because that meant they had no bread to eat. Chuck commented that for a dime to buy a loaf of bread, $27,000 had to be a substantial fortune. Jacob nodded. That made it all the more mysterious why Otto would not only have stashed the money, but why he never reclaimed it. The only reply was, "Well, he was a character, wasn't he?"

Jacob took Chuck to his bank, and got him established. Jacob and the bank president were old buddies, so even the immediate provision of a debit card for the account was not a problem. They transferred the few dollars remaining in his Chicago account, and Jacob gave Chuck his business card. "Be careful, my friend," Jacob told him in parting.

Chuck's first reaction after discovering he had some jingle in his jeans was to think of a nice hotel to stay in. That reaction was immediately followed by the consideration that he needed to keep his spending under control. So it was that he found himself a decent housekeeping room that was still better than the place he'd lived in Chicago. Then, he bought some groceries, and while dinner cooked, finished picking the cactus out of his legs. Not all that much later, but after he showered most of the grime off, he managed to get some deep, dreamless sleep.

The next morning over breakfast, he considered his next step, and finally made three lists. One was of things he needed now. The second was for things he needed, but could delay getting. The third was for anything else. Then, he observed this approach was useless. Items changed groups depending on his objectives. So the objective controlled everything else. For instance, if he were to follow Jacob's counsel, and abandon the visions, he would essentially abandon the search for LaGrange the pirate, unless he turned himself into a thorough-going genealogist. It didn't seem like he had the resources for that kind of a project. That would mean doing something else, at least for now. One option might be to go back and enroll in college. A second possibility going with abandoning the search was to look for a job.

Finally, it might be that having experienced these visions and finding they were real, perhaps he was obligated to follow them, in this case, to Oregon. These visions had so far proven to be self-financed, after all. Still, as Jacob warned, the visions were not without dangers. Just with these visions he'd been totally wrung out. He figured his pants size had dropped four to six inches. A beer belly he'd noticed developing lately, and without benefit of beer, had largely disappeared, leaving only some wrinkled skin behind.

The way the visions replayed was an additional problem. Jacob was right. The visions could take over. Still, Chuck thought, the same focus that gave the visions could also keep him grounded in present reality. If he went after the visions, that focus on the present had to be his safety net. Going after the visions meant going to Oregon. Who knew where the trail might lead after that? Mr. Sherman, or, since he no longer worked for him, maybe Lee Sherman would be the way to think about him, seemed to believe that if there was a French pirate, there had to be a connection to New Orleans.

How should he do such research? One way was to use public facilities all the way: that is, fly between places, rent cars, and stay in motels. A slower but lower cost alternative was to drive between places. That would involve trading his car for one more likely to survive the trip. Also, it would mean always staying in motels, and he already knew those costs added up rapidly. In addition, there was the cost associated with eating out a lot. He had already solved that by renting housekeeping rooms, but didn't know if such things were even available in smaller towns. There was, in addition, the problem of hauling his stuff, such as it was, from one place to another.

There were other possibilities, most too outlandish to consider. One approach that appealed to him was buying a used RV, a small one, maybe. Night before last, for instance, he could have slept in the comfort of his own bed. Since, as he understood it, RVs had generators, he could have had air conditioning in the daytime. Heat, too, when he needed it. So there it was, he knew his objective and had decided on a way to take care of it.

That settled, he went in search of a hot spot to make himself an instant expert on the subject of used RV's. Even a cursory search taught him that an RV had all the problems of a truck, plus all the problems of a trailer or house, plus other totally unique problems. Even so, he thought this strategy was the way to go. After enough study, he thought he'd at least have an idea what everyone was talking about, and began making the rounds of local RV dealers, as well as checking online for prices and availability.

He did what he thought was due diligence, looking at some high-end rigs with marble sinks, and low-end ones that didn't even look like they could drive off the lot without disintegrating. He sat in the driver's seat of quite a few of them, and tried to imagine what it would be like driving such a thing. The larger ones sent him off mumbling to himself.

After a good deal of thought, he settled on a gas-fueled class C rig that had a few years on it, but not a whole lot of mileage, and an interior that seemed acceptable. Everything worked, and his test drives seemed to show he could handle it without too much difficulty. Also, it wasn't terribly expensive, meaning he still had money after the transaction.

Chuck then sold his car, and with a couple days rent left on his room, got familiar with how the RV drove, as well as getting it loaded with his personal stuff and buying groceries and supplies. When his week's rent was up, Chuck had already gotten the place as clean as he could, and got his security deposit back. Things were working out all around. In any case, he saw the local weather was forecasting really hot weather for the next week (yeah, it was a dry heat). The cool pines of Oregon, as he was visualizing the state, seemed very inviting.

3: Blodgett

One reason for going with a Class C RV was to minimize the new skills Chuck would need to learn. That was a point made on several web sites. While this rig was small by RV standards, and although the place he bought it from did give him some training, Chuck was neither comfortable nor competent driving when he started north. The interstate was crowded heading toward Phoenix, and Chuck was perpetually nervous about where he was in the lane, not to mention the clearance behind him the few times he was actually passing slower traffic. Further, he found to his dismay that the turn for San Diego was not at Phoenix, but quite a number of miles south, at Casa Grande. He pulled into a truck stop just before the routes separated, and proceeded with the planning he should have done before leaving Tucson.

His original idea was to go to San Diego, and then just head up the coast. That would have meant dealing with the entirety of San Diego, not to mention all of Los Angeles, and Chuck was a nervous wreck already with this traffic. He had experience with a sedan in Chicago, but could not figure out the drivers in this part of the world. The truck stop had a hot spot, so he hauled the laptop inside. His computer recommended going on I-5, but a TV news report talked about very heavy traffic that way, along with a major accident. A final way he looked at went through Las Vegas to Reno, where he could cut across Northern California, intersecting with the interstate just south of the Oregon line. That sounded like a winner, so after Phoenix, Chuck set course for Reno by way of Las Vegas. The air conditioner kept the cab in reasonable condition, and he managed to reach Las Vegas, where he parked at a truck stop for the night.

Along the way, he tried to keep his focus, which consisted in keeping the RV under control. There were some times when high-speed semi trucks going past him made the control issue a real question. Most of the time, it was just the RV rolling down the road. Very often, there was nothing much to look at. Then the visions would start playing their program. For a period of time, Chuck let them play, which now included his more recent vision of Otto. He realized what was happening, though, when the vision started motoring through Tucson toward Gates Pass. When 1938 Tucson started to overlay the highway, he had to regain focus, fast.

Chuck noticed that as he got tired, it took more effort to keep his focus on the present and greater likelihood of the visions starting up again. So, he tried to make sure he got plenty of rest before heading on up the road, and decided he would no longer try to push the driving. While he would have driven the five hundred plus miles to Reno as a matter of course, now he decided to shut it down after about four hundred miles. He was doing whatever it took to keep the visions under control. It did seem like he'd been going through desert forever, though.

The fuel consumption figures seemed theoretical things, but translated into real money in a hurry with this gas-hungry rig. Chuck found the sales price was only the down payment. He was paying for a higher education at every fill up. No wonder it didn't have much mileage. On top of that, steeper grades translated into both slower speeds and higher gas consumption. When he was at truck stops, or travel centers, as people called them, his ears began to listen a bit more carefully to the truck drivers. He found out there were now semis getting better mileage than his little rig.

He imagined being in pine forest before he reached Reno, but he was well into California before that happened. The pine trees came at a cost, with him having to climb endless grades, not to mention the downgrades and some really noteworthy winding roads and hairpin turns. The wisdom of coming this way was more and more in question. Finally, I-5 came up, and that section of the trip was behind him, for better or worse. At least with his going relatively short distances each day, Chuck was running in full daylight and in a fully awake condition. So he stopped for the night when he got to the interstate.

The next morning, he found he was leaving the pine forest behind, which had him double-checking the map, but he was indeed heading the right direction. Some of the grades on the interstate were about as bad as any he'd seen, but at least here, traffic could go around him. Further, the curves were nowhere near as bad as on the two-lane road. Late morning started getting him to what he thought Oregon was all about: well-watered and lush. It kept looking better as he proceeded onward. Chuck considered his ancestors had good taste, indeed, coming here. If Otto hadn't had to deal with asthma, maybe Chuck would have been from here, too.

Later in the day, he pulled into Corvallis, and found an RV park. He needed to dump waste and refill with water. Before that, though, he needed to restock a few groceries. Living this way was wasn't all that bad, he supposed. Soundproofing in it could have been better, but many of his apartments had suffered in that regard, as well. After shopping and getting checked in and parked, he walked around, looking at everything and smelling the air, which was such a change from the desert. He was able to get some flyers for the area, some of which mentioned Blodgett. Evidently, it was pretty small, but at least he had directions for getting there.

✡ ✡ ✡

Chuck spent a comfortable evening, happy to sleep away from traffic for a change. He was also pleased with himself for being able to tune out the visions for extended periods of time. He had a leisurely breakfast, and filled his garage sale air-pump thermos with coffee before getting his RV ready to roll. He tried to be careful, and to follow the manual, but was so obviously unsure of himself (gray water tank? black water tank? one, then the other? one into the other?), that it attracted several more experienced owners, who were instrumental in keeping Chuck from having a complete disaster.

Finally behind the wheel, he drove slowly westward out of Corvallis into Philomath. It wasn't that easy to tell where the one ended and the other began. Looking around, Chuck was marveling that his ancestors had indeed lived in this area. Not only that, he recalled Philomath was one of the places Otto said was associated with the pirate, and might need research. He finally became aware of horns blaring behind him. Looking in his mirrors, he saw a long line of cars, no doubt late for something important somewhere, and in any case, not much inclined to stop and smell the roses. Well, he hadn't been smelling roses, either, but maybe thinking about ancestors qualified.

Chuck saw a place just ahead to pull off. The line of cars roared on by, some slowing slightly just so they could emphasize their opinion using rude gestures. Chuck reflected that he would probably have been doing the same thing not very long ago. Now, it just seemed useless, somehow. Still, he wondered, if he'd been in that line now with someplace he should have been five minutes ago, would he have been anywhere near as calm as now? If his research kept him here long enough, he'd have to get a job. Maybe he could get going five or ten minutes sooner, and wouldn't need to be tense. What a concept!

Looking to his right, there was the Benton County museum. He recalled the library in Chicago telling him the Benton County Genealogical Society was near it. Those were places he could do research after doing a little first-person investigation in Blodgett. Speaking of Blodgett, it was quite a stretch to think he was going to just drive up to a village and get useful information about people who lived there a hundred years earlier. Actually, he guessed he would probably be back to start working historical documents later today. It might even be before lunch.

Chuck felt a wave of despair roll over him. What could possibly be in Blodgett? At most, he'd find a head stone in a cemetery with an inscription nearly eroded into nonexistence. With all the people seeking fame, someone trying to stay out of the limelight could usually accomplish it. What did he hope to find? Would the local newspaper have a headline, "LaGrange the Pirate Moves to Blodgett!" with a picture of the mayor giving him the key to the city? It was time to get real. It had been a long trip to suddenly have a reality break. Still, this was pretty nice country. If he had to be a dishwasher, at least he could do it in a pleasant area.

After a few minutes, he put the RV in gear, and checked for traffic. Evidently the Philomath rush hour lasted just a few minutes. Back on the road, he was out of Philomath almost immediately. The traffic thinned, and he got into some dense pine forest. He rolled down the window to enjoy the cool, pine-scented air. Abruptly, he noticed that he was there. In fact, he had to turn around and come back to the Blodgett Store. Either the town was hidden in the trees, or ... Chuck couldn't imagine what would go after the 'or.' All he saw was a highway intersection and the store.

Evidently, several generations of his family lived here. Otto was born here. How could this be? Chuck wondered what on earth he could hope to learn here. Still, here he was, and it didn't look like that bad a place, so he got out of the RV, and was about to go inside.

☆ ☆ ☆

Outside the RV, it came to him that it would only be polite to buy something while he was there. He went back into the RV and surveyed his refrigerator and pantry. His trip to the store the previous night had stocked him up pretty well. He shrugged to himself, walked into the store, and after a minute, found a snack. Taking it to the counter, he saw the cashier sitting at a table behind the register, working on a laptop PC.

After a moment, Chuck said, "Excuse me?"

She was startled. "Oh. I'm sorry. I didn't see you."

"That's okay. I'm not in any hurry."

She got up, brushing back dark hair as she turned to face him. She brought up a small smile, which faded. "Do you need anything else?" she asked.

Chuck was pulling out his wallet, and decided that was about as good an opportunity as he was likely to get. "Well, yes. That is, maybe. Dumb question: Have you been in this area a long time?"

"Well, no. I've only been here about a month. Why?"

Chuck sighed. This was going downhill in a rush. "Well, I'm looking for relatives who lived in this area a long time ago. My great grandfather was born here in 1898, or so I'm told."

The girl finished ringing up the sale, and then favored Chuck with a full dose of attention. He knew focus when he saw it – he'd been practicing steadily now for several days. "What was your great grandfather's name?"

"Otto LaGrange."

"Do you have parents on him?"

Chuck was astonished. She almost sounded like the genealogist.

"Yes. His father was Andrew Tyra LaGrange. His mother's name was Phosa, but I've never been able to find out much about her."

It looked like a light bulb came on. She went back to the table, sat down, and woke the laptop. She started speaking while hitting keys. "I came here to work on my own family, and I think I may have something of interest." A few keystrokes later, she smiled. "Okay, you said the family name was LaGrange?"

"Well, yes. Same as mine."

"Phosa must have been Otto's mother's nickname. Her real name was Tryphosa."

"Tryphosa? What kind of a name is that?"

"I looked it up. It's a very old name from the Bible, listed in the New Testament. Some of the people really got into biblical names in the 1800's. Her maiden name was James. Her mother's maiden name was Fuller. You got all that?"

Chuck was standing there in shock. "Uh, no. In fact, my head is spinning. I walked in here fully expecting to find out nothing more than the price of snacks at a country store, and get handed a whole new branch of my family tree." Chuck's mouth took off on its own at that point. "I might add the information's coming from the most attractive person I never expected to meet."

His main experience in trying to talk to girls was that he'd end up with his foot in his mouth, and he must have gotten a little red in the face, since she giggled. He was saved further embarrassment, at least for the moment, since the door opened, and an older lady strode in.

"Hey, Melissa. Thanks so much for watching the store while I was out back. Were there many sales?"

Chuck's own focus was total. Melissa. Memorize the name, Chuck. Melissa.

"Just this one. Hope I rang it up right."

"I don't know how you could do it wrong," then to Chuck, "So are you east-bound or west-bound?"

Chuck was about to say something...he didn't even know what, when Melissa answered for him, "Actually, it turns out he's here researching his family tree, like me. It actually looks like we may have some common ancestors going back to not long after Blodgett was founded."

The lady laughed. "Well, if you both have relatives from here, it's very likely that you have common ancestors. It's a benefit of small towns. Okay, why don't the two of you go have a family reunion or something?

✲ ✲ ✲

Chuck remembered some manners at that point. "If you like, we could have a snack, or lunch, or coffee somewhere?"

Melissa waved it off. "Actually, all my notes are over at the cabin I'm staying in." She wrapped up the power cord, and picked up her laptop. "Why don't you come over to the cabin? I think I've got enough lunch for the two of us. I can give you copies of some of my notes on your family line."

"Okay, but I don't want to impose." He followed her out the door. "Where's your car? I could follow you."

"Actually, it's not far, and I walked over."

"Well, at least I can give you a lift."

She had him take a gravel road that headed out behind the store, and then to the right for what seemed like a couple of blocks, to a small cottage that looked like it had been there quite a long time. Inside, it turned out to be two decent sized rooms. The front room was a combination living room and bedroom. The kitchen and bathroom were behind it. Melissa looked at him appraisingly. "Big enough for my needs, cheap enough to stretch the funds as far as possible," she commented.

"I understand completely," Chuck replied. "The RV represents my own answer to the same question. So, are you a professional genealogist?"

"Well, no. I have an MBA, and scored a decent position out of college. That led to a second, better position. I thought it was ideal, having a great job that exactly fit my professional credentials right in Denver, so I could stay close to my ..." She paused a moment. "Anyway, about a month and a half ago, we were the subject of a hostile takeover. Make that a very unfriendly, very hostile takeover. Most of the management team at my firm then became the object of some equally unfriendly - make that hostile - streamlining, to create more efficiency, they said. Well, creating efficiency is what an MBA does, but there was nothing we could do. Nearly all of us got our walking papers."

"It sounds like you've got plenty of credentials to get in somewhere else."

"There's the theory they teach about what an MBA does, and then there's the reality. Quite frankly, I'm really upset about the whole thing."

Melissa continued talking as she made lunch, and it turned out, much to Chuck's dismay, that he knew the firm she'd worked for as well as the firm that took it over. It was his first project after he joined the M&A firm, and he felt pangs of guilt about the whole thing. The fact that his only contribution had been to crunch numbers for some of the team members was beside the point. He found himself wanting to make a good impression on Melissa, but at the same time, not wanting to give false impressions. The sensible thing to do was to not say anything.

Chuck found his mouth moving. "I hate to admit it, but I know about that takeover."

Melissa looked at him briefly before turning back to the stove. "Oh?"

"I worked for an M&A advisory firm. We were retained to give advice on the takeover."

Melissa served up two plates. "What things were you to advise?"

"I did some asset valuation. Stuff like that."

"Well, then, it wasn't up to you to determine what kind of assholes took control. Anyway, they paid me off fairly well, considering that I wasn't high enough to get a golden parachute. Anyway, it gave me a chance to pursue a dream. So, how did you get into the M&A game?"

Chuck considered what to answer, and once again found the truth coming out of his mouth instead of a convenient, believable cover story. "I got into it accidentally, frankly. I was out of work, and had been sending résumés everywhere, and not getting any response. I got desperate, and started padding the résumé. Finally, I was running out of unemployment, and sent out some really outrageous stuff. This job offer came out of the blue attached to a very nice rate of pay, so I took it."

"What happened then?"

"I was totally out of my depth. Still, they seemed to be okay with my analyses. Maybe I could have cut it, but they started verifying my information. They shouldn't have hired me in the first place, but there it was."

"So how did you get here?"

It seemed like once the truth started, it was hard to keep a handle on it. "I had a vision. Not a religious vision, but one that told me to leave Chicago for Tucson. Another vision in Tucson gave me the resources and advice to come here." Chuck shook his head, and looked at Melissa. "You probably think I belong in a rubber room now, but I did have visions. They were visions of my ancestors."

Melissa reached across the table, and took Chuck's hands. "I called them dreams, but I think I had some of the same experiences that you call visions. You know what else? I've had some partial visions right here, in this house. Tryphosa, or Phosa, used to live here." Melissa whispered, "I've seen her."

✲ ✲ ✲

Chuck remembered something Aunt Millicent said, that she heard Phosa referred to as "that red-headed Dutch woman." "I was told you could only connect with direct ancestors, but it sounds like you managed it anyway. What did she look like?"

Melissa looked a little bit nervous at being asked to bring back the vision, but went ahead. "She's got an oval to round face, and red hair," she started.

Chuck cut in. "No. You don't need to replay the whole thing. That's her, the red-headed Dutch woman. So it appears you don't need to be a linear descendant. You only need the focus."

Melissa was a bit shaken, but gratified someone was confirming what she saw. "Thanks for not making me go through the whole thing."

"What can you tell me about her, keeping to generalities? If your experience was like mine, you could repeat verbatim, and even describe the bugs in the area."

"You're exactly right. What is this thing we've stumbled on, anyway? Do you think other people know about it?"

"Other people do know about it, and have known about it. There was an older fellow in Tucson who knew it, and warned me not to use it, or at least not to use it much. The visions suck energy from you, and if you stay in them too long, he said they can kill you, and I believe him. Also, in one of my visions, I asked Otto about it, and he called them touch stones. As I understand it, everything a person handles absorbs the memory, attitude, and personality of that person. By focusing attention, we can detect that, and play that person back in our own mind."

It was evident Melissa didn't care to expand on her vision of Phosa at this point. Chuck didn't understand why, but was gratified that his trip to Blodgett had not only turned up useful information, but had also brought him someone willing to help him pursue his family. Whether she'd be willing to chase the pirate was another problem. He thought he might be interested in her personally, as well, but had such a rotten history with the opposite sex, he didn't dare think about it.

Chuck brought in his information, and they started comparing data. He felt good, being able to provide information that filled some gaps in what Melissa had. It was obvious that whatever his analytical skills, Melissa was the real deal, thinking both wide and deep with such speed that he was getting writer's cramp taking notes. He started out trying to input directly to his software, but the information was coming from so many directions, and his skill with the genealogy software was so minimal, that he went to manual note-taking, intending to input later. He considered that maybe the freeware he was using might not have been the most efficient for this kind of thing.

Melissa started cross-checking census data, and concluded that yes, this had been the LaGrange house. A.T. LaGrange, Otto's father, was shown. Why a vision of the house only turned up Phosa might indicate Andrew Tyra owned the house and was maybe married to Phosa, but for some reason didn't actually live there. At least that was the conclusion Melissa arrived at on the basis of known information. Further searching seemed to confirm that Otto was born in 1898, but Phosa and A.T. were married in 1900.

It was a strange situation, especially given what they knew of attitudes in 1900. Then again, Melissa considered, maybe they only thought they knew what social attitudes were in 1900. By that time, they had pretty much burned through the afternoon, and Melissa offered to make dinner. Chuck asked if there were any supplies he could help with, seeing as how he was pretty well-stocked (at least by his lights). After consideration, she gave him a small list that would be very helpful in making dinner.

Many of the items looked familiar, and Chuck went out in the late afternoon sun to get what he could. While he was there, he noticed the auxiliary battery was getting down a bit, so he started the generator, which coughed and sputtered before getting cranked up. That sounded like some maintenance on the horizon. He glanced at Melissa's cabin, visible out the windshield, and had the thought to take a picture. Whatever the danger might be, maybe using a picture for a vision would be productive.

Inside, Melissa declared the supplies he brought to be perfect, and proceeded to demonstrate a talent for multitasking Chuck never knew could exist in real life. Along with making dinner, she was forwarding her own research, and helping Chuck with his genealogy. She only shifted gears as she served him a plate, and hoped it would taste okay. Mostly living on whatever crawled out of the freezer, Chuck was overwhelmed. She said she had just sort of invented it as she went along. Chuck had no idea such things were possible.

By the time they were done eating, both of them continuing to work in the meantime, Melissa had become satisfied about an additional point. "If you go back on Phosa's side, it seems quite certain that we have a common ancestor, Sarah Ann Fuller. That makes us fifth cousins." She seemed pleased with the discovery.

Chuck was thinking about what he could say, when his mouth just opened itself and started talking. "Would that make us kissing cousins, do you think?" he heard himself say, thinking how he probably just messed up everything. To his surprise, she kept smiling, and maybe smiled a little wider. Oh, she had a nice smile.

"That might be," she said. Then she abruptly got up. "I heard you start your generator earlier," she observed. "If you'd like to work on the project some more in the morning, and have an extension cord, I'd be glad to let you plug in overnight. If you do it now, you won't be burning fuel, and you can run the line while there's still daylight."

That suited Chuck extremely well, as he was having visions of having to go back to Corvallis. While the RV Park was okay, this was far and away a better thing to do. Later, in the RV, Chuck printed the picture he'd taken of Melissa's/Phosa's cabin. Andrew Tyra LaGrange seemed to be both here, and not here. If he could keep the vision under control, maybe he could answer a question or two.

4: Harlan

In the RV, Chuck lay back in the recliner, and focused on the picture while he thought about Andrew Tyra, Phosa, and Otto. Almost immediately, he saw it – the same house, but looking much closer to new. There weren't many trees in the area, and he saw that Blodgett was at the entrance to the mountains. That was something he couldn't see at all with the full-grown pines in the area now. A red-haired woman came out of the house. Chuck found this surprising, since previously, all the scenes had been static. Perhaps it was the combination of things he had focused on.

The woman was carrying a laundry basket, and there was a dark-haired boy, maybe ten years old trailing behind her.

Chuck asked, "What is your name?"

"I was born Tryphosa Belle James. I go by Phosa. My married name is Phosa B. LaGrange."

"Does Andrew Tyra LaGrange live here?"

"This is his house, and I am his wife, but this is not home for him."

"Do you see him often?"

"He comes around now and then. If I need something, he leaves me money. Then he goes away again."

"How does he get the money?"

"I don't know. He never says. He's kind of puny, and always claiming to be sick. I've never heard of him working. I think he gets the money from his father, somehow."

"He doesn't sound like much of a husband. Why did you marry him?"

"I didn't want to, but he is little Otto's father. My family looked at the baby and went up the mountain and spoke with the Lillard and LaGrange bunch. They all came down and looked at Otto, and said the baby needed a name. Finally, A.T. confessed, and the families declared we had to get married."

"How did the Lillards get into it? Didn't Minerva divorce Charles LaGrange and remarry?"

"Minerva had two children by LaGrange, and came to hate them because of their father. Minerva's brothers, and there are a bunch of them, were more than happy to disgrace the father through the son."

"What about A.T.'s father, Charles? Is he still around?"

"People say they see him now and then, but nobody's completely sure."

Chuck found himself fumbling for questions, although he could ask the same question a number of times in a slightly different way without having any repercussions. He was reminded, too, that he needed to get in, take care of what he needed, and get out, minimizing problems with the vision.

"Did you ever meet Charles?"

"Yes, I encountered him a number of times."

"What do you know about him?"

"I don't really know much of anything. Sometimes, he said he had a gold mine. Other times, he claimed he'd been a pirate, and only just got to Oregon ahead of the British. He never told the same story twice, other than that he was French. Maybe that part is true. He sure sounds French. He's a fancy dresser. The man likes to wear a white shirt and a red sash at his waist like he's some kind of dandy."

"Where would I find A.T. and Charles?"

"From what people tell me, A.T. spends time up around Harlan, which means that's where Charles is, as well. They wouldn't actually be in Harlan, since that's Lillard country. The Lillards are in and around Harlan, and a lot over toward Burnt Woods and further west. That leaves A.T. and Charles wandering around in the woods. I think that's kind of funny – a dandy living in the woods."

"Where did A.T. grow up?"

"Oh, in Harlan. A.T. told me they had a house not far from the store. That was while Charles and Minerva were still married."

"What about the Lillards?"

"The Lillards and Mulkeys were related clans who came from Missouri. They say they founded Harlan, but others say they moved in on some folks who were already there. They're very clannish hill people, a lot of them, anyway. Most of the Mulkeys settled near the river around

Corvallis, but this bunch, well they were hill people in Missouri, and they're hill people here, too. Not folks to be on the wrong side of. That's exactly where Charles is, on the wrong side."

"So why didn't he pack up and go?"

"I don't know. I only hope it's because he's got enough decency in him to take care of A.T. and us."

Chuck thought he might as well cut it off there, and get some sleep.

✡ ✡ ✡

It seemed like he had no sooner ended the vision when he heard knocking on the RV door. He opened the door, and there was Melissa, who had a big smile that faded to shock and concern as she looked at him.

"You've still got on the clothes you had on yesterday, and they're soaked with sweat. And you ... you look awful! Are you all right?"

"Oh yeah, I'm fine," Chuck replied, except right then the cool morning air got to his skin below his sweaty clothes, and he staggered. "Or maybe not," he concluded.

"Can you make it to the house? I've got breakfast ready."

She helped him into the house, and sat him down, feeling his forehead and studying his face. "Well, you don't have a fever. I think that's good. Can you make it to the kitchen?"

Chuck wasn't sure he'd be able to eat, but one bite rapidly led to an empty plate. Melissa didn't say much while he was eating, but kept looking at him out of the corner of her eye.

"So what the hell happened to you?" she demanded when he was done eating.

"I did a vision based on the house, and got Phosa mainly, but also Otto when he was about ten years old."

"You got a vision just sitting in front of the house?"

"No, actually, I took a picture of it yesterday afternoon."

"I thought that guy in Tucson you talked about said it was dangerous. From the look of you, I'd have to say that guy was exactly right. Still, after finding out you did visions, I was wondering how this house would affect you. I've had dreams about her nearly every night, kind of fragmentary visions. I never asked any questions. I was hoping that if you did a vision here, you'd be able to reach A.T."

"That's exactly what I was hoping, but it didn't turn out that way." Chuck went on to describe the entire vision to Melissa, together with the fact that it seemed like her knock on the door happened just after he stopped the vision.

"I think your time sense must get distorted in these visions," she observed. "I'm not sure what you would look like to a real-time observer. My guess is that you would seem unconscious. You're obviously burning energy at an incredible rate, speaking of which, stand up a minute."

Chuck stood up, and Melissa stuck two fingers behind the waist line of his pants and pulled out. She whistled. "These pants actually fit you last night. Now, they're way too big. If you can show people how to do the visions, you can make millions and billions of dollars. Do you have any idea how much women will pay to knock off a couple of dress sizes overnight?"

She pushed him back into the chair. "If you're to be any use at all today, we're going to have to feed you some more. Make that quite a bit more."

After a while, she decided he might be able to travel, and that a field trip to Harlan might be a good thing for both of them. The condition was that she would be driving, and they wouldn't be doing any side trips. It would only be to Harlan and back. Further, she told him that he wasn't to be doing any more free-lance visions. She was going to supervise any such ventures.

So she sent him out to get changed, with strict orders ringing in his ears. He was only to change his clothes and come right back out. They would take pictures in Harlan, and they would try to talk to a few people. That was all. Melissa told herself that it wasn't as if he were on drugs. After all, there weren't any chemicals involved. On the other hand, his appearance had changed drastically overnight. Despite what she said about the weight loss, it wasn't all that good a change. Really, he could have been used in the old anti-drug ads: This is you when you're not having visions. This is you with visions.

She shuddered, and decided to hang around the RV until he got ready. She needed some fresh air, anyway. Happily, he got changed quickly, and returned with a shave and appearing about as ready to go as he could be without a good deal of rest and recuperation. She got him into her car, and keeping an eye on him, drove on out.

☆ ☆ ☆

4: Harlan

Chuck leaned back, and watched the scenery. It really wasn't very far to Burnt Woods, and when Melissa turned onto Harlan-Burnt Woods Road, it looked like a nice paved country road. He was presently disabused about it being paved, although Melissa informed him it was considered a pretty good country road. Yeah, okay. He'd seen lots worse holes in paved streets. The road began winding through an incredible green maze of tree-covered hills. He felt like he was physically going back in time.

"Melissa, I'm trying to imagine how the first settlers, that is to say, my ancestors, found this place."

"For one thing, they got here in the early 1850's. The family we're both related to got here in 1845, and even then the best spots had been taken out in the valley – Corvallis, and all that. In 1845, they eventually found, after looking all winter, the place that bears their name, King's Valley. The Lillards came about 1853, and ended up out here. The thing for them was, they actually succeeded in finding land they could farm. Not everybody was so fortunate."

They drove on, Chuck soaking it all in. Finally, he saw that the little valley they were following was starting to open up, and they passed a house. The road came to a "T" and Melissa pulled over to the side. "Welcome to Harlan," she said.

Chuck was awe-struck. It was a hamlet sited between a tall forested hill and fields that extended across a verdant valley. Chuck got out, and Melissa turned off the engine. The silence was a physical force. The crunch of the gravel as he stepped suddenly was unacceptable, and he quickly got onto the grass.

"This is beautiful! Why would anyone, having found this kind of paradise, ever leave?"

Melissa's voice was as soft and sweet as ever, but it sounded harsh at the moment. "From what I've read, they left for the usual reasons, opportunity and money. This is a great place for subsistence farming, but they needed to get surplus crops to market. The road we came in on started out as barely a trail. They could hardly get a horse down the trail, it was that narrow. Wagons were out of the question, at least at first. Even with a wagon road, it's a long hard way to market. What kind of profit do you get if you have to take off from farming for a week just to go to town?"

Chuck stood there, ready to shoot some photos, but not sure what the subject should be. He let his attention wander just a bit, and realized the visions were still there, just pushed to the side. He refocused his attention, but in spite of it, a bit of his awareness now consisted of the visions. He wondered if they would finally go away, and decided he'd better hope they would. The alternative was that these visions might eventually overwhelm him.

On the thought that Harlan had been a notable town at one time, Chuck just shot overlapping pictures for a full circle. Melissa watched him, a puzzled look on her face.

"You're thinking that you'll be able to do a vision based on a structure having been there?" she asked.

"Yeah. Something along that line, anyway. I went into vision using a picture of your cabin in the present. The cabin in the vision was almost new, with a clothes line to the side." Chuck turned toward her, and pulled up for a shot. "Smile. Maybe this way I can get a vision of loveliness."

"That's as good a line as you can come up with? You're more tired than I thought." Still, Melissa was smiling when she said it, although Chuck had to admit it was a pretty lame line, even for him.

They walked around and drove around. They tried talking to a few of the people in the area, but got even fewer results than they had already gotten off the internet. Chuck did two more panorama shots, and they headed back to Blodgett. Melissa let Chuck print pictures in the RV, but made a point of checking on him frequently, usually on the pretext of either having found something, or else to define something a little more precisely. Chuck managed to keep his head in the game either because of her attention, or maybe in spite of it. It was hard to tell. He did seem a bit preoccupied, which concerned her.

Finally, the printing was done, and Melissa was running out of make-work, so she looked at his prints, and decided they'd be harmless enough. She figured there'd been enough excitement for one day, and took Chuck off to a favorite place she'd found to watch the sunset. He was a strange guy, she thought, but she also felt like things between them could get personal. She wasn't exactly sure how she felt about that prospect.

✲ ✲ ✲

After dinner, they talked for quite a while. Then, Melissa went in the other room and Chuck leaned back on the couch, thinking he'd relax just a little. The next thing he knew, Melissa was nudging him.

"Hey there," she said. "Maybe you need to go catch up on all the sleep you didn't get last night."

He started to get up. "Yeah, you're right. I'm sure sorry. You ended up with a less than exciting guest, this evening."

"Don't worry about it. One thing: don't do any more visions. Okay? You promise?"

"Sure, that's an easy promise. My only problem will be walking the ten feet out to the RV. Gee. Couldn't I just take a nap here?"

"Not this evening, mister. You've got your own bed. Go use it," she replied, pushing him out the door.

In the RV, he drew the privacy curtains inside the driver's compartment, sighing as he shut out the view of the cabin. Then, he turned around. There were the prints he'd done. He was pretty tired, and suddenly the visions, which had been on the periphery of his consciousness, began to expand, until those pictures were his only focus. He went from one photo to another until on one, a shot of a hay field, a ghost of a house appeared.

The image of the house solidified, and then he saw a scrawny looking guy, who looked a great deal like what he'd seen in the mirror when he shaved, with dark hair and a dark complexion. A major difference from what he saw in the mirror, though, was his attire. Out in the little hill town of Harlan, Oregon, he had on a white shirt with a period tie, a formal-looking jacket that was unbuttoned, and a red sash at his waist. This guy looked like Phosa's description of Charles L.F. LaGrange.

"Who are you," Chuck asked the man, who gave him the reply he expected. Chuck gasped, coming out of the vision. He went back to the front and peered out. Melissa's lights were still on. Evidently, not much time had passed since he came into the RV. As tired as he was, he didn't want to take the chance of looking at the photos again. Melissa was exactly right. His visions had to be in a more controlled environment. Chuck turned off the lights, and felt his way past the doorway to the toilet, and finally to the bedroom, where he took his clothes off and slid into bed, feeling like he'd accomplished something.

Then, as he fell asleep, the visions came swirling in from the sides, and there, right in front of him, was Charles L.F. LaGrange waiting to give Chuck answers to this quest he'd been on. He tried to refocus, to wake up, to force the visions back to the side, but there was Charles, he would not go away.

"Okay, Charles, what year is this?"

"It's 1908."

"Do you take care of Andrew Tyra?"

"Yes. Someone has to do it. I'm his father."

"Do you get along with the Lillards?"

"Not even a little bit."

"So why are you in Harlan? This is their place, isn't it?"

"It's where some of them live. Most of the people here now arrived recently, and have nothing to do with them. Anyway, the Lillards are off at a dance in Eddyville."

"Since they hate you so much, how did you end up married to Minerva?"

"Ah, her brothers were most persuasive. They thought I looked prosperous, and they knew they could beat me physically, so they ran off her first husband and told me how it was going to be."

"Didn't she divorce you for abandonment?"

"I did the best I could, but there was to be no satisfaction for anyone. Her brothers later got together, and they all decided our marriage was a bad idea, and were telling her that I was a bad person. So, after the children were grown a bit, I slipped away. A.T. was always sickly, so I kept close, to keep an eye on him, and help as I could. Minerva hated me for leaving, but she already hated me for being around."

"You supported him out of the cache of gold, both before and after he married Phosa?"

"Yes, I did."

5: Civil War

Chuck tried again break free of the vision, but was unable to, so he asked the big question: "Were you a pirate?"

Charles answered without blinking. "No, I wasn't. My grandfather, Philippe, sailed with Lafitte. There are those who say Jean Lafitte was a pirate. There is a family story about an ancestor being a privateer who turned pirate. I borrowed the family story to disguise how I really came to have the gold. Some people would probably equate how I got the gold with piracy anyway."

"Where and when were you born?"

"I was born in New Orleans, in 1830."

Well, Chuck thought, score several points for Lee Sherman. If Philippe sailed with Lafitte, then he knew Lafitte. In all honesty, however, the reverse didn't necessarily hold true. Lafitte might not have known each and every crew member personally. Bonus points for LaGrange originating in New Orleans. "What of the story of you being French, and from France?"

"My parents are French, so I am French. I have never been in France."

"Tell me about your family."

"After Philippe sailed with Lafitte, he became a tradesman, and had a mercantile in New Orleans. My father Jean, named to honor Jean Lafitte, took over the store, and specialized in imports from France, which he mainly sold to the French living in and around New Orleans. I became a partner in the mercantile. My grandfather Philippe was retired from actively running the store, but continued to give us valuable advice."

"Why did you leave New Orleans?"

"New Orleans was always a French city, even though a number of countries claimed to rule it. During my lifetime, it was the Americans who claimed New Orleans. Then, the Americans fell to bickering about who should rule Americans, and in 1861, Louisiana seceded from America, along with a number of other American states. We in New Orleans, the second largest port in America, viewed it all as a form of political theater, and of no possible personal impact. Then came the Yankee blockade of New Orleans, and it became very personal, since we could no longer get stock from France.

"My father came to know things would be extremely serious, and gathered the family in December, 1861. He had information there would be an attack on New Orleans, and decided to send as many of the family in different directions as possible. Several family members had already enlisted to fight under the new flag, and had reported to their units. I had listened to my father and grandfather. My grandfather was born in Cap Francais, Saint Domingue (Chuck had to frame several questions before he found the current name was Cap Haitien, Haiti.). The entire family was forced to flee when Napoleon was not able to protect his own citizens from a slave revolt. They went to New Orleans, a French city ruled by the Spanish. Then the Spanish flag was replaced by the French flag, only so that it could be replaced by the American flag.

"The choice came down to choosing between flag and family. I said that I would prefer family. Father approved. His idea was that I should go to Canada, to Quebec, and stay there until the Americans sorted this all out. The most direct way was to take a steamboat up the Mississippi to St. Louis, and to make my way on to Canada from there. He had just found out, however, that the Yankees had a second blockade, about where the Ohio River joined the Mississippi, and it didn't seem feasible to go overland. The short way now blocked, that left a long way, going across Texas, dropping into Mexico if that looked safer.

"Once on the Pacific coast, I could catch a ship going to Canada, and then make my way east to Quebec. If I found a sanctuary anywhere along the way, I should stay there. In any case, I should contact the family to advise them of my safety. Whenever the war was done, the family could get back together. My parents and grandparents would stay in New Orleans, and try to protect family property, such as might be possible."

Chuck mused that the ancestor he'd always heard was a pirate, bringing pictures of eye patches, cutlasses, and parrots, turned out to be a shop keeper specializing in luxury imports. Bravery in battle was not his forte, either. Still, he'd ended up with gold, obtained in a way people might not approve. A pirate in the family tree was already an old family tale by the time Charles came along. Chuck had established the ancestor named as a pirate was no such thing. So let me out of this vision, already.

☆ ☆ ☆

Chuck was absolutely unable to stop the vision, and began to wonder what it would take to break out of it. While he thought about it, he asked for more on the French experience in New Orleans and Saint-Domingue/Haiti.

"In both Saint-Domingue and New Orleans, we considered ourselves French. After the American take-over, we still considered ourselves French. When all the squabbling was heating up, not many of us really considered ourselves Confederate even though a number joined their army. Almost no one thought of themselves as a Yankee. Jean Lafitte was our great hero. He was a leader, and a commander, and a merchant, and a genius. He got things done when the kings and nations playing at governing the area wanted to do nothing.

"When the British and Americans came to blows, it was Jean Lafitte who decided who would win the contest. He volunteered his crews to save New Orleans, and it was their artillery experience together with Jean's reordering of the battle lines that won the day. What was the result of his sacrifice? Andrew Jackson, who would have lost the battle without Jean Lafitte, was declared a hero, and went on to become President of America. Jean Lafitte, instead of being given credit, was declared a pirate, and hunted by any number of navies. So it suited me far more to simply be French, and to swear allegiance to my family and friends.

Chuck asked Charles about his trip into Texas, continually trying to break out of the vision. That had been so easy before.

"In January of 1862, friends of the family took me from New Orleans to Barataria Bay, which had been Jean Lafitte's headquarters at one time. While I was there, we talked about whether the best course would be for me to just stay with families in the area. After all, it wasn't as though they'd be looking for me. On the other hand, if spotted by either side, I could very well find myself an unwilling soldier. So, there being good arguments on both sides, my father's wishes prevailed, and we headed out in two pirogues. I was entirely too visible in my normal city clothes, so I packed them, and wore borrowed clothing to look like a fisherman.

"We made it into Texas without incident, and stayed with Cajuns living there. The plan had been for me to switch to horseback at that point, but we got the news that Texas was grabbing any and all men for their cause, of whatever nationality. Any man unfortunate enough to be caught in Texas would be in the Texas army. After some further discussion, we continued down the Texas coast by pirogue. There was great temptation to swing out into the Gulf now and then, but they told me the pirogues did not do well in rough water.

"So it was that we'd have to portage from time to time. I felt ashamed that I was not able to carry a full load, but these were life-long boatmen, big and tough, and getting me through safely was a duty they said was owed to my father and grandfather. They would never say how it was they came to owe such a duty. We would stay in fishing villages along the coast, when it was safe to do so. Otherwise, we got our own food as we went. There was more food than a city boy like me had any idea about, so we did not lack for food along the way, especially at the beginning.

"As we got further south, things changed, and finding food was more challenging. Locals often showed us what to look for, and what to do with some of the items we got. It was a terribly long trip just to get to Mexico, taking us 45 days. I was amazed at the willingness of these men to take me all that way, and to be separated from their families. We began to joke that the war might be over by the time they got me to Mexico, but that never got beyond a joke, since we could see Yankee blockade ships sitting off the coast the entire way.

Chuck's thought processes were still running through all this. He knew every single step of the three hundred miles along the Texas Gulf Coast. It occurred to him that it was entirely likely that this was a terminal experience. Could anyone save him from this vision? Had he locked the RV when he came in? Yes he had. He always locked up wherever he stayed. There was probably nothing that could save him. This might be a great story, but what good was it if he couldn't pass it along to someone else?

✲ ✲ ✲

Charles continued his story, not that Chuck had found any way to stop him. "The men left me on the south bank of the Rio Grande, and headed back to Louisiana. Being with them all that time had made me feel that they were family and not just friends of family. They had gone far beyond what they said they were going to do, and needed to get back, concerned about what the war might have done to their people and property while they were gone. I stood on that beach, watching them head away. As they disappeared, my isolation and the extremity of my situation fully sunk in."

Chuck considered that at this moment, he'd match ol' Charles isolation for isolation and extremity for extremity, plus the fact that the Charles odyssey obviously did not end there, and it looked like Chuck's story would end soon. However, Chuck's participation in the Charles epic was now mandatory and not voluntary, and so he went in lockstep, trudging south along the beach only to find impassable tidal pools and having to cut inland. Having run out of water, he had to go all the way back to the Rio Grande, which he knew had fresh water.

Casting back and forth, he finally found a faint fresh track, and was able to catch up to an ox cart. At this point, experiencing it wasn't enough punishment. Charles started up what amounted to a voice-over narration to go with it. Chuck considered this was reality TV with bionic fittings, and worse, he couldn't change the channel. "In New Orleans," Charles was saying, "Spanish was my second language, with English a poor third. With this man, his first language was that of his Indian tribe, but he could speak Spanish. We talked a while, and he gave me a ride to the next village."

Chuck found some small control: he was able to tune out the speech for periods of time, but the dust, heat, thirst, and fatigue seemed to go on forever. Oddly, though, Chuck found he understood the local Spanish as well as Charles. In fact, whatever Charles understood was what Chuck understood. What made it more puzzling was that Chuck only knew a few words of Spanish, most of which were either slang or else not repeatable in public. Chuck reflected that most of what Charles had been saying was in French. Certainly the conversations in the pirogues with the Cajuns were French, and he understood those men as though it was his native tongue.

There was a total of one road out of the village, and it went northwest, exactly the wrong way for Charles' purposes, but he was able to get a ride to the next town going that way. This process continued until he arrived at Matamoros, the biggest city in the area. The difficulty for Charles was being on the Rio Grande, and more than that, "Texians" as they called themselves were all over the place, looking for wayward citizens who needed to be in their army. Fortunately, Charles being slight of stature and with a dark complexion, wearing workmen's clothes, was about as invisible to the Texians as the Indios among whom he moved.

Charles joined a wagon train bound for Victoria, far to the south. He found that coming into Mexico had gotten him away from the American war, but that wars and rumors of wars were still abundant. Evidently, the French had invaded Mexico. So, he turned inland to San Luis Potosi, not pleased with going over mountains, but happy to get out of the desert. He hitched a ride to Aguas Calientes and Guadalajara. Finally he got to Manzanillo, on the Pacific coast.

This was where he got the good news that ocean shipping did go out from Manzanillo. Then, there was the bad news, which was that no shipping went north from there. As Charles got acquainted with the local people, he discovered that they were much like his Cajuns back home. The local working people did what they needed to do to get by. There were people involved in trading and shipping. The authorities regarded it as smuggling since they weren't getting a cut of the action. The locals spent little time worrying about it, since they knew they were simply making a living.

As time went on, Charles had made no effort to hide the fact that he was French. This caused the locals to have reservations about him, because French naval vessels began making port calls at Manzanillo. Charles, they found, wanted nothing to do with these ships or the people on them. After the first few days, when he found there were no ships going north, Charles wanted nothing to do with the town officials, either. So he began to fit in with the local ways of getting things done. Soon, the locals would let him hide in their homes, or find him someplace to be out of town whenever the French showed up, or whenever local officials started getting too nosy.

☆ ☆ ☆

Chuck remembered when he was very young, visiting somewhere, and being told they were all going to watch a slide show. There was a sheet tacked to the wall, and the old slide projector humming while voices kept up a commentary. No one asked whether he wanted to be there, and the slides of unknown people doing boring things just kept going click, click on the screen. Eventually, the slide show was done, but

Chuck had fallen asleep long before. This thing with Charles was along that order of things, except it didn't seem allowable for Chuck to just sleep through it. Chuck just wanted to go to Melissa and find out everything was going to be okay. He was aware, of course, that things were not at all okay.

Charles arrived in May of 1862. This was after he'd left New Orleans in January. His conclusion was that Manzanillo seemed like a place he could wait out the American war. The French military was more of a nuisance than a difficulty. He seemed to be avoiding them with little difficulty, especially considering they weren't looking for him. Even if they discovered him, what could they do? He'd been born in a French territory thirty years after France gave it away.

Then, there was an American consul in town. Charles assumed he belonged to the Yankee faction. Actually, which faction the consul bowed to was of no consequence to Charles. His entire focus in that regard was to avoid that individual. Even if the consul saw Charles, he wouldn't have thought of him as American, anyway, dressed the same as the local pobres, and not having a physical appearance that different from them. Charles had studied him from afar, and did not have much regard for him.

Chuck, while the life of Charles was droning along was voting to consider whatever strange thing happened between here and Oregon, he'd be more than willing to mark with a big red pen "A miracle happened here," and let it go at that. Might it at least be possible to just put up a power point slide stating "Nothing happened today," instead of having to actually relive the whole damn thing? At least then, everyone would know up front, and he wouldn't have to drag through the entire twenty-four hours, step by dusty step.

On Monday afternoon, July 28, the customs boat came into the harbor with survivors of a shipwreck. The next day, the harbor was a beehive of activity, bringing in both survivors and the dead. Charles, along with everyone else did what they could. Unlike most of the locals, Charles was able to talk to the survivors, who told him they were from the Steamship Golden Gate. The ship, one of the most modern, fast steamships, was on its way from San Francisco to Panama, when there was a fire in the engine room, and the captain ran the ship aground about fifteen miles north of Manzanillo to save the passengers. This had happened on Sunday.

They knew Manzanillo was not that far away, and the intention was to walk to town, but they were blocked by a headland called White Rock, and ended up spending a miserable time on the beach. The SS Golden Gate was carrying a major amount of gold. Also, many of the passengers were carrying gold. In order to get to shore, most of them dropped their gold. Charles shared this information with some of the locals, and in appreciation, they included Charles as part of their salvage effort. It may have helped when Charles pointed out that he was no stranger to steamship salvage. New Orleans, as a major port, had its share of wrecks.

The survivors had not found the way to town because it was a very rough, unmarked trail. Not many of them were in good enough condition to have made it on the trail even if they had been able to find it. It was certain that whatever gold was recovered would not be going back on that trail. Charles showed them what he knew about salvaging in shallow water. In exchange, they showed him some tricks about building a cache, and also about working in surf. They were able to salvage quite a lot of gold before the several navies with an interest in the matter showed up, followed closely by people interested in heavy salvage.

At that point, Charles and the locals simply pulled back into the woods, ensured the anonymity of their caches, and went back to town. They hoped that after an initial surge of interest, everyone would go on about their business, but it seemed the official-looking population increased on a daily basis. Charles and the locals talked about it. They all agreed Charles was not nearly as invisible as he had been, and the moment someone decided he was suspicious, it would not bode well for any of them.

It had gotten to the point that a French picket ship was stationed outside the harbor, looking for suspicious activity. So, Charles walked to Playa de Oro, Gold Beach, and keeping inside the tree line, got up to his cache. Meanwhile, some of the locals got a boat, loaded nets and supplies, and for all intents and purposes, were going fishing. A month later, the boat, carrying Charles and his "supplies," sailed into San Diego Bay, slipping past the town itself. They kept going up the bay, offloading Charles and his gold at the mouth of a creek. They wished him well, and sailed for home.

✡ ✡ ✡

Chuck was in a mode of "I Have No Mouth, And I Must Scream," with apologies to Harlan Ellison. He now had a handle on the infamous gold, and why he wouldn't have been eager for people to know where and how he'd actually gotten it. Big deal. From this point would be a narrative on how he made the long trek up the California coast. There were about eight years for Charles to accomplish that feat. Judge, defense is willing to stipulate Charles LaGrange did in fact make it from San Diego to Oregon. Chuck was beginning to feel light-headed. Was this is how it felt to die, while a vision, spider-like, sucked out the last of your vital juices? It didn't seem to matter. All the while, the story meandered on except for a time as Charles approached San Diego, when everything just stopped. It only stopped momentarily, but Chuck wondered if his body was giving out.

Charles dug a temporary cache, depositing the gold along with some other items he didn't think he'd need right away. He already knew this location would only be temporary. Then, he heard horses and voices further up the hill, and amended the use of this cache to no longer than absolutely necessary. Still, he wasn't going to take all that much with him now. Mainly, Charles took his good clothes, which had been packed ever since Barataria Bay, along with what he thought would be enough money for a while, and headed toward where he heard the noise. He found a road, or more to the point, a wide path, and followed it north. He kept his eyes on the ground, and, dressed as a pobre, was universally ignored.

There wasn't much traffic, but he kept his ears open, and found he was on the Camino Real, and it wasn't all that long before he got to town. San Diego was considered a major center for this area, even though the population was less than 800 people. Manzanillo was a major metropolis, relatively. The town was located at the base of a hill. Protecting the town from the top of the hill, there had been a fort. The fort was no longer protecting much of anything, having fallen into ruin.

Wandering around town, he noted there were some Yankee troops, but they seemed to keep to themselves, mostly. Keeping on the edges of conversations, he picked up additional news. There had been an earthquake in June. Earlier than the earthquake, around the New Year, there had been flooding that was bad in San Diego but catastrophic elsewhere, especially up around Sacramento. There were some concerns about a smallpox outbreak. Charles finally decided he'd heard enough, seen enough, and knew enough, to get by, and found himself a private place, where he changed clothes.

The vision stopped again without releasing him, and Chuck wondered if this was the end. The light-headed feeling went away, and Chuck considered this might not be the worst way to die. Then, however, he felt the vision starting up again. There was more torture for Chuck.

In his city clothes, Charles suddenly became visible. Not only that, he was a person everyone wanted to meet and greet. He got a haircut and a shave, and rented a room. He wanted a bath, but decided that needed to wait until after he moved the cache. That in mind, he rented a wagon, and headed back south. He drove around until a likely spot suggested itself. All the while, he was considering his options, and whether this might be a place to stop, at least for a while. He considered it nearly certain there would be coastwise shipping to San Francisco, and from there to Canada. On the other hand, he was now traveling a lot heavier than he had been.

If necessary, he could get a wagon, and drive all the way to Canada. There was much to consider, and perhaps he could stay here long enough to make an intelligent decision. From what he could tell, the war was still going on. He wondered how his family was doing, and whether New Orleans had suffered damage and death. He heard mail between the two sides was stopped, and in any case, Charles didn't dare try to send a letter since he was telling everyone that he was French.

In the morning, Melissa looked outside at the RV, but the privacy screens were still drawn. The poor guy was really tired last night, and must be sleeping in, she thought. She had watched him go out to the RV, and when she looked a few minutes later, his lights were out. That was a good sign to her, since he seemed to have to stare at a picture for a while for the visions to happen. At the same time, something gnawed on the back of her brain, telling her things weren't right. She thought about it for a bit, and the rational side won out, and she went to make some breakfast.

An hour later, there was still no sign of life at the RV, and she went outside and knocked on the door. There was no response. The bad feeling increased. She walked around the RV, and peered in a window. She was able to see enough to know he was not in the living or dining areas. She knocked yet again, and finally listened to her rational mind enough to give it another hour. At ten, she pounded on the door, and then tried the door. It was locked, of course. The doors to the cab were also locked.

Melissa wondered if it would be too forward of her to have Chuck leave a spare set of keys in the cabin "just in case."

By eleven, Melissa knew it was time for action. She knocked on the door. Then she pounded on the door. The windows in the little bedroom area were too high for her to see in, but she did have a stepladder. Up on top of it, she could see the bed, and Chuck was in it, flailing around, and seemed to be talking, though his eyes were tightly shut. The covers were on the floor, and he was nude. Besides that, he looked awful, almost like the old pictures of Nazi concentration camps. This was terrible! What could have happened?

She had to get inside the RV. Melissa pulled on the door handle, and there seemed to be a bit of give. She had heard these older models were often not all that secure. She remembered a pry bar in the trunk of her car, and hauled the ladder back to the house as she went to get her car keys. Melissa glanced around involuntarily as she took the pry bar to the RV. God knew what people would think if they saw this. She put the pry bar behind the flange on the door, and after some effort, the door popped open. She was greeted with some fairly rank air, going inside. Three steps brought her beside his bed.

He was jabbering rapidly, and after she tuned in to it a bit more, it was real language, predominantly French, but also Spanish, and an odd variant of English. Even as she watched, his flailing got weaker. She yelled at him, "Chuck! Wake up!" She slapped his cheeks, which were so sunken it made her cry to do it, but he did not respond. For reasons that escaped her, Melissa bent over and kissed Chuck. It had an immediate calming effect, but didn't last very long. She kissed him longer and deeper. The calming effect was more pronounced, though she also noticed his arousal otherwise. She also saw that his body, which had been soaked with sweat during the previous vision, was cool and dry now.

Could all this be him trying to get her in bed with him? As wasted as his body looked otherwise, that was hard to imagine. Speaking of which, how did that thought enter her mind? He was becoming agitated again, and she gave him a long, slow, penetrating kiss. His arms and legs relaxed, and Melissa turned around, and closed the RV door. Looking at him, her heart went out to him. Even while the rational side of her mind was asking if she was really certain she wanted to do this, she was undressing.

Later, she was lying beside him, stroking him as he was now fully relaxed and sleeping. She wondered if he needed medical attention, but had a feeling he would be all right. There was no way to know for sure, but these feelings had suddenly come in bunches, pushing her MBA rationality out of the way like a dust bunny in a hurricane. There was absolutely nowhere else she wanted to be at this moment, anyway. After a couple of hours, Chuck started to come around a bit, and she softly got up and into her clothes. By the time his eyes opened, she had heated a can of chicken noodle soup. She'd have preferred broth, but that wasn't in the pantry, and she wasn't going into the house.

Chuck lay there, just looking at the ceiling for a while. Then he looked over at Melissa, wonder in his eyes. "Am I alive?" he asked.

She nodded and smiled. Melissa propped him up in bed, and slowly fed him some of the broth from the soup. His eyes kept glancing from side to side, a smile slowly coming. "They're gone! The visions are gone, and I'm still alive."

Melissa shushed him and gave him another spoonful of soup.

"But you don't understand," Chuck continued. "The visions were controlling me. Ever since the first time, they were controlling me. Now, maybe, just maybe, I can control the visions."

She fed him some more. "What I can't figure out is what broke the vision, and how everything changed."

"I think I know," Melissa replied softly.

Chuck looked at her, a thoroughly puzzled look on his face.

6: California

"If you know how the vision was broken, why don't I know?" Chuck asked finally.

"Oh, you know. Think about it."

Chuck lay back and considered. "Well, Charles was just going around, into San Diego Bay, when the vision just sort of stopped momentarily, and started up again. A bit later, the vision stopped and started a second time, but, more slowly. After that, there was yet another stoppage. That time, it didn't really start up in as coherent a way as it had been. Finally, the vision stopped altogether. Now, I don't have to concentrate on keeping focus. The visions that were always running in my peripheral vision have gone, too. Then I think I slept briefly."

Melissa nodded. "I was pretty sure before. Now I'm certain. Oh, two things: You're moving into the house so I can keep an eye on you. Also, you're going to give me a spare key, so I don't have to break in here again to save your life. Make that list three things. You really should upgrade your locks. I broke in far too easily."

"Um. Duly noted. You saved my life? You broke the vision? How did you do that?"

"Examine the evidence, and listen to your heart, young grasshopper."

Chuck shook his head, absolutely mystified. There was one thing he heard from his heart– Melissa was still around. Hallelujah!

Melissa looked at Chuck and shook her head. "I'm going into the house. Get dressed, clean up your place, and get over to the house. If you're any more than five minutes, I'll be out with a club."

Chuck caught the tone, and replied, "Well, that's something to look forward to."

The following three days got Chuck rested, reasonably well-fed, and more questions about his motivations than he was accustomed to. He found he kind of liked it. In that time, he regaled her with the entire Charles L.F. trip. Well, it was the trip without the step at a time routine. Melissa immediately had questions: Was Charles married? Where was his wife? What about children? He was over thirty at the start of this odyssey. Also, Otto said he spent the last of the cache. Was there more than one cache? Might they still have something in them?

Melissa finally decided he could do a trial run. The vision would be for no longer than an hour. Chuck would go in, ask the predetermined questions, and get out. He was completely agreeable with that. She was about to go out to the RV to get the photos, and Chuck told her not to bother. Remembering how he fell into that terminal vision, he was sure he could call up the initial vision of Charles without it. Melissa considered that to be pretty scary, especially considering her entire plan was to protect him by separating him from the pictures. "I don't know for sure, but I think it will be a whole different situation from here on," he told her.

Chuck was just going to lean back sitting on the couch, but she had him lay on the bed. Further, she didn't want the bed dirty, so he disrobed, and crawled under the covers. Chuck could not imagine why she insisted on this specific approach. It seemed a little kinky, somehow. Melissa came in, and stood next to him, looking down at him nervously. She held his hand, and her other hand kept fiddling with the top button of her blouse, which he considered an odd nervous habit. He told her he was ready, called up the image of Charles in Harlan in his mind, and was in vision that easily. One difference he immediately realized was that he was still conscious of what was going on in the room in real time. The questions came, and Charles answered.

Yes, Charles said, he had been married. He had courted Madeleine in his late teens. She was from an old-line Cajun family, and everyone was delighted with the match. They were married in 1849, and had four children. Charles became a partner with his father in the mercantile in the summer of 1856. As part of celebrating the partnership, his father, Jean, gave Charles and his family a holiday at a hotel on an island just off the coast, a place called Last Island. They went in August. Three days later, a hurricane hit the hotel. The hotel was destroyed, along with everything on the island, and, indeed, the island itself. Charles barely survived, but his wife and children were all taken from him.

His family let him mourn for a year, but then began pushing him to remarry. Charles said his heart had drowned with Madeleine, but he began to court a lady anyway. That was late 1860. A couple of months later brought Secession, and the lady's family definitely did not care for his point of view. As for the gold, there were a number of caches, only one of which he ever made known to A.T. As far as Charles knew, the rest of the gold he brought from the Golden Gate, together with the other silver and gold, were still in place.

Chuck saw Melissa was getting really nervous, so he stopped the vision at that point, and was personally overjoyed when he was able to do it. He looked up at Melissa, and grinned. "Did I do okay?"

"Yes you did. Did you actually get answers? You weren't in the vision very long. Also, it didn't seem to have cost you anything, physically."

"I posed the questions we discussed and got answers. I was going to follow up and get the locations of the other caches, but I was also watching you. It looked like you were about to have a fit with that button."

Melissa realized what she was doing, and blushed. For his part, Chuck had no idea what brought on the blush, but he liked it.

Melissa checked him over, and decided he was no worse for wear because of this vision. On his part, Chuck didn't think it was any more of a problem, or stressful, or draining than going to the office. He thought that it was definitely less stressful than going to the office and getting fired. So they made a new plan. Right after he'd have a vision, they would discuss what he learned, and decide on the questions to ask the next time. After some further discussion, they decided to pursue the story starting in San Diego, and Chuck would go for the general idea rather than all the details.

Melissa kept a journal of the discussions, even though Chuck proved he could access any of the information at will. According to the visions, Charles went to work as a clerk in a mercantile. This enabled him to fit in to the community, and to keep up with news from all sides. This was January of 1863, and the war between the secessionists and the union continued. It astonished Charles how bitter the fight seemed to be. The French continued trying to impose their will on Mexico, but were only partially able to control the country. It did not seem safe for Charles to say where he was really from, so he said he was French, and spoke English with a French accent.

One day, when he was getting a little bit comfortable with his existence, one of the Army people came in. Charles saw stripes on his sleeve, and thought he might be a sergeant, but didn't really know. In any case, this Army guy instantly disliked him, and Charles had no idea why. For the Army sergeant, personal dislike evidently translated into conviction that Charles had to be a Confederate agent. Because of this, he questioned Charles endlessly, trying to trip him up. Charles saw several attempts to trick him into saying he wanted to create an insurrection.

A couple of weeks later, a French warship made a port call in San Diego, and Charles' tormentor went and hung out with the ship's crew for several days. This suited Charles, and he began to hope the Army guy might go on to other interests. Then, the day before the French ship was to sail, the Army guy came back into the mercantile, with one of the crewmembers in tow. The sergeant had the sailor start talking to Charles in French. Maybe he thought Charles couldn't actually speak French, which might prove him to be an enemy agent.

Charles, of course, spoke French, so the plan failed from that perspective. On the other hand, Charles didn't get along with the French sailor any better than the sergeant got along with him, and it wasn't long before they ended up swapping insults. The sailor maintained that if Charles were a real man, he'd have joined the French military to help increase the glory of the new French empire under their glorious Napoleon III. Charles responded, observing Napoleon III was neither glorious nor Napoleon, and that even the great Bonaparte couldn't control the slaves on a small island, and was forced to sell half of North America to finance his military misadventures. They continued on, the sailor insulting Charles' French, commenting that he not only spoke Popular French, the language of provincials, he didn't even speak that very well. Charles responded that the sailor only proved that even a sewer rat could be taught Standard French, the language of Paris.

It went back and forth for quite a while, all of it in French. Their interchange attracted a pretty good crowd, none of whom understood a word being said, but all agreed it was a hell of a show. The two were about to come to blows, which Charles would almost certainly have lost to the younger, larger, and stronger sailor. Fortunately, the store owner showed up, along with the French ship's Captain. The Captain hauled his sailor off, with apologies to the owner. The crowd dispersed, and the owner wanted to know why he shouldn't fire Charles. Charles decided he'd overstayed his welcome, and said he'd quit, if that was all right with the owner.

He bought a wagon and two horses, and got some lumber which he used to construct a false bottom in the wagon. The contents of the cache went in the secret compartment. Then he went back to the mercantile where he'd been working, and bought a good selection of trade goods that he thought he could sell north of there. He also bought himself some clothes more likely to blend in, and parted with the store owner on good terms. He allowed as how he might go to Sacramento, where they were still rebuilding after the flood, and headed north on the Camino Real.

Melissa had to bring Chuck back on task. Charles had long since specified he was not a pirate, and his story confirmed it. Lacking a pirate, they would be interested in some of the gold Charles presumably had stashed in the area. That is, of course, if that gold had not already been located. They were a century beyond where any of this happened, so the existence of the gold was questionable. Now, the details of local color were interesting, but could only be used to fill in between existing documents. Melissa admitted, though, the story was fun. The argument with the sailor in San Diego was a nice touch.

Chuck agreed to cast an even wider net in questions. If at some point, he needed to get additional information, it would be easy. Recovering time wasted on trivia would be impossible. They worked the questions as best they could, and began to feel they were getting the hang of this search technique. So, instead of the details of every little town where Charles stopped, Chuck was able to simply confirm that between January and August, 1863, Charles travelled north, looking at each town along the way. He would stay anywhere from a few days to several weeks before deciding the town wasn't going to work.

Late in July, he reached San Jose, in Santa Clara County. A week into August, he decided this was probably as good as it was going to get, and that he could survive pretty well. The fact that he was tired of being constantly on the move figured in the decision. He sold the goods in the wagon to a general mercantile store for a junior partnership. Then, he built a cache for the gold in the nearby mountains, and settled down to what he hoped would be a quiet life. He even dropped his French accent as best he could in an effort to blend in.

Between August of 1863 and spring, 1864, his concentration on staying out of the public eye appeared to be working. The only thing really bothering Charles at this point was not being able to let his family know that he was okay. He had known for quite some time that the Union had taken New Orleans shortly after he left, so mail delivery was possible. Still, nosy postmasters would have been the doom of his efforts to keep everything about himself quiet. In fact, such correspondence when he was keeping a low profile could have really stirred things up.

In spite of all his efforts, he became aware of people watching him. He tried to write it off to being overly sensitive, but the idea just would not go away. Finally, it became really obvious he was being followed. Specifically, there were two men he didn't know who always nearby, no matter where he went. So he became even more careful. It didn't help, though, because one afternoon, he walked into his room to find two strangers waiting for him. These weren't the same men who'd been following him. They were both seated, and each had a pistol in his lap. Charles got the impression of them as relaxing rattlesnakes.

"Is that him, George?" the one said.

"Yes sir, Captain. That's him. He and his family have a store in New Orleans, talking French, selling fancy stuff."

"Okay George," the one identified as Captain replied. He looked at Charles. "Do you care to call my man George a liar?"

"I guess not."

"There's a wise man. I am Captain Ingram, CSA, late of Quantrill's Raiders. You've heard of us, I presume?"

"By the letters CSA, I'm guessing that 'C' must mean Confederate. As for Quantrill's Raiders, lots of people say lots of things. It's hard to know the truth of it." Charles was temporizing, trying to figure out how to live another day.

"We've watched you. You've been staying low, trying to keep out of sight. You're pretty good, but not as good as my guys. Congratulations. You've just been drafted into the Confederate Army, known around here as the Knights of the Golden Circle. If you don't follow orders, notes will appear in various places about how you are a Confederate spy. I guarantee the Union Army will take those notes very seriously, and they won't hesitate to stretch your neck on the nearest gallows."

With that kind of encouragement, Charles saw little recourse but to join them.

When Chuck reported all this to Melissa, she started working her computer, finding that a Captain Ingram claiming to have ridden with Quantrill's Raiders did in fact organize a robbery theoretically in support of the Confederacy. As far as she could tell, it had not all been recovered. So maybe this was the additional gold and silver Charles alluded to. They agreed this would be a point that could stand some extra detail from Charles, and it might clear up a detail of history, if only in their own minds.

✡ ✡ ✡

Ingram had said only that Charles should await his orders, so he kept to his normal routine. He noted in the newspaper that someone named George had been shot by persons unknown. Shortly after that, Ingram showed up in his room again, this time by himself.

"Here are your orders," Ingram told him. "You are to act as though you are not in the KGC. In fact, it is important that no KGC member knows about you."

"That's except for George?"

"Ah, George, That was a pity, wasn't it?" Ingram didn't sound in the least sorry. "Now, we must speak about your part. I've followed you long enough to be quite certain you have a cache hidden somewhere in the mountains. Frankly, I was going to let you donate it to the cause, but I couldn't find it. This tells me you are quite good at erasing all evidence of your cache. Now, my lads in the KGC are as loyal as any, but they might be tempted to wander from the straight and narrow by the sight of too much filthy lucre.

"We are going to relieve the Union of some of its unneeded wealth, and use it to finance our beloved Confederacy. Initially, my troops will create hiding places for it. Then, I will come back and together, you and I will ride out there and move the funds to more secure locations until arrangements can be made to ship it south. After you have helped me secure it, you and your cache will be free to go, and both the Confederacy and I will be eternally grateful for your services."

Charles considered it far more likely that he would die as soon as the last cache was closed, and considered he'd better follow his own course.

Ingram was obviously talking about a robbery. It was public knowledge where KGC meetings were held in town, so Charles watched the place, and noted the ringleaders ride out of town after the meetings. He got his wagon, and followed carefully. He discovered they were on a ranch not far from his cache. They must have picked up on him not long after he placed it.

He kept an eye on the ranch, and finally watched the group head out to the east. By that time, it was hard to tell who was actually running the gang called an army unit. Charles unloaded his cache, having decided he wouldn't be back. He was no tracker, but a blind man could have followed this bunch. They were headed for Sacramento, but they were trying to stay off the roads, so he was able to keep them in sight, at least often enough to reassure himself he was still behind them. When they got near Sacramento, they circled around, and headed east, finally camping outside Placerville.

Charles went on into town, and stayed at a hotel. He heard some folks still called the place "Hangtown," which didn't sound propitious for Ingram and his bunch. The next morning, he rented a horse, and took the wagon and horse on east. When the country started looking rough, he found a spot to hide his wagon, and took the horse on ahead. Further on, he saw that he was catching up to them, so he went off the road. Leaving the horse at the bottom, he carefully and quietly climbed up a ridge.

He watched them rob two stages. Being this far away, he couldn't hear much, but it was still prime entertainment. The gang split afterward, and Charles was most attentive to where they put the booty before hightailing it away from there. He continued to watch for the next act of the show. The stages predictably had run on to Placerville as quickly as possible, resulting in all available law enforcement coming back with the intention of doing justice. The posse halted briefly at the site of the robbery, then continued east.

When the coast was clear, Charles collected the horse and his wagon, and drove up to where the loot was buried. He transferred it to the wagon. That's what Ingram ordered him to do: transfer all this 'filthy lucre' to a more secure site. Well, Charles would follow orders. Ah, Ingram not being in on the new location. Well, now, if George's end was a pity, then this must be more of a shame. Unbeknownst to the authorities, the treasure arrived in Placerville a few hours behind schedule, in a weather-beaten wagon driven slowly by a dark-haired fellow who looked like he only wanted to be done with his journey.

Hanging around town, Charles heard about a deputy getting killed, and a number of the gang members having been rounded up. Watching as they were brought in, he saw that Captain Ingram was not among them. The newspapers estimated $3,000 in silver on the two stages. Charles knew what he picked up, and it was way, way more than $3,000. There seemed to be no lack of liars in this country. On the subject of his personal safety, Charles knew that while Ingram was on the run now, he'd almost certainly be back, especially with the money involved. He'd never know who helped himself to the loot. Still, if the face of Charles LaGrange showed up, Ingram would no doubt want to have a very long chat.

Where could he go? Charles already knew things didn't really suit him further south. San Jose wasn't healthy for him, as several of the gang had gone back there. East of him was both the ongoing war he'd been trying to stay away from all this time and Captain Ingram, the person he specifically wanted to avoid. West of him was the ocean. That left north, the direction he'd been heading ever since Manzanillo. Oregon was the next spot he'd heard about. Maybe he would try that. It was now July, 1864. From all reports, the Union was going to settle the argument on their terms. Maybe then, he could go home.

Melissa put Chuck in her bed the first several days while he recovered. She still had him do the visions lying in her bed, thinking that if she had to take extreme measures again, it would be easier. To her surprise and chagrin, she found that she was actually looking forward to such extreme measures. It was most embarrassing when Chuck, now be in control of the visions, observed she was playing with the button on her blouse.

The bad, long vision had Chuck looking like he had been starving for months. Fortunately, his digestive track had not been impacted in that fashion, and he was able to eat normally almost immediately. She was careful to enforce a three-hour break between visions, and tried to use at least an hour of that time to get Chuck exercise of some kind.

They would go out for walks, and she would challenge him to throw a rock or stick further than she could (or would).

He came back faster than she thought would happen, but it was hard to say what might have been injured in that near catastrophe. His clothes just hung on him, but he claimed he was feeling as healthy as ever. That may have been so, but she was quite certain his stamina couldn't be up to where it should be. While Chuck was actively doing the visions of Charles, Melissa would rest on the couch as best she could. She was also enforcing at least eight hours of down time for Chuck, and after a couple of days was seriously contemplating joining him in bed.

The story about the Bullion Bend robbery got her attention, and she was researching the event. As was the case with most of the vision, while what Chuck brought back from Charles might not necessarily contradict documentary evidence, there was no real way to confirm it, either. Chuck told her about Otto's mason jars full of money, and had been straightforward about thinking the whole vision-thing was imaginary until he physically located the jars.

Studying the Bullion Bend information, Melissa concluded that, considering Charles could not lie about it, there was obviously treasure being shipped that was not official, and maybe not legal. The most likely scenario was an inside job. So Charles had made off with treasure hidden by thieves who had stolen it from thieves. Charles seemed to have nailed it with his observation about there being no lack of liars in this country. Also, she agreed with Charles' thinking that going along with the Ingram plan would have gotten him killed. Still, as it turned out, Charles could have ignored the whole thing, and lived his life in San Jose. What few reports she found indicated Ingram went to Missouri. Even though most of the rest of the gang lived out their days in California back around San Jose, evidently only Ingram knew Charles was involved at all.

Neither of them saw much point in further visions of Charles. He went to ground in the Harlan area, and married Minerva Lillard, according to him, at the insistence or at least encouragement of her brothers. It was not a happy marriage, and he bugged out after having two children with Minerva. His son was evidently sickly, and Charles didn't go too far away, supporting himself and his son. The trail to a pirate in the family tree evidently led next to New Orleans and Haiti, which before the slave revolt, was the center for French privateering and piracy in the Caribbean.

As they went for walks, conversation turned at times to the way many cultures had cults devoted to the dead, and how it was possible, and perhaps even likely, that these cults had a basis in reality. It was reasonable to consider that people throughout history found this thing that Chuck and Melissa were calling visions. Further, people like Chuck, who had experienced these visions, might themselves become extra special resources for those who knew what questions to ask.

Chuck brought up the point that most of Otto's stash had been spent, and perhaps they should tap into at least one of the Charles caches. Melissa questioned his motivation, noting that most of the money had gone on the RV, and was spent before he even left Tucson. Chuck just grinned and did a shrug with a flourish. Melissa wondered where he learned that. It looked like something from Italy or maybe France. It was likely, she reflected, that living in someone else's head for that many miles, habits would rub off.

Remembering Chuck jabbering in different languages, she tried to recall some college French, and commented on his gesture in French. Chuck automatically answered in French. She phrased a second question in French, inquiring how long he had studied the language. His immediate response was that he had never taken French in school, never studied the language, and found what little he knew of French pronunciation utterly incomprehensible. "And might I ask, in what language did you make that comment, sir?" Melissa asked with a grin. Evidently, a vision of a person gave not only that person's thoughts, but the means by which the thoughts were expressed, namely language.

Later, they decided to go ahead and get the locations of all the caches, to see if any still existed. They were spending very little money in Blodgett, but New Orleans was likely to be another situation altogether. This time, in a demonstration of his control, Chuck just leaned against a tree, called up Charles, and got the location and situation of all seven caches, including the presumably empty one used to support A.T. and Otto. He did that while Melissa held up differing combinations of fingers, and he mirrored the combinations of fingers back to her.

"See, I did it!"

"Well, now that's assuming you were actually in vision at that time."

"We can go to the places, and see if something is there, or at least was there. That will prove it."

"That's also assuming you hadn't already gotten the cache locations, and were just shamming here."

"I'd have to be a real rat to do something like that," Chuck protested.

"Thou sayest, Monsieur Rat."

At that, Chuck launched into an extended oration in French defending his integrity, and calling on all of his noble ancestors to witness his innocence. Melissa couldn't really keep up with the speech, but was getting the gist of it, anyway, and finally burst into laughter.

7: The Girl, The Gold

Back in the cabin that evening, there was a lot of cuddling and no visions. Chuck still gave no indication he knew how Melissa had broken the "terminal" vision. At the same time, Melissa couldn't imagine that Chuck didn't know, at least at some level. All of the time and emotional support given so he could explore how his ancestor of the same name had tap danced around the Civil War had to have its reward. She thought he was, basically, a good person, and probably capable of doing any number of things. Further, it didn't seem to her that he was putting on an act, at any level.

Meanwhile, Chuck was certain good fortune had decided to hit him on both sides of the head. Tonight, he was with a girl who thought he was okay, and tomorrow he might be quite wealthy. Oh, yeah, and all of a sudden, he was trim and even reasonably fit. Memories of the kind of person he'd been were rapidly fading. Andrew Tyra lived his entire life from part of one cache, while Charles had lived the last half of his life from it, and enough was left to give Otto a running start. Six more caches, and if Ingram couldn't find a cache Charles had near San Jose, maybe nobody found these caches around Harlan.

The next morning, they found a guy in Blodgett willing to lend them a tow bar, and they hooked Melissa's car to the RV. They locked the cabin, and told the owner (the lady running the store) they'd be away for a while. Chuck gave her an extra month's rent, just in case. Then they were off to Harlan. One of the locations wasn't that far from the hamlet. They drove slowly, Chuck peering all around, and occasionally stopping to confirm their location, and about five miles out reached what seemed to be the right spot. He carefully checked for anyone in the area.

Finding the spot was difficult, Chuck told Melissa, because the forest had grown up a lot, making the outlines of the hills really tough to make out. Also, there was erosion and everything else that happened with time. Melissa agreed, remembering comments from early settlers about the hills being covered with ferns, the result of a fire some years before the settlers came. Still, as far as he could tell, everything seemed to be right, except they needed to go toward the hill. They took two backpacks, a shovel, and a mattock, and slowly went in the indicated direction. Every few steps, he would check their position. At last, they were there. Such was Chuck's hope, anyway.

"If this works, it'll sure beat any old pirate map with an "X" marking the spot." Melissa observed, as Chuck started to carefully cut the sod.

"If no one beat us here, this will work, and I can personally authenticate the source," Chuck replied. "Anyway, you like seeing me do this, since you want me to increase my exercise."

"Here I was, being so subtle about getting you to work out. You're just too smart for me."

He took a ground cloth out of a backpack, laying it flat. Then, he removed the sod, and carefully laid it in order on the ground cloth. The area he'd chosen to excavate had, to Melissa's eye, absolutely nothing to distinguish it from anyplace else around there. He then dug out the subsoil, laying it on the ground cloth beside the turf. Melissa wondered if she was watching Charles rather than Chuck, or whether Chuck was running the show with knowledge from Charles. If Charles was in charge, how would she know? After a time, she had to admit there really was little way to know, although his reversion to French seemed awfully automatic.

Chuck struck rock after about one and a half feet. Melissa thought the whole effort was in vain, watching the shovel scraping across a rather large rock. In spite of that, Chuck didn't even slow down. He continued the careful removal of dirt, finally disclosing the rock was just slightly smaller than the hole he'd dug. He then stuck the blade of the mattock along one side, and pried it up, like a manhole cover, disclosing the fact that the rock was not all that thick.

With a fair amount of effort, Chuck and Melissa got the rock out of the hole, and on top of the dirt. Beneath was a rock-framed cavity with multiple golden glints. Chuck knelt down and carefully examined the contents. Finally, he whispered, "It's all here. The cache is untouched." He brought out a gold bar, marked 100 troy oz. Then he reached for another. There were four such bars.

"Talk about your nest egg," Melissa said. She did some fast math. "At $1,300 an ounce, these are worth over $500,000. Actually, last I heard, gold was higher than that."

"We're not done yet," Chuck said, as he brought out gold coins, silver coins, and a nice collection of what appeared to be Civil War era paper money. The items went into the backpacks, which they took to the RV. Following that, Chuck and Melissa replaced the rock and the dirt, following with the turf. On the way back to the RV, Chuck brushed the area with the ground cloth, including footprints around the RV. When he was done, Melissa couldn't tell anyone had ever been there.

They drove on, and finally got back to the highway by a different road than through Burnt Woods. They had already discussed the next step, which was to go to Eugene, where they thought they might sell some of it. On the way, a thought occurred to Melissa, which she held back for a while, but finally asked anyway. "So, Chuck, what are you? Are you an heir? Are you a miner, like Charles claimed to be? Are you a thief? If I'm going to hang out with you, I need to know, so I'll know what role to play."

Chuck was silent for a few minutes. Finally, "Well, I guess I'm all three of those things, and maybe more besides. My official public position has to be what I told them in Tucson: It's a legacy. I was just able to discover or decipher the directions. Digging it out of the ground makes me a miner. I haven't a clue who owns the property where we found it, and we certainly didn't get permission, so that might make me a thief."

Melissa smiled. "Well, at least that makes you an honest thief. Would you give it back?"

Chuck thought about that a while. "Who, exactly would I give it to? Who has more right to it? The landowner? The successors to whoever owned the SS Golden Gate? The stagecoach company? An insurance company? Nah. Probably not."

☆ ☆ ☆

"Okay," Melissa responded, nodding. "I'll hang out with you some more. Not having Elliot Ness after us is helpful in that regard. I've never fired a tommy gun, anyway. That your basic public position is that it's a legacy sounds about right. As it happens, some of my extended family fell into old money not long after I got my MBA. I hardly knew them while I was growing up, but they decided I was now a financial wizard and I should help them out pro bono. Well, I helped them, as best I could, and although the situation was way less than this, the general principle should be the same. Your tax basis would be your ancestor's basis, which is to say zero. I guess you could make a case for a basis of the value of the metal in 1870. The tax rate on precious metals is, as I recall, 28%. That still leaves you 72%, which isn't bad. It's not bad at all."

They checked places in Eugene, and were able to sell a fair amount of the smaller items. For the bullion, they were given a few names of places in Portland that might be able to handle a transaction of that size. Still, they got enough cash to make it a nice day, and after looking around a bit, found a hotel with a room overlooking the Willamette River. When they got to the front desk, Chuck came down with a sudden case of nobility, and asked if they should get one room or two. Melissa gave him what he thought was an extremely strange look, and asked him why they needed two rooms now.

In the room, Chuck admired the view, and how nice everything was, even while a voice in the back of his head was commenting that it should be nice. He'd just paid more for a night than he used to pay per month. Melissa told him he should go check the security of their stuff, which Chuck already knew was about as secure as it could be, seeing they'd unhooked Melissa's car, and parked it so tight to the RV that the two vehicles were almost touching. She also said he should go for a walk along the river for an hour or so, as she had some things to do that couldn't get done properly with him under foot. So, off he went.

It was a strange and rather insecure feeling, being without her beside him to keep him on task. Chuck leaned against a railing, looking at the river going by. His mind, no longer needing to stay focused to fend off unwanted visions, and undirected by Melissa, began to wander. He began thinking about all the great things he could do with this money. He imagined getting a really nice place for Aunt Millicent and Irv, and how much they would like it. He imagined buying the old home place in Tucson, tearing down the great ugly apartment edifice in the back, and returning the house to its former glory.

His feet started walking, as he imagined buying the M&A company, with the sole purpose of firing everyone he didn't like. He went on to imagine actually doing all the things he told people he had done, and actually going all the places he'd claimed to have been, and imagined doing all of it first class. That would be great. Actually having a pilot's license, and able to fly a multi-engine aircraft and a jet, and maybe get ten thousand hours. Oh yes, the possibilities were endless. Then all his imagining started to shake apart as he shivered, and realized it was getting dark.

He realized at that moment the one thing he hadn't been imagining was Melissa. He didn't have to imagine Melissa. She was real. She said maybe an hour, and he'd been lost in his daydreams for nearly four hours. This was awful. He started walking back to the hotel, only then realizing he had gone quite a distance. He walked and walked, and shivered, and worried that he'd messed up the one good thing in his life actually helping him to be somebody.

Finally, he got back to the hotel, and hurried to the room. In the room, he saw a table, set with candles and a white tablecloth, and two chairs. The candles had gone out. A magnum of champagne was on the table, mostly gone. Melissa was on the bed, in a sexy negligee, sprawled out, evidently asleep. Glancing back toward the bathroom, he saw a plush bathrobe. She'd organized quite a tête-à-tête, and Chuck managed to mess it up big time. He staggered against the wall, with a kind of dry sob, realizing the enormity of what he'd done.

There was an easy chair and ottoman near the window wall giving access to the balcony. He planted himself there, and gazed at her in the moonlight, wondering what on earth he could do or tell her that would make up for this. He thought maybe getting out of the terminal vision hadn't been a blessing after all. Maybe it would have been better for him if the vision just sucked him dry and let him go. Then he thought maybe the vision had not let him go. Maybe it was a vision within a vision, that let him see how totally pointless and futile his existence was. After that came the thought of there being no visions. He'd gotten an overdose of something, and was actually expiring in a back alley in Chicago. Good things never happened to him, so he only imagined being in Oregon. Finally, darkness closed around him.

☆ ☆ ☆

Chuck thought and hoped the darkness marked the end for him. There would be no more awakenings. He was almost looking forward to it. Then, without explanation, a flash of light stabbed his unwilling eyes. He opened them to see a reflection of the early morning sun in a mirror. As his eyes came into focus, they beheld an empty bed. Well, it wasn't completely empty. He slowly rolled out of the chair, went to the bed, and looked at the note on the pillow. It was from Melissa, and all she wrote was, "Chuck - I have to get back to the cabin. There's work I have to do. Melissa"

The bed was cold. She'd been gone a while, maybe quite a while. Maybe she hadn't been asleep at all when he came in, and was just waiting for him to go to sleep so she could leave. He checked the parking lot, and found, not surprisingly, that her car was gone like it had never existed. He wandered around the hotel, and looked up and down the street going from it without seeing her, though he really knew he wouldn't. He alternated between panic and depression, with depression eventually winning the contest.

He thought about the breakfast which was of course included with the room, but couldn't stand the thought of food. Actually, the smell of the dinner from the previous night he hadn't touched made him nauseous. So, he finally loaded the few things he had in the room, and checked out. He nearly lost it when the front desk clerk hoped he'd had a pleasant stay. The clerk no doubt thought he was a head case, and at the moment, he had to agree.

Out in the RV, he half-heartedly checked that the gold was still in the tiny wardrobe. At the moment, he thought it would serve him right if it was gone. If Melissa wanted it, he'd have loaded it in her car. Turning around, he noticed her necklace on the bed. She hardly ever took it off, but removed it when they got the tools to excavate the cache. He remembered her saying it was a keepsake necklace, and had to do with her grandmother Sara Jane, whose great-grandmother Sarah Ann Fuller was their common ancestor.

Holding the necklace, Chuck's depression deepened. He seriously thought about heading for Blodgett. He also thought about throwing the gold in the Willamette River, or handing it to some homeless person. He finally decided Charles used it for his family. So Chuck could keep his act together for a day or two, and follow the plan. He'd haul this stuff to Portland. It was a long, sad drive. He was near the edge as he came up on the exit for Corvallis, but he managed to keep the RV going.

In Portland, he spent several days talking and negotiating, trying to ensure he got the best deal, and doing everything possible to keep from getting ripped off. The amount of his transaction was so large, his customer wound up being a consortium of organizations. In addition, the IRS was there, palm upward to accept their just due, though they'd done absolutely nothing to earn it. Melissa was pretty much on time with her estimate of what the taxes would be. The paperwork seemed endless. Being the recipient of most of the required forms and other dead trees, rather than the generator of it, was not all that huge an improvement, actually.

When all was said and done, he had bank accounts in several Portland banks, all close to the FDIC insurance limits. He had both debit and credit cards, along with hot and cold running bankers eager to have his business in any way, shape, or form. He had become everybody's darling, and discovered he couldn't care less. The only thing he bothered doing for himself was to buy some clothes the right size, and even then, he just got some jeans and outdoor-style shirts at a big box store. Investment counselors were lined up to give him advice about how to best use the funds, but the prospect of dealing with it just pissed him off now.

There was one expense he was going to have to deal with presently. That was the RV. He'd been parking overnight at truck stops, and the generator was becoming increasingly uncooperative. There might be other issues with the little rig as well. Chuck guessed he'd like Portland a lot if he'd been in a passable mood. In the right company, he was sure he'd love it. But as it stood, there was absolutely nothing in Portland he cared about. Now he had to deal with the saddest thing he'd ever have to do, which was to return Melissa's necklace when she would most likely invite him to slide it under the door, or else leave it up at the store.

Still, the day was getting on, and if dealing with that task in the daylight wasn't bad enough, trying to cope with it in the dark was definitely more than he could handle. Darkness, Chuck thought, intensified emotion, and the combination of darkness and hate was not a thing he could drive into.

✲ ✲ ✲

With the generator's functioning becoming questionable, Chuck went to an RV park. His was about the humblest rig there, which wasn't of much consequence; except for finding his spot was between two behemoths, whose owners were standing in his assigned spot, debating features on their coaches. They looked at him, jointly sniffed, and moved away. Chuck considered that if they didn't care for the neighborhood, they had wheels, and could move. He'd only be there for the night, and found he had absolutely no desire to go run with the breed of dog they represented. So he hooked up utilities, and went back inside.

It occurred to him it wasn't that long ago when he would have made himself the center of that conversation. He couldn't imagine bothering with it now. It came to him there was truth in the old saw that those who had nothing to say always seemed to be the ones saying it loudest and longest. Evidently, he'd made some personal progress. Nearly dying could do that, he supposed. Still, he hadn't progressed enough to hang on to the one thing that could make a real difference in his sorry ass life.

Speaking of which, (and on what other subject did he even want to speak?) there was something approaching a religious ceremony he needed to do. Whenever he was driving, Melissa's necklace lay in the middle of the bed, with a seat cushion on it, to protect it. Now stopped, he needed to put it back in its place of honor, hanging toward the cab on a wall where he could see it even when he was laying in bed. He carefully removed the seat cushion. Then, he reverently picked up the necklace and carried it forward to the hook that previously held a cheap picture. Chuck's palms tingled from contact with it.

He sat in the dinette, staring at the necklace, considering this was the last night it would hang there. Tomorrow night, it would be back on Melissa, where it belonged. Chuck knew he'd be lost without it as a reminder of her, who he'd already lost forever. There was one thing he could do, though. He could take a picture of it. He made small adjustments in it, so it would be just right, and then he took a number of shots from every angle he could imagine. Loaded on the PC, he tweaked the pictures just a bit, and printed some of the best shots.

Sitting there looking at the pictures, and comparing the pictures to the actual necklace, Chuck found himself going into a vision of Melissa. That, of course, couldn't be, because you could only get visions of direct ancestors. Then, he thought about the fact that Melissa had visions of Phosa. In any case, there she was, wearing the necklace. Still in shock at seeing her, or at least the vision of her, he started out asking her name, and heard, "Melissa Ann Duncan." Yes, it was her voice.

He obviously had not intended to be in this vision, and had no questions prepared. He wasn't really sure he could have come up with anything sensible in any case. Chuck recalled that general, open-ended questions had gotten him into terminal results, but then considered if he had a terminal vision of Melissa, there couldn't be a better way to go.

So, he simply asked about her experience with him, and found that she had been studying him from the moment they met.

When he was trapped in the vision with Charles, she had been thinking about him, and later worrying about him. Then she was doing everything she knew or could conceive of, to save him. There were her impressions of his wasted body. Then there were the increasingly passionate kisses. She was quite certain he had to be aware of their lovemaking on some level. He considered maybe he had been aware of it, but swiftly convinced himself it was all a fantasy needing to be kept in a corner, and only brought out in case of cold, lonely nights. He couldn't imagine it happening in real life. Her embarrassment at his noting that she was playing with her button was crystal clear now.

He understood now about her relief that he recovered from the nearly terminal vision, and her distrust of his claims that he now could control them rather than before, when the visions controlled him. While he was pursuing Charles through California, Melissa was pursuing what made Chuck tick; resting little, and continually reassessing her observations. Chuck thought he did okay on analytical work, but Melissa was an analytical machine on the one hand, and a very caring, feeling, emotional person on the other hand.

She didn't have the necklace on going to Eugene, so he couldn't ask the vision about any of that. Still, he could now piece it together. Melissa had committed to him, and set up the romantic rendezvous to celebrate their being a couple. She had trusted him, but he betrayed that trust. Chuck recalled someone coming back from a seminar, and quoting the speaker as saying that trust is earned slowly, but can be completely lost due to a single misstep. Listening to his better angels was not his strong suite, obviously.

It was clear, now, what he had to do in the morning. When he returned the necklace, he had to find some way to let her know. Okay, he had to let her know what? That he was an ass? She already knew that. He had to let her know that he knew it as well.

And then?

And then?

And then nothing.

Melissa would go on being wonderful, and, he hoped, get everything she deserved.

For himself, nothing. He'd been a dishwasher pretending to be an executive big shot. Now he was a dishwasher who happened to have a wagon load of cash. Big deal. It was time to get dishpan hands, and let the world go on its merry way.

☆ ☆ ☆

Chuck was up with the sun the next morning. He tried to be careful getting everything ready for the road, but his mood was favoring the "move it!" side. He had no idea why there would be a rush to arrive at what promised to be the unhappiest moment of his life. Nevertheless, there he was pulling out before there was any activity in the coaches on either side of him. He hoped they would appreciate his efforts to improve their view. Actually, he didn't hope that for more than a moment as he inched out from between the titans, craning his head trying to get enough visibility to not get smacked by other early birds.

The necklace was, of course, back in its place of safety for the drive. Chuck had no illusions about what would happen if he had a problem, but putting it on the bed with the cushion to protect it made him feel better anyway. Once he was on the highway, and had gotten into somewhat less dense traffic, he replayed the vision, knowing he'd replay this vision any number of times in the days, weeks, and years to come. It somehow seemed appropriate. The best moment of his life happened while he was unconscious. More than that, it was the moment that literally saved his life.

When he got to within a mile of Blodgett, he pulled over and picked up the necklace. Sighing as he carried it up to the driver's seat, Chuck tried to console himself with a saying that made the rounds on the internet: you shouldn't be sad about it being over, but that you should be glad that it happened. Comfort like that, he thought, is only effective long after the event. In his case, maybe it never would be. Still, this was something he had to do, so he might as well get on with it. He took a big gulp of air, swallowed a sob, and pulled back onto the road.

Pulling up to the cabin, it felt like he'd come home, even though he knew he'd be gone again in a few minutes with his tail between his legs. Chuck made sure he had a good grip on the necklace, and stiffly got out of the cab. As he closed the cab door, he heard the cabin door open, and there was Melissa. Surprising Chuck, she didn't look mad. She looked concerned and maybe hopeful, though he figured he was ascribing emotions to her out of his own need. Suddenly, he found himself rushing toward her, and saw she was coming to him.

"I didn't know!" they both said in unison, and both began talking at once. They both stopped, and then laughed.

Melissa asked, "Can I have my necklace back before you squeeze it to death?" Chuck gave it to her, and helped her with the clasp.

After that, he just kind of blurted out what he'd discovered about the necklace, together with his foolish walk in Eugene. He knew she could never forgive what he'd done, because it was beyond forgiveness, but he wanted her to know that he realized what an ass he'd been.

She responded, "Sweetheart, I don't think you're an ass. Well, not now, anyway. When you disappeared, I felt sad, betrayed, angered beyond words. I was awake when you came in. Watching you in that chair, looking so sad and vulnerable about broke my heart. I thought about staying, but ended up leaving because it seemed so hopeless. Back here, I was still mad, but I was mad at myself, kicking myself that I hadn't read the situation better, trying to figure out what I did wrong. Finally, I thought I might as well get some sleep, but the result of lying on the bed was to have a vision of you.

"You really didn't know how I saved you. I must admit I asked your vision some other things, as well. Anyway, I thought, or at least hoped you'd be coming around. Now, it's a fact that you're a bit screwed up, but I think I love you."

Chuck looked at her in wonder. He'd come expecting a confrontation and got reconciliation. More than that, she seemed to be a vision of herself, beautiful beyond belief. His mouth was dry, but he managed to stutter, "I do love you."

They went into the cabin, after a while, and discovered a whole new world of lovemaking. Looking in each other's eyes, they found themselves having a joint, present-tense vision. There was no past or future or anywhere else; there was only here and now. When, finally, they were through, neither had to ask or even wonder whether, or how good it was for the other. Each of them had the vision of the other's experience in addition to their own experience.

Later in the day, they went out to "their" spot to watch the sunset. Chuck thought that anything with Melissa was wonderful, but all of a sudden, he thought maybe watching sunrises would suit him better. The end of the day can be breathtaking, but at the moment, he thought beginnings more closely matched his style. He hadn't actually said anything, but Melissa had been in vision with him. She playfully punched his arm, and said, "Sunrise might suit your style better, but are you sure about getting up that early? Are you tough enough, buster?" Then, hand in hand, they wandered on back to the cabin.

8: New Orleans

It was several days before either of them cared to think about much beyond the moment. Interest in the past or concern about the future faded away when the present was all-encompassing. It was inevitable, however, that some subjects would come up eventually. It started with observing they were almost out of food. The last groceries came when Chuck arrived at the store. They finally drove down to the supermarket in Philomath, and when they passed the museum, Chuck related his experience causing a traffic jam there. Melissa said both the museum and genealogical society were excellent, and that she had been in both places.

On the way back to the cabin, they talked about what they might do next. Melissa still thought she'd like to see New Orleans. Chuck thought that would be just fine, and wondered if they should pursue the family history while they were there. Melissa definitely thought they should, so Chuck offered to question Charles in vision to find out where the family store was located, on the off chance it might still be there, and he could then use it to get visions of some of the rest of the family.

Getting the address (actually it ended up being a description of the location) was a relatively simple matter, but when Melissa looked up the location, she found the building no longer existed. The Louisiana Supreme Court building now occupied its former site, along with the rest of the block. They then discussed going there, taking pictures, and seeing if he could get a vision. Chuck got another idea, and in vision had Charles give him a mental picture of the building, which had the store on the first floor, and living quarters on the upper floors, typical of structures in the neighborhood. The problem was that Chuck had minimal artistic ability, and his drawings were not usable.

Another of Melissa's talents showed up then, as it turned out that she was an excellent artist – she said that she was okay, but not that great. Chuck maintained she was equal to the masters. Melissa suggested Chuck get an eye exam. Nonetheless, she went into vision with Chuck, and Chuck gave her the mental picture of the place. Melissa said drawing it was simple at that point, almost like tracing over a photograph. When she was done, Chuck saw a place typical of the pictures he'd seen of the French Quarter, with red brick construction accented with what he thought of as wrought iron pillars supporting a balcony.

Chuck got nervous at this point, considering the possibilities of another terminal vision. Because of that, Melissa had him get undressed and get into bed. She got in bed with him, "just to be safe," and looked into Chuck's eyes as he attempted to get a vision from the drawing. The vision came more easily than he expected, and in short order, he was looking at an older man, whose features marked him as clearly related to Charles. This was clearly not the usual vision, because where the individual viewed would ordinarily be indifferent to his presence, this individual turned and looked back at Chuck.

"What is your name?" Chuck asked.

"I am called Jean LaGrange, son of Philippe," the man replied. "Which of my children gave you birth?"

Chuck nearly stopped the vision then and there. Nobody in a vision questioned back. They couldn't. This must be a whole new thing. Melissa told him to continue.

"I am descended from Charles, who left New Orleans at the beginning of the Secession, and headed for Mexico," Chuck replied. "Can you see me?"

"Yes, but only your face. You do have some of the look of Charles. But I can see a woman's face with you. Is she your wife?"

Chuck smiled. "She is my wife in spirit now, and soon in the eyes of the law as well." Chuck felt Melissa's smile.

Jean LaGrange smiled, as well. "You do well. I like the look of her, too," he said. "She looks like a good addition to our family. All the more, since I've never heard of a woman able to use touch stones."

"I appreciate that. You are the first person in the family to learn of our betrothal."

"I am honored, and I am overcome with joy, to finally learn that Charles survived the war. We had hoped he would contact us after the war, at least. I tried to show him how to use touch stones, but his wife persuaded him using such things were against Holy Ordinances. Tell me, what sort of touch stone did you use to reach me, and how did you obtain it?"

Chuck related a bit about how he used photographs, and a very little about Charles' adventures. "It would be better, though, if you simply used my mental picture of Charles (and Chuck showed Jean what he used). You can get as much detail as you can stand. I would guess you're aware of the dangers of these visions taking over your consciousness."

"Yes, I am aware. It is good that you know, as well. I find it humorous that you use photographs as touch stones. Charles' wife loved to get her photograph taken, and would have been horrified to know they could be used in such a way. She might have had a different opinion if she used touch stones herself."

"Charles told a story, a fable I have now discovered, that he had been a pirate. Charles in vision tells me that he wasn't, but his grandfather was a pirate. Is there any truth here?"

"My father, Philippe, sailed briefly with Lafitte. Tell me, are you considered a large man?"

"No, I am considered not quite average height."

"Ah. Some aspects of breeding stay true. As you know, then, the entire LaGrange family is slight in stature, and the physical requirements of such a life were more than he could handle. He knew Jean Lafitte, and was known by him. Our family has had contact continuously with the Lafitte family and organization since before I was born. In fact, my father named me after Jean Lafitte."

✲ ✲ ✲

"What year are you?" Chuck asked.

"It is now 1870. The war over the secession has been done for five years. What year are you? And what descendent of mine are you?"

"I am in 2011. I am the fourth great grandson of Charles, which makes me your fifth great grandson."

"You are so far into the future! That's more than 140 years. Has mankind been perfected?"

"There have been all manner of clever gadgets invented, many of them concerned with improvements in how people kill each other. Up to this time, at least, mankind's tendency toward procreation has outpaced its tendency toward self-destruction. Earth is becoming somewhat crowded."

Jean shook his head. "Some want to think things will become so much better. Obviously, things only change. That's too bad, but for the race to become perfect by the end of the millennium there would have been changes I could have noted in my lifetime. That is such a pity."

"Well, we haven't destroyed ourselves so far. I don't know about being perfect on Earth, especially, but it doesn't appear we've gotten worse. At the moment, I think there's hope."

"I'm glad to hear that," Jean replied. "If Charles had returned, he would have had the business. Speaking from his future, I am hearing that he will never return to New Orleans."

"Not as far as we know. He might have left Oregon, except a son from his forced marriage was sickly, and he stayed in the area to do what he could for him. That son did eventually marry, and had a single son of his own."

"Charles was honorable, then. That is good. As I said, Charles would have inherited the business. Now I know he survived the war, and did some good things. At the very least, he was not among those who were attempting to kill their fellow man. Perhaps I can use your method to understand more of my son. You have done a very good deed, and I must reward you. I will establish a trust, perhaps leading to a corporation, and I will capitalize it appropriately. You can consider it my marriage present to the two of you."

"Isn't this changing the past, or something?"

"Not in the least. The only person doing changes is me, and I am doing them in the present. The Bible commands us to provide for our families, and that is all I am doing. What I will do is to establish "Jean LaGrange & Sons." What you will do is to journey to New Orleans in the stead of Charles, my son, in order to claim your marriage present."

"How will I identify myself to the trustees, or whoever is running it?"

"Can you recite your chain of ancestors?"

"Well, I am Chuck ... Charles, actually."

"So Charles is coming home. That will be wonderful. Proceed."

Chuck took a mental breath, and started again, feeling like he was reeling off biblical 'begats.'

Jean then repeated them back, exactly as Chuck had given them to him. Then he continued. "I will also have Jean LaGrange & Sons safeguard my touch stones. I have touch stones for Philippe, Gaston, and

Jean Baptiste. You have found ways to use touch stones that I had not imagined. Frankly, I never thought it possible to have a two-way conversation in this fashion. If I'd known of it, Charles would have never left New Orleans without the means to do it as well."

"It may be his failure to get in touch had as much to do with his situation as anything else. Nonetheless, you will have to decide yourself as you view his life, whether his motivations and actions had merit. In all honesty, I did not view the part of his life that would have included when he might have contacted you."

"You are saying wise things for a person so young."

"I have no idea where the words I just spoke came from. It certainly has nothing to do with any wisdom on my part."

"Regardless, use your ancestry, starting with yourself, and ending with me. That will be your password."

Chuck agreed, but had a question. "What did you do that enabled us to communicate like this?"

"I was thinking about Charles, and about what might have been his fate. I was thinking that I would like to know before I die. Then you appeared, just as easily as that."

Then Chuck saw purpose firm Jean's face. "Thank you so much for the news about my son Charles. Contact me when you get to New Orleans, and let me know what you find." Jean's face morphed into an incredible leer as he said, "I shouldn't keep you, seeing as how the two of you are in the midst of your honeymoon."

The vision faded, and Melissa snorted. "He is an old fraud! 'I can only see your faces.' Ha! He was having a peep show the whole time."

Chuck laughed. "It looks like being a dirty old man is in my DNA."

Melissa giggled, pushing Chuck over. She straddled him, and started tickling him furiously. "That's only if you live that long. I distinctly heard you telling him that we were married in spirit, and you hoped we'd soon be married in the eyes of the law, as well."

"Did I say such a thing?" Then, as he fended off increased tickles, "Well, if I said it, I must have meant it."

"So are you proposing to me, Mr. LaGrange?"

Chuck relaxed and caught his breath as he gazed at Melissa and smiled. "Yes I am. Melissa Ann Duncan, will you marry me?"

She suddenly jumped off the bed. "What? You're proposing while I'm here without a stitch of clothes on? Whatever will the children say?"

Chuck laughed, and jumped up after her. She ran behind the couch, and kept it between them as he tried to catch her. She suddenly acted like she saw something on the floor, and Chuck caught her. As he lay her on the bed, she whispered, "Oh please be gentle, sir. I'm just an innocent girl, I am."

✲ ✲ ✲

"The computer says we should go this way?" Melissa looked at the routing, and Chuck stared over her shoulder.

"Well, it's all paved, and it's pretty much a straight line, landing us on the Interstate not far from Boise. It doesn't seem that bad."

"Not that bad? Do you know what's out there? There's lots of desert. There's lots of bad desert. Our ancestors, our common ancestors, nearly died in that very desert. That is a bad place."

"Okay. But didn't you also tell me a lady in the family did a reenactment of it at the age of 80, and in period dress? I'm sure people drive it all the time."

They left the cabin and Melissa's car, and started driving east in the RV. The country did become more arid as the sun got higher. Finally, it was the real deal, reminding Chuck of his drive north through Nevada. According to the computer, they should arrive in Boise in time for an early dinner. Long before that, however, Chuck was getting an object lesson on the subject of Melissa's premonitions. The RV started running rough and losing power. It always had problems with grades, and now they had to make multiple attempts to get over what should have been fairly easy ascents.

They ended up spending the night in the same Malheur desert Melissa had worried about. Once they were in the situation, however, complaints from Melissa evaporated. She was totally focused on their resources, and what they needed to get to Boise. "Okay, we've got full tanks of water. We've got plenty of food. We're actually most of the way through this desert. We're going to make it." She had him pretty much fired up, and ready to take care of business. Then there was the generator. Chuck was muttering to himself. Do you remember the generator you didn't get repaired? Yeah, Chuck, we're talking about that generator. Well, Chuck, you genius, it ran for all of ten minutes after a hard start, before it proceeded to seize up altogether. In the words of the immortal

Lee Sherman, Chuck, "You're smart enough, but you just aren't using it right. I hope you're able to figure it out someday."

So, there was no power overnight. In spite of the primitive conditions, they made it to the morning, and Chuck got the RV moving once more. It very nearly achieved the definition of a committee: the unwilling, led by the unknowing, to do the unnecessary. The RV fully made the unwilling part, and Chuck qualified for unknowing. But as for unnecessary, no: it was extremely necessary they get out of this desert and on to Boise. Where yesterday, they were mostly looking forward to a meal cooked by someone else as their reward, now all Chuck could think about was getting this thing running again.

As it turned out, Chuck got to focus on an RV repair for quite a while, as it was afternoon when they finally limped in. Melissa had long since decided where they should go, and had called, so the place was expecting them. She had even set up for a tow, just in case the RV died totally. For a while, it looked like the tow might be necessary, but they kept on going, with only the prospect of a two-hour wait for a large tow truck keeping them from parking it and waiting. They managed to coax it on in, with a reception committee to take it off their hands. The owner, who was also the chief mechanic, took one look at it, and shook his head. After a half hour, he came to them bearing news.

"The entire chassis was snake bit from the beginning. The reason you got this cheap is because the maintenance snowballs after only a few miles. These power trains seem to be a combination of various low bids, none of which have ever been allowed on the road, and absolutely should never have been put together. Frankly, I'm amazed it's gotten this far."

Chuck told him what the mileage was when he bought it, and what he paid for it.

The owner shook his head. "Spending a few minutes on the internet did not make you an expert. It only qualified you to get ripped off. And you did get ripped off. Some salesman saw you coming, and made damn sure you only looked at units that would lead you to think this thing was your best bet."

Chuck nodded. "You're exactly right. But if there's no way to become a subject-matter expert, then I'd have to learn who I can trust. That leads me to wonder why I should trust your statements."

The owner smiled. "Well, actually, you shouldn't. You don't know me. Still, I'll tell you this flat out: if you want me to work on your rig, I can get it running. It might even get you wherever you're going, although there's no way to guarantee even that. For me to get it running is going to be expensive. It will be very expensive. Finally, when I'm done, you'll still have a piece of junk."

"You wouldn't be making this speech unless you've got just the solution for me."

"Actually, I don't. Frankly, the closest thing to a solution for you may well be to call a taxi and go to the airport. I do have a rig that would do anything you need to do. It's been sitting behind the shop for a while, the result of a corporation paying me in kind for working on their equipment. Frankly, the unit is way more than you'll either need or appreciate, but I could show it to you. I'll tell you right now, though, it won't be cheap."

Melissa had been observing the conversation closely, and when he glanced at her, she gave him a "Why not?" so they trooped around to see it. At a glance, it looked like a Class C, same as what he had, but this was larger. The cab looked like something off a semi that had been reduced in height, and the rig was quite a bit longer than the RV. Overall, it had the appearance of a person who was extremely wealthy, dressing in plain clothes custom-made for them by a tailor. It was a statement like, "Look at me. I'm so rich I can afford to dress plainly. None of you nouveau riche need apply here."

The owner opened the door, pointing out dual awnings, and the deadbolt door with combination lock. Melissa specifically approved. Inside, there was granite everywhere possible. The owner opened the slide outs, and showed them the king-size bed, and satellite TV that could be used while in motion. It seemed a transportation company had purchased it for executive use, but had downsized radically and instead used it to pay for truck maintenance. His information was that nobody had ever taken it out overnight. His cell phone rang, and he excused himself to take care of an issue, but told them the price as he left.

Chuck had a thought, watching the owner leave. Okay, this thing was expensive, but Melissa looked right in it, and they had the money. The question, as the man said, was trust. Was this rig, impressive as it looked, any better than what he had, which was unquestionably junk. If visions worked with Melissa, could he use visions with this owner? Chuck focused, and presently had a vision of the owner. Chuck asked him for the truth about the rig, and the vision gave him some minor details that were questionable, but said it was one of the most solid units he'd ever seen. Chuck also asked the vision what he'd really take for it.

While they waited, they looked at everything, sat on the leather sofa, checked the TV, and bounced on the bed. The owner finally came back, apologizing for the delay. Chuck shrugged it off, and proceeded directly to the minor details he'd learned about in the vision. As expected, that got the owner's undivided attention, especially since one of the points would have involved a detailed technical inspection underneath.

"A little birdy tell you, did he?" the owner asked, smiling, but clearly reevaluating the situation.

"More like straight from the horse's mouth," Chuck replied.

"Or a reflection thereof," the owner finished.

The owner had a sales sheet with him, and Chuck wrote the number the vision had given him. "That's what you'll take for it, and that's what I'll offer," Chuck said.

The owner looked at it and nodded. "While I was checking your RV, I was checking you, too. You're the real thing. We've got a deal."

They brought it around and parked next to the RV. Chuck and Melissa moved their things in. The owner plugged them in for the night, and took them home to have dinner with his family. After dinner, they exchanged notes on how they used visions. Later that evening, they went back to sleep in their new bed. Well, they slept some.

✲ ✲ ✲

In the morning, they had a leisurely breakfast, trying out the kitchen. Everything worked as advertised. Somewhat later, the owner showed up, and gave Chuck some driving instruction. Chuck discovered he needed all the instruction the owner was willing to give, and commented several times about how his concerns about driving something that big had sent him to the smaller RV. The owner just smiled, and advised Chuck the little RV was there for the taking, assuming he could get it to go at all.

Finally, his comfort level got to where they went out on the street, and practiced intersections, corners, and getting through tight places. It turned out the owner had been a trucker for a number of years before starting his truck repair business, and had trained his share of drivers. He further claimed a number of them were less proficient than Chuck. Chuck told him he was glad for the vote of confidence, but frankly thought the owner was stretching the truth considerably. Chuck added that he was speaking as a professional in the area of truth stretching. The owner commented that being able to tell jokes and continue driving meant he'd passed the driving test.

Finally on the road, Chuck went fairly rapidly from trying to get some level of comfort driving the big rig to astonishment at how bleak it was going across that part of Idaho. Evidently, there was green down along the Snake River, but the highway went nowhere near any of that. After some grassy areas as they went into Utah, they got into salt desert. It all made Chuck think maybe that run from Las Vegas to Reno wasn't so bad after all. Getting into the Salt Lake City area, traffic kept him so occupied that he wasn't even thinking about the scenery. By the time traffic thinned a bit, they were heading up into mountains, and even saw a few pine trees. It had gotten late, and they were both tired, and a roadside rest area gave them all the excuse they needed to pull off for the night.

The next day, they got out of the pines almost immediately, it seemed, and Melissa gave Chuck geography lessons, courtesy of their joint ancestors who had gone this same general route, heading the other way. Those folks managed twenty miles on a good day, mostly on foot, to save the oxen and cattle used as modes of propulsion. It almost seemed like they were cheating, rolling along at seventy-five miles an hour. Melissa took over driving periodically to keep Chuck fresh for what lay ahead.

The computer claimed their best route lay in going south from Cheyenne, and bypassing Denver. Melissa again declared the computer was out of order, and their best bet was to continue into Nebraska on I-80. Unlike the shortcut in Oregon, however, Melissa didn't seem to have any specific premonition. She simply didn't want to go that way. Chuck flipped a mental coin, and again decided to go with the computer. Melissa didn't argue further. She just sat there, obviously tense and unhappy.

Chuck again decided he should listen to Melissa more often. It turned out the computer didn't tell them a few crucial bits of information. First was the bypass, while it avoided the city center, was still well within the heaviest traffic zone. The second was what they would find to be the definition of heavy traffic in the Denver area at what some people called "rush hour." There was absolutely no rush to it. They turned on a radio at one point to hear jokes about the "I-25 Parking Lot." Fortunately, their route turned off I-25 before it got to that part. In spite of Chuck's best efforts to get into tight situations, they survived the ordeal, getting past some fender benders and a couple of vehicles that ran out of gas.

Finally on I-70, going past the airport, they discussed the fact that if they had caught a plane in Boise, they'd have been in New Orleans already. Still, Melissa commented, Chuck now had a real feel for a good piece of the Oregon Trail. Chuck was relieved at how Melissa's normal upbeat mood was returning. Heading across the eastern Colorado plains with a Technicolor sunset in the mirrors, they both started wondering whose deadline they were trying to meet. They were not professional truckers, and there would be no welcoming committee in New Orleans. In fact, there was no telling what was in New Orleans, if there was anything at all.

Having reached that conclusion, they called a halt in Limon, Colorado. Neither of them felt like cooking, so they parked at a truck stop and ate at the restaurant. The food wasn't bad, and was certainly filling. Later, Chuck reflected that if they'd been at the same place in the little RV, they'd have been disturbed all night, as trucks came and went. This rig was big, and pretty soundproof, and the king-size bed was very comfortable. Still, he had strange dreams of pirates, slave revolts, and trudging across endless deserts trying to keep up with a wagon train which just kept getting further away.

The next day, considering his dreams and Melissa's stories of the previous day, Chuck reflected that whatever was going on now was still better than an ox cart in northern Mexico. It was also better than those times he (as Charles) had to portage across areas of Texas coastline. It was certainly better than the experience of Charles in California, with his wagon heavy with gold, trying to encourage a couple of weary horses over one more hill. It got down to his body knowing what to do and doing it, while his mind was just kind of experiencing a blur. Melissa said he was driving well, though he didn't think she qualified as an unbiased observer.

The time went by without particular notice, although it kept getting greener and warmer until it hit a maximum of green and warm, and transformed into wet combined with hot. The rig's air conditioning did manage to keep up with the load, and TV reports started featuring speculation about this year's hurricane season, and how forecasts for this year compared with the year that saw Katrina. It seemed like everything involved wind and water. Up in those deserts, there was wind and no water. Here, there was sometimes wind and often too much water.

Speaking of which, Chuck suddenly realized they were on I-10, physically driving over Lake Pontchartrain.

They went past the airport, and turned into a street lined with motels serving the airport. They decided it was time to give the rig the night off, and checked in. They told themselves it was so they'd have a base of operations to figure out where "Jean LaGrange & Sons" was located, assuming, of course, that such a thing existed. If not, they could get a rental car from the airport and go enjoy New Orleans. In celebration, Chuck scooped up Melissa, and carried her over the threshold of their motel room.

☆ ☆ ☆

What things they figured they'd need in the room were piled on a motel baggage cart, and Chuck scurried out to bring it in after trying to carry Melissa all the way to the bed, and stumbling just before he got her there. He did manage to get her onto the bed as he went down on his knees. She pivoted, striking a queenly pose as he was feeling stupid. "Thou doest well to grovel in my presence, varlet," she told him. "Now go attend to my baggage train."

A few minutes later, she was getting her laptop plugged in and turned on, and Chuck was paging through the hotel phone directory.

"Huh. Lookee here, Melissa. Jean LaGrange & Sons, Inc. They put it under 'J.' I guess that would be because it's the legal name of the corporation."

Melissa was not to be outdone, however. "Okay, smartass. Here's their address and phone number. The map link shows the location downtown. Where does your link go?"

"It goes back in the drawer. But I found it first."

Melissa stuck her tongue out at him, and the wrestling match was on. Later on, Chuck called the front desk to inquire about parking downtown. Their rig was currently a prominent element of the parking lot, and the front desk clerk advised that parking was marginal where it was, and somewhere between "really better not" and "nonexistent" downtown. Chuck was duly thankful for the vote of confidence, and told the clerk that in exchange for such great advice, they thought they would stay at least one more night.

The next morning, Chuck called the number for Jean LaGrange & Sons, Inc. A receptionist answered the phone, and Chuck asked, "Is this the Jean LaGrange & Sons that was founded in 1870?"

"Yes sir, it sure is. Can I help you?"

"I certainly hope so. My name is Charles Louis LaGrange, though everyone calls me Chuck. I need to talk to someone about my family tree."

He heard a gasp, and the receptionist stammered, "Can you hold for just a moment, sir?"

After a couple of minutes, a man's voice came on the line. He seemed cordial enough, but a good deal of suspicion and perhaps a touch of fear seemed evident to Chuck, although he couldn't think where that feeling came from. Chuck took a deep breath, and asked, "Would you be interested in my ancestry?"

"I might be, if it is of the right sort."

Chuck took an even deeper breath. "Okay. Well, as I told the receptionist, my name is Charles Louis LaGrange. My father is Jack Edward LaGrange. His father was Kenneth Otto LaGrange, whose father was Otto S. LaGrange, whose father was Andrew Tyra LaGrange, whose father was Charles L.F. LaGrange, whose father was Jean LaGrange, who founded this company as a marriage present to me."

There was a moment of silence. "Jean LaGrange left a handwritten note in 1870 with a list of names, and the message that someone would show up in 2011 claiming those names as his ancestry. All shares of the corporation are in your name." The suspicion was still there, but the fear had overwhelmed it.

"I am told that my coach might not be able to park in your area. I'll get a rental car, and stop by after a while."

"Oh, that wouldn't be appropriate. We'll send a car to pick you up at your convenience. If you could give me your location, we'll have transportation there within the hour. Will there be anyone with you?"

Melissa and Chuck were a bit concerned when he got off the phone. Neither of them had any clothing appropriate for the corporate world. With a car coming in less than an hour, about all they could do was to get cleaned up. Suddenly, Melissa brightened up. "You don't have to look professional. You don't work for anyone. You're the owner. It's up to them to look professional. If you show up looking casual, you're only demonstrating how far you are above the rat race."

"You are right, as always. Still, if we had business-grade clothes, we'd wear them."

"Transportation" turned out to be a limousine. The driver came into the lobby, and asked at the front desk, who pointed to Chuck and Melissa. He was not at first inclined to deal with them, but after Chuck produced his driver's license, the driver led them outside. Inside the limo, presumably for the purpose of conversation, or, more likely, to determine what they were up to, was a man who identified himself only as Armand. Their destination was what appeared to be a high-end office complex, though, as Chuck well knew, such an address and profitability often had little to do with one another.

They were escorted directly to a meeting room, and shown to seats at the head of the table. Armand turned out to be the managing director, and had been the voice on the phone with Chuck. A series of briefings commenced, concerning how Jean LaGrange founded it in 1870, capitalizing it with $10,000, and leaving instructions for how the company was to be managed up until the recipient and owner should appear in the year 2011. All investments were conservative and long-term, with an additional intention of keeping the corporation's profile as low as possible. Current valuation of the corporation was more than $100 billion, even after several down years.

A substantial binder was brought out and given to Chuck. They said it summarized the operating results for the corporation for the 140 years. They also brought him a corporate credit card. As the owner, anything he used it for was considered valid company business.

Chuck thanked them for everything they had done, and advised he would get back to them after he had a chance to review the books. Melissa whispered briefly in his ear, and Chuck nodded. "Isn't there something else you've been holding for me? It might be a box, or maybe even a bag of some kind?"

Armand's finger tapped rapidly on the table several times as he chewed on his lip. There was wide-eyed silence around the table. Armand finally got up and left the room. When he returned, he brought a small carved wooden box in one hand, and a key in the other. A second person brought in something looking like a sample case. The documents went into the sample case. Chuck casually admired the box for a moment, verified the key opened the lock on the box, and after glancing inside, placed it in the sample case as well.

Armand and his people then did their best smiley face routine, which reminded Chuck of the old joke of what the top monkey in the tree saw when he looked down. He was mindful of the rest of the joke, of what the monkeys lower down saw as they looked up. The merry group took Chuck and Melissa on a VIP tour of the offices, which turned out to be the entire complex. Chuck and Melissa both noted a lack of friendly interaction between Armand's group and the bulk of the organization. Further, there seemed a tendency on the part of Armand's group to try to keep conversation between Chuck and a number of staff personnel to an absolute minimum, although obviously they couldn't forbid it.

9: Family Business

Armand rode back to the hotel with them. As they got out, he gave Chuck a corporate smart phone. He said the phone already had everyone in or connected with the company. Chuck thought the timing of that presentation was odd, along with the absence of anything personal in their conversation up to that point. Chuck stopped as he was getting out, and asked Armand his last name.

"Why, my last name is LaGrange, of course. What did you suppose it would be? We are cousins, after all." They were cousins? In addition to their being cousins, Armand presumed Chuck already should have known. That was astonishing information, and made the lack of any family or personal conversation even more interesting.

The driver dutifully followed with the sample case as Chuck and Melissa strolled to their room. The driver looked around the room, as though trying to decide on the appropriate place to set his burden. Chuck shook his head and told him to just leave it on the desk. The driver sort of saluted, and left.

"My," Melissa said. "The driver's attitude certainly changed from when we first saw him."

"I believe we're seeing fear rather than respect. He appears to be Cousin Armand's puppy dog. For some reason, Armand is afraid, so his driver is, as well. I think the driver was, among other things, scoping us out. They are trying to figure out our agenda."

Melissa pulled the document out of the sample case. Paging through it, she observed, "It looks like they're trying to overwhelm us with data. That's a possible indicator of them trying to hide something."

"Meanwhile, we get to deal with a major fortune that, according to the records, has been growing for 140 years, but did not in fact exist a week ago. What in bloody hell are we supposed to do with this?"

"Well, it's not that major. The company isn't such big potatoes on the world scene. Now, I'll grant you're suddenly ahead of Carlos Slim and Bill Gates. However, since Fortune magazine doesn't know about you, it's not official. If Fortune doesn't know about it, then it didn't happen. Also, the corporation is generally referred to as JLG&S, for your information, and has been since the 1950's."

"JLG&S." Chuck tried out how it felt on his tongue. "JLG&S sounds like a municipal utility company."

"That may be part of the plan, actually. It doesn't appear many people have ever paid the company any mind. It's of course closely held, namely by you, with widely diversified investments that appear to be world-wide. JLG&S does not have significant holdings in any one company, keeping outside scrutiny to a minimum, as well. I see an exception to the 'no significant holdings' rule, but that's been the situation for a lot of years."

Meanwhile, Chuck opened the box, and was examining the touch stones inside. Each had a custom-made slot, for its specific shape. The first was a flat stone on a rawhide thong, with the name of Jean Baptiste LaGrange engraved on it. Next was an ivory carving like a rook chess piece, with Gaston LaGrange on it. Third was a pyramid-shaped copper item identified with Philippe LaGrange. The final item was a piece of carved wood in the form of a sunburst. There was no engraving, but its association with Jean LaGrange was evident. He wondered what he would find in these four touch stones.

Melissa quickly got down to cases. She found a number of times where the corporation invested in names that later became really big. Curiously, they usually sold the stock just as the price began to really move up. She was beginning to get a feel for it. JLG&S had first-rate talent, and was capable of nearly astronomical growth. However, if they got too big too fast, that would attract unwanted attention.

A great deal of work went toward reducing their down-side risk, and it appeared they had nailed it. Corporate growth just continued sailing at a steady pace, whether the economy was good or bad. Even the great depression didn't change the rate of growth very much. While Melissa knew the last few years had been difficult, there hadn't been anything that should have been able to slow, much less stop this massive freight train of an operation. In addition, profitability began to flat-line before the current economic problems began. She was about to start delving into the source of that when the shiny new corporate phone buzzed.

When Chuck figured out how to answer the thing, Armand was on the other end. Dear cousin was now doing his utmost to be genial. It came across hollow to Chuck's ear. Armand said when his wife heard Chuck and Melissa were in town, she insisted on them coming to the house for dinner. He said he wouldn't take 'no' for answer. This comment came even though Chuck hadn't given any indication he would decline. Oh, and the car would be by at six o'clock.

Melissa wondered, when Chuck told her the substance of the call, whether they should have been getting clothes instead of analyzing the books. Chuck sensed she was throwing up a straw man and replied that their priorities were exactly right. "As you pointed out," Chuck told her, "it's up to them to impress us, not the other way around. What we're seeing comes from the fact that he and his paycheck can be made to go away."

"That's undoubtedly part of it. I'm seeing a few things in these books. Somehow, I don't think they were expecting anyone with real expertise to show up right away. Between us, we may be able to dig a lot further into the company than Armand might expect. We need to be careful, though. He's been running things for a while, now, and we need to stay alert for whatever booby traps he may have laid for us."

Since their getting ready would mostly just be walking out the door, they spent a little time playing like they were filthy rich. Although, since they were filthy rich, they no longer had to play at being anything. "So what sorts of things do the really, really rich want to do?" Melissa asked.

"I have no idea what they might want to do," Chuck replied. "I only know what I want to do with you."

☆ ☆ ☆

In spite of their best efforts, Chuck and Melissa were in the lobby when the driver showed up at precisely six p.m. He made no effort at conversation going to Armand's place, but did ensure he let them out of the car like royalty on arrival. Armand's house looked like a palace to Chuck. If the intent was to impress, this place definitely did that. Chuck whispered to Melissa as they walked up to the front door, "We need to find out how much we're paying this guy."

They were half-expecting a liveried servant to open the door, but were greeted by Armand's wife, Madeleine, who was dressed like she was receiving the queen, and obviously, even to Chuck, intended to make their 'honored' guests feel just as shabby as possible. Since it was just the two couples, they were seated for dinner not long after they arrived. Chuck was not at all familiar with society, and found a good deal of discomfort as it became evident he was expected to say something trivial and light. He finally came up with an appropriate light subject, he hoped.

Addressing his hostess, he said, "You have a beautiful name. Interestingly, in my study of the family tree, my ancestor Charles L. F.'s first wife was also named Madeleine. That's quite a coincidence, don't you think?"

Madeleine became pale, as she stared at Chuck, and she nearly dropped her fork. Armand finally spoke up, "More of a coincidence than you could imagine, cousin. My Madeleine is a great niece of that Madeleine, and was actually named after her. The thing is, nobody told her until after we had announced our engagement. It's very odd that you should have brought up the subject."

"Not all that odd. I've noticed family lines seem to cross every few generations. Still, there was no intention to shock anyone, or cause discomfort, and I do apologize."

"Apology accepted, cousin. Why don't we go into the library? I have some very fine brandy."

So it was that Chuck left Melissa to comfort Madeleine, and followed Armand into the library. This would be a major test of Chuck's intestinal fortitude, since he didn't smoke, and brandy was a long way out of his league. Nevertheless, he endeavored to hang in there. Chuck asked Armand if he used the touch stones, to which Armand replied he did use them, though perhaps not all that often. Chuck then asked why he covered for his wife like he did, since anyone exploring the family history had to have known that fact, and the tragedy of it.

Chuck noted Armand's eyes darting around. "Ah, yes, it was terrible, the way she died in the war." Except, the moment Armand said 'war,' he glanced at Chuck, and saw he just failed a test, and instead of finishing the word, suddenly had a coughing fit and excused himself. When Armand left the room, Chuck immediately did a vision of Armand, and from the weakness of the vision, could tell Armand did not have very much contact with this house. Chuck asked the vision why Armand feared him, and was told he was certain Chuck would "end my good thing."

Chuck asked a second question, "Do you use the touch stones?" The answer came, "I used them twice. I don't dare let Madeleine know even about those two times, since she equates anything outside her experience with voodoo." Chuck considered the two Madeleines had more in common than their name. "Why did you use them the two times?" Chuck asked the vision. "I had to use them to prove that I qualified to be the Managing Director. The most important job of the Managing Director is to ensure the company is run in accordance with Jean's wishes, and the touch stone ensures it happens."

Armand came back into the room at that point, and Chuck dropped the vision. He thought he had enough for the moment, however.

"I imagine you must be tired after today," Armand said jovially, in an obvious move to change the previous subject.

"Ah, yes, I am, actually. I want to tell you, though, while we have this private moment, that knowing the family tree, I understand the need to keep a low profile. My impression, at the moment, is that you are managing the company pretty much along the lines that Jean would want. I will, of course, go to Jean for counsel from time to time, and compare his counsel to your results. Still, you should know that I will support you just as long as nothing gets out of hand."

Armand got all oily and obsequious. "Oh, as you can tell from the books, everything is exactly in order. You can come in and examine everything you like, whenever you like, because everything is in order. Yes sir, everything is exactly in order."

Chuck had put down the cigar when Armand left the room, and never picked it up again. He put down the brandy snifter, and allowed Armand to guide him toward the door. Chuck didn't need a vision or a lifetime in high society to discern those reassurances meant exactly the opposite. He also made himself a mental note that with Armand patting him on the back, he needed to check for daggers. He walked into the front hall to see Madeleine and Melissa exchanging farewell pleasantries.

☆ ☆ ☆

They watched Armand and Madeleine wave as the limo pulled out of the circular driveway. Out on the street, they kissed with open eyes, joining each other's vision, and found their separate impressions of

Armand and Madeleine largely matched. Being certain the driver was Armand's stooge, they said very little on the way back to the motel. When Chuck got out, he made a point of shaking the driver's hand and gaining momentary eye contact. Chuck had plans for that eye contact.

In the room, Melissa explained, "I know we're doing real communication when we vision each other. Still, though, I just don't feel like we've really exchanged points of view until we do it verbally."

"I have no problem with that," Chuck responded. "Armand basically pisses me off, because he is the same kind of person I've just quit being. Or at least, I'd like to think I've quit being. He lied to the company to get the Directorship. He lies to his wife about using the touch stones. He lies to himself because he doesn't see himself as the asshole he really is. It wouldn't irritate nearly so much, but he's managed to be successful at it."

"He only looks like he's successful. His wife spends money like there was a "use not later than" date on the currency, and that date was today. She's kind of ignorant, on top of it. All the while, she's quite certain of her arrival in high society, even while whining about how they are never invited to the really quality affairs. By the way, she's terrified of you, and has talked herself into the notion you must be a voodoo priest, and must be the reincarnation of Charles L.F."

"Well, I walked in his shoes far enough to look like his reincarnation. Now, I'm no expert on such matters. Still, being an anglo voodoo priest might well be a first of some kind. Shouldn't I be sacrificing a chicken about now? Or maybe a virgin. Yeah, a virgin would do. I'll pick you."

Melissa sidestepped his grab. "Not so fast there, mumbo jumbo. I've got some accounting jive talk to do here on these twice-cursed books. Your thought to cross-check Armand's salary with his house is an interesting exercise. In the past, the policy was for company executives to stay in homes owned by the corporation. Armand bought his own house. More interesting, he bought it for cash about six months after he became the director. And, no, his financial statement prior to that shows nothing like enough assets to get that house, and his wife has no personal source of income."

"There wouldn't happen to be any correlation between his becoming a director, and the sudden lack of profitability of the company, would there."

"There would only a perfect correlation. The company shows a growth rate that makes it double every six years, and they kept the rate year after year, rain and shine, boom and bust. So, lessee, that's about $420 million a year that didn't happen. In addition, he authorized the company to acquire this one outfit. It's the only time the company has purchased more than a 2% stake in anything. It was owned by Armand's father. It was profitable, actually, but Armand's father wanted to go fishing, so his dutiful son caused his father's burden to be lifted from his shoulders."

"Nice. Of course, that immediately elevates JLG&S visibility."

"Naturally. There's a note here talking about a move by the legislature this session. If it passes, they'll require public audits of large private enterprises. The idea is to ensure private enterprises are in fact paying their share of taxes."

"Beautiful. That would put audits of the company out in the public eye. What are we doing about it?"

"I'm looking. There doesn't seem to be much. Legislators are suddenly concerned the company has changed its game plan, and might now simply buy a good part of the state."

"Okay. Well, I promised Jean that I'd contact him after we got here, and let him know what's up. It may be he'll have some words of wisdom for us."

Chuck considered using Melissa's sketch of the store, and then realized all he had to do was to visualize Jean LaGrange. First, though, he wanted to confirm a thing or two about the driver. Chuck found his memory for faces had improved dramatically, and he was shortly in a vision of the driver. The driver was Madeleine's nephew, earning a six-figure salary driving the limo. While theoretically a chauffeur, his real job was to record what his passengers said, and give the recordings to Armand. Chuck considered that quite a racket, sounding more like a gangster's operation.

Then, in vision with Jean, Chuck related what they found so far. Jean considered the situation for a bit, and while he was thinking, wondered if Chuck's clothing was an example how men of affairs dressed in that age. Chuck admitted it wasn't, and promised to correct the situation presently, but it was what they wore in the woods. "In any case, I'm dressed better than the way you saw us last time." Jean laughed, and said he tried his best not to look, but, well, he was a man after all, and Melissa was very comely. Chuck thanked him, and said he'd pass along the complement. Jean just shook his head.

Finally, Jean seemed to have come up with a plan. "You know, it is a sad thing when family members cheat each other. Here's what you should do: set up Armand in his own company, without mentioning what he's already stolen. Whatever capitalization you give will be less than he's already stealing. Armand will have to pretend to be grateful. Also, perhaps you can make a deal with the legislators. You could offer to get out from under that company he bought, if they will vote against this measure, or at least amend it sufficiently so we can get back on an even keel."

"I'll have to make sure Armand's allies go with him. Most of them were probably in the board room. They'll give themselves away, one way or another."

✲ ✲ ✲

The next morning, Friday, Chuck had an idea. If he could vision people he didn't know just by eye contact, and if he could vision someone by focusing on a picture of where their house used to be, why couldn't he vision someone based on a phone call? He started by calling one of the numbers at random, exchanging a few pleasantries, and ending the call. After the call, he did a vision based on the number, and tried to determine where the individual really stood.

He got the vision readily enough, and asked, "What is your opinion of Armand LaGrange?" An answer came, readily enough, but Chuck suddenly realized that would not be a real indicator of loyalty. He tried another question, "If Armand LaGrange got a position elsewhere and offered to take you, would you go with him, or stay with JLG&S?" That appeared to be more predictive, so he worked through the list of numbers in the phone, making notes as he went. He had a thought after several calls and visions, and went back to the ones he'd already done a vision on, and asked, "What would be the reasons you would go or stay?" Now he was starting to get definitive replies.

After going through the list, Chuck thought he had a pretty good idea of those who would leave with Armand. Looking at the organizational structure, the so-called box-and-string chart, Chuck saw that by removing Armand's people, he had simply eliminated an artificial layer of management superimposed over the real organization. In further checking those who would leave with Armand, a very good predictor turned out when they joined the company. Armand hired all of them after he got into power. Chuck knew there were probably lower ranking people in the organization beholden to Armand and concluded such people would have to identify themselves by their actions.

In thinking about who might be best suited to replace Armand, Chuck kept coming back to one name: Andre Moniteau. Chuck considered some new questions, and brought up the vision of Andre Moniteau.

"Do you know about visions?" he asked the vision. Again, "Have you done any visions?" The vision of Andre Moniteau answered "yes" to both questions. Then Chuck asked, "If I told you I had a vision with a person pertaining to JLG&S, would you keep the information in confidence?" The answer came, "Absolutely." "If I told you I had a vision with Jean LaGrange about the company, would you find that persuasive?" The vision answered in length, indicating the strength of the feeling about this. "No other vision pertaining to the company would mean anything. It is Jean LaGrange who has kept JLG&S on a steady course all these years. The problems caused by Armand and his hatchet men only prove how much we need Jean's guidance, since Armand never used Jean for anything besides an excuse." A final question: "Would you work with Chuck LaGrange?" The vision answered, "I know nothing about Chuck LaGrange, but that isn't the point. If I am persuaded that he follows Jean LaGrange, I will work for him."

Chuck went over what he'd done with Melissa, who thought his approach sounded workable, at least. Melissa also declared her brains and eyeballs were fried, and wondered about them maybe playing tourist for a while. That sounded good to Chuck, and through the front desk got several tours over the weekend, fully aware the company could have booked them on any kind of extravaganza imaginable. Still, it suited his sense of the situation to go just like a regular tourist. He had a feeling their just being folks (as Aunt Millicent and Irv would put it) might not be possible after Monday.

Truth be told, they did have a great time. However, they never quite managed to be just regular tourists, since everyone else was keeping an eye on their budget. One cache providing an abundant supply from Charles, together with an evidently bottomless credit card from the company, anything Melissa saw that might be fun, they got after it. By Sunday evening, they were both exhausted.

Monday morning, they drove the coach to the company offices. The security personnel were all in a dither, since they had no instructions about a forty-five foot vehicle parking there. Chuck drug out his phone and looked up the head of security, who he knew was not part of

Armand's circus, and requested that he have these fine folks look after his coach while he was in the building. Immediately after Chuck's call, the security people's radios started buzzing. Chuck and Melissa strolled into the building, simply nodding to the receptionist as they passed, proceeding on to Armand's office.

Chuck still had on jeans and a short-sleeved snap-down cowboy shirt with jogging shoes. He and Melissa ambled on with total serenity, as though all the "Who ...?" "What ...?" "Where ...?" coming at them were a babbling brook they happened to stroll beside. Finally, as they approached the inner sanctum, even Armand stuck his head out the door to check on all the commotion, and blanched when he saw them.

"Hi cousin!" Chuck said cheerily. "Could we could have a word with you?"

Melissa recommended they do it that way, figuring the news of their entrance would be all through the company nearly immediately, which was part of the plan. In Armand's office, Chuck requested the presence of the corporate attorney, chief financial officer, and a couple of secretaries. When they arrived, Chuck announced that he was extremely grateful for everything Armand had done for the company, and as a token of his gratitude, Chuck was setting Armand up in his own company, and financing it to the tune of $500 million. This was to be treated as a gifting, not an investment. Further, Armand was welcome to take with him any JLG&S staff he wanted, and who desired to go with him. By the way, this was effective immediately, and remember, we're all family as well as friends. The corporate attorney and CFO were to work together right now, and come up with a short, clear statement of this agreement.

Chuck directed one of the secretaries to work with the attorney and CFO, and asked the other secretary to spread the word of a mandatory all-hands meeting as soon as the agreement was on paper, say in an hour, at ten a.m., looking at the two responsible for getting the document together, and raising his eyebrows. They hurried out of the office.

At the meeting, Chuck repeated his message to Armand. Presently, Armand was off on the side, talking to the coterie Chuck had expected to go with him. Interestingly, there were a few who didn't go over to join their lord and master, and Chuck made a special note of them. By the time the meeting was done, the CFO had managed to get a deck of checks cut from various accounts for the full amount. Chuck thought the CFO would stay, but since he missed the meeting, made a point to let him know he could go if he wanted. He declined, as expected.

With Armand's bunch sliding out the door, Chuck and Melissa made the rounds, getting better acquainted with all the folks who were staying. Chuck also had asides with the head of security, to make sure he got all company property from those leaving, and to give him a heads up on the few who didn't go.

☆ ☆ ☆

Things started happening in a rush, and they began even while Chuck and Melissa were making the rounds with the glad hands. Fortunately, none of Armand's cronies cared much for either real work or the effort of acquiring technical expertise, so physical security, information technology, and finance were essentially intact. Andre, having been informed of his selection, spent some time creating new department heads where necessary. In many cases, the Armand crony holding the title hadn't really been the functioning head anyway, and it was simply a matter of elevating the people who were actually doing the work.

Almost immediately, bank accounts, locks and other physical security, and computer security changes and upgrades began happening. The department heads, together with Chuck and Melissa had a working lunch in the board room. The remark was made that the board room hadn't seen so much real work and progress in years. After a substantial number of operational items were addressed, and policies that governed the company prior to Armand were reinstated, Chuck decided it was time for him to take the floor. "How many of you know about touch stones?" Chuck asked. Nearly every hand in the room went up.

Chuck turned to Andre. "Do all of the department heads need to at least be aware of this, do you think?" Andre said he believed so, and Chuck continued on. "For the benefit of you not familiar with touch stones, our policies are based on principles given by the founder of JLG&S, Jean LaGrange. Unlike documents, whose words can be twisted and reinterpreted to suit the whims of those currently in charge, we get our marching instructions directly from the mind of Jean LaGrange. This is based on something I have personally come to think of as viewing, or a vision. Anything a person has been in contact with over an extended period absorbs the personality and memories of that person. These can be discerned later, once you learn how.

"I am self-taught, having stumbled onto having a vision accidentally. Not knowing what I was doing, the visions nearly killed me, but Melissa saved my life. Later, I had a unique experience. In his older years, Jean LaGrange turned his view to the unknown and the future, wondering what became of his son Charles. I attempted a vision of the LaGrange Mercantile. Our visions coincided, and we actually had a two-way communication. We've had several such communications, now. This morning was based on specific advice given by Jean. It is certain I could never have come up with this plan on my own."

Chuck looked around, seeing a mixture of disbelief and some little awe. Andre had a certain gleam in his eye, but seemed to be withholding judgment for the moment. After his visions of Andre, Chuck knew he had to do something more to sell his position. What came to him was to simply use a comment Jean made to him after talking about getting Armand out of the way. He was careful to use Jean's exact words and intonation. "The question at this point, is whether we have rid ourselves of the serpent which was trying to choke the company. The answer is, and must be, no. Still, to kill a serpent in your kitchen, the first step is to get it out of your house. This we have done, but do not be deceived: the serpent is out there, is angry, and will bite and poison anyone foolish enough or inattentive enough to get in his way."

"That right there," Andre proclaimed, "That was Jean LaGrange. You, sir, have just convinced me. I will follow you, and if the rest of these don't follow you, they'll follow their noses out the door."

"Thank you Andre. That means everything to me. Now I'll give all of you an instruction ... no, I'll make that an order. If I give anyone here any requirement that does not square with what Jean LaGrange would give in the same circumstances, I require you to nail me on the spot. We will have some challenging times ahead of us, and we need to keep ourselves straight." Chuck then went around the table and shook everyone's hand, ending with Andre Moniteau, who appeared absolutely happy with the direction events were going.

Andre stood with Chuck and Melissa as the department heads filed out of the room, and then asked if it might be possible for them to move the motor home. Chuck replied they could have it gone in five minutes. They still had their room out at the motel. Andre shook his head. Now that he was a person with social standing, that motel simply wouldn't do. They walked to the Director's office, (now Andre's), and the new incumbent had his assistant get them lodging at a more appropriate address. Andre relieved Chuck and Melissa of their motel room keys, and sent another assistant to get their possessions and take them to the new address.

"Now," Andre remarked, as they sat in his office. "You will want to make the social rounds. I will first host you, in a private dinner, tomorrow night, at my home. Dress will be elegant casual. Here is a list of stores for you, sir, and another list of stores for you, madam." Chuck didn't have a clue of what 'elegant casual' might be, and evidently his confusion showed. "If you advise the clerks in these stores of the mode of dress required, they will be glad to help."

Andre considered for a moment, and then said, "On another subject, we will get you an estate appropriate to your social level. The company will purchase the estate, and it will be a company asset, which is something Jean LaGrange would have done."

"I certainly agree with that."

In Andre's front office, the IT Manager was there, along with the CFO. The IT Manager relieved Chuck of his company cell phone, and gave him another, saying most numbers had been changed, and his, specifically, so Armand and any others of his ilk wouldn't bother him. The CFO exchanged his credit card, and gave Melissa a credit card as well, in the name of Melissa LaGrange. Sitting somewhat primly, as though at attention was a woman that Chuck thought might be a forty-something. Andre beckoned to her, and she rose and was taking a first stride all in one motion. "This is Margot, who will be your personal assistant. While your cell phone is absolutely the top of the line, it is Margot who will really be your personal information manager. She will let you know what you need to be doing, where you will be going, and details about any person you need to talk to. She'll also run your life."

"That sounds like a terminal vision," Chuck said, before he really thought about it. Andre chortled softly, and Margot gave Chuck a look like she might rap him on the knuckles if he didn't watch it.

"I'll have an adjoining room at the hotel. I also have an office here. When a suitable property is located, I will reside there. Now, you'll go to the hotel. A car is waiting outside. I'll give the keys to your motor home to a trusted employee. The motor home will be at a safe site until you need it. You and your lady both have appointments separately with style consultants at four pm." She started moving both of them toward the door, and as they went out, Chuck heard Andre's voice, full of merriment float after him, "A terminal vision, indeed!" Margot did not break stride as she guided them to the waiting car.

Later, in the room, Chuck told Melissa, "This social thing utterly appalls me. What is the point of it?" He continued complaining, and Melissa, who had simply been smirking, finally burst into laughter.

"Gee," Melissa replied. "Just think how much less unemployment there is just because of you, sweet cheeks!" She pinched him on both pairs of cheeks. "Remember all your daydreams about what great things you would do and be? Well, here you are – another victim of getting what you asked for. You don't care for the lap of luxury? What do you want?"

Chuck looked her straight in the eye. "A cabin in Blodgett, Oregon would suit me just fine."

"That is a nice cabin, isn't it? So, what are you going to have to do about the company here in order to let you go back? While we're on it, just what expertise do you bring to the company, anyway? Can you be replaced? If so, who or what would it be?"

"I made some brave statements today. Still, from the amount of pure action we've seen, it's evident to me the company can run itself just fine. I can't really plan how to work myself out of a job, because I don't have a job, nor do I have any expertise to get one."

"That sounds a great deal like your position with the M&A firm. Of course, when they sent you to my door, they didn't even kiss you good bye. They just booted you out the door."

Chuck wandered over, and stared out the window.

10: Society & Politics

Chuck's style consultant showed up a couple of minutes early, and Margot made him cool his heels in the hall until the precise time. At that moment, Margot requested Melissa to step out into the hall with her so the style consultant could do his job. She then escorted Melissa to her room next door. Melissa's consultant attempted a flamboyant entrance a couple of minutes later, and Margot made it exceptionally clear to that individual such tardiness would not be tolerated. There were many other consultants both more than qualified and more than willing to take over the contract, so the product had better be worth every penny.

Chuck's consultant looked at him from all sides, while Chuck wondered what sort of person got into style consulting, anyway. He hadn't felt such a complete lack of privacy or need to hide since the closed-office interview with the M&A Personnel Director. The consultant made extensive notes, periodically going out in the hallway to confer with Margot. After some apparently tense exchanges, he came back in and made more notes. Finally, he stayed out in the hallway, and it sounded like he and Margot were making phone calls and finalizing schedules. Then, Melissa's consultant started through some of the same process, after which Melissa finally got to come back in the room. Before they could relax, however, Margot came in and briefed them on what turned out to be a total makeover for both of them.

After Margot finally left them alone, Melissa had an idea. She reminded Chuck of when they were in Blodgett, and he proved he could vision and communicate with her at the same time. She speculated about whether he could talk to someone while in vision with them. He tried it, and she decided that maybe it wasn't workable. She noted that trying to talk to him while he was in vision was like having a conversation with someone while they were talking on the phone. After thinking about it a while, she suggested he try doing the visions between conversations. For instance, when someone was talking, but then said something to a third person. So, they talked for a while, and then Melissa walked over to the window for a moment, giving him some time for a vision, but not a whole lot. While that worked, Chuck observed it didn't give him much opportunity to frame questions the way he'd become accustomed.

"Okay, then you could have questions ready to go," Melissa suggested. "You might have generic questions that might give you an edge, and more specific questions tailored for particular occasions."

It had been a trying day, and she was ready to move on to other topics. Anyway, the whirlpool tub for two was calling. "I know just the thing to enable you to contemplate truly cosmic questions." Later, Chuck had formulated one question: Why hadn't they gotten in the tub sooner?

The next morning, Chuck tried the conversation plus vision routine on the stewards bringing their breakfast. He got some amusement, while improving his questions and procedures. At a quarter before nine, Margot knocked on the door: in fifteen minutes, they would experience the tender mercies of the style consultants. Chuck had no idea how to prepare for it. They were to make him look like whatever he was supposed to be now. Nothing he did at this point would impress the consultants anyway. Anyway, maybe his jeans and cowboy shirt would enable them to point with pride, like "See what I started with, and just look at him now!" Another voice did counterpoint, "Yeah. Look at him now. He looks pretty good for a goddamn dishwasher."

When they got to the front door of the hotel, Chuck saw there were two limos, the first one evidently his. Chuck and Melissa kissed and wished each other good luck before they went their separate ways. Chuck whispered to Melissa that this all looked like a circus. The whole thing did attract some small amount of attention, with a few people evidently certain they must be high rollers of some kind. Chuck wondered if the company could do better at maintaining a low profile. One way might be for everyone to drive a fleet sedan, for instance.

On their way to the first stop, Chuck asked, "Why did they hire you folks anyway. They already gave us a list of stores."

"That's an easy one. The store clerks are paid commissions, so they'll sell you anything, and are happy as long as you buy a lot of it. I only get my pay if you look good. The final quality check is if you pass muster with Mr. and Mrs. Moniteau. Actually, passing you by them will be easy once I get an affirmative nod from the dragon lady."

"Margot, you mean."

"Yes. That's who I mean," he growled back.

Chuck leaned back, and smiled. Then, he did a vision on the consultant, and smiled some more. The consultant, meanwhile, kept up a steady patter about the importance of looking good, and how people judged others based on their first impression. Chuck had a flash-back to his office days, with the worn pants with no crease, his shirts left to hang until the wrinkles got discouraged and went away, and the well-scuffed shoes, not to mention how long he went between haircuts. If he'd dressed a little better, he might still be working there, also assuming he hadn't done something else causing Lee Sherman to find reasons to get rid of him.

It came to him everything happening to him recently added to the list of reasons for his stay at the M&A firm to have been even shorter than it was. Chuck didn't believe Lee Sherman was a candidate for sainthood, but in hindsight Lee tolerated Chuck far better and longer than logically should have been the case.

Back in the present, Chuck could do these surreptitious visions for entertainment. If he'd known about visions sooner, he'd have known what people thought of him. Maybe then he could have changed his ways, or most likely not. It was certain if he'd been spending more time in vision with other people, his jaw might have been spending less time flapping. Oh well, he had to go through quite a lot in order to get to this point. He didn't think there were alternate realities of 'if only." That is, where he might have been something or somewhere, if only some other thing occurred.

The day showed clothes were the easy part of the makeover. His newly slender body seemed to be made to order for fashion statements. Clothes were ordered and sent back to the hotel. Then Chuck found himself in a styling salon, his hair cut properly, or 'styled,' as they termed it. They did things to his face, the details of which he didn't really want to know. They worked on his fingernails and even toenails. They were making an effort to tell him how he could keep it all going, so he could always look like whatever they were doing.

Finally back at the hotel, Margot kept the two of them separated, while the consultants, together with teams of specialists, buzzed back and forth, and finally had them dressed, and the last hair in place. Then, a half hour before they were to meet the Moniteaus, they were allowed to see each other. Chuck had to admit there were some notable changes in Melissa's appearance, but beneath the new hair and cosmetics was still Melissa. That was the most awesome part. Chuck saw that clearly, and he told her so. Melissa smiled, and commented he cleaned up pretty well. Margot checked the two of them closely, and finally declared until they said something, people might actually mistake them for people.

Following Margo, Chuck asked Melissa in a whisper if Margot's statement was a complement or an insult. Melissa just smiled and shrugged.

✲ ✲ ✲

Andre did not arrive in a limo. He and his wife Charlotte drove their own car. That agreed with Chuck's assessment of how a low-profile company should be. Chuck saw Margot stiffen, realizing this would not be a Personal Assistant affair. Still, she soldiered on. Andre came around and let Charlotte out, and there were introductions all around. Meanwhile, Margot stood at attention while the two consultants fidgeted. Finally, Andre and Charlotte looked at each other, and she smiled. Andre then glanced at Margot and nodded, and that was it. Chuck and Melissa were satisfactory.

Melissa already made it clear small talk would be the order of the day. Minus the braggadocio, Chuck always did poorly in the conversation department. Still, on the drive to the Moniteau's home, the conversation revolved around New Orleans, and with the previous weekend's outing, Chuck was able to make some reasonably intelligent comments, aimed at not insulting anyone or anything. Since Melissa and Charlotte were in the back seat, there wasn't any way she could give him clues by way of nudges.

The Moniteaus had a comfortable home, but not one that was ostentatious. Andre said they were put in the place when he was quite a few steps lower in the pecking order, but it suited them. They stayed in it when they could have easily moved upscale. With his new position, Andre thought they might have to move, but hoped Chuck might stay in the area, perhaps allowing the Moniteaus to stay where they were. Chuck had no problems with New Orleans, and certainly didn't want to strain relations, so didn't answer directly. Instead, he wondered about the part social gatherings played in the conduct of company business. Andre explained the company and its executives were considered "old money" and needed to fulfill certain expectations. Chuck, with some trepidation, then inquired how well Armand had fulfilled that role. Andre responded they tried to play the role, but never seemed to get it right.

Chuck kept viewing his hosts, and it turned out that Melissa was, as well. So, when Andre and Charlotte left the room at one point, Chuck and Melissa checked with each other to see if they were both getting the same thing. It turned out they were. Andre and Charlotte were concerned about Chuck and Melissa's marital status, to include repercussions if they now got married. There was a significant amount of fear the situation could turn the social situation against the company. There was worry the situation could get as bad or worse, than with Armand and his wife. Compounding that fear was concern that losing the social support would become a political liability.

They had only enough time to formulate something resembling a plan before their hosts came back in. "You know, Andre," Chuck began, "your comment about the company being considered "old money" and needing to fulfill certain expectations reminded us we need to have things right. We've been talking about fulfilling a few obligations with my great-aunt Millicent, who is a LaGrange. She lives in Missouri. We could quietly slide out of town in the motor home, go up to Missouri and while we're there, have a small private wedding. We should be able to avoid any publicity. When we return, we'll act like we've been married for some indefinite period of time. Do you think that might work?"

Both Andre and Charlotte approved the plan, and Charlotte went so far as to give Melissa an engagement and wedding ring that had been in her family a long time. Melissa wondered how to explain her not having worn the rings before this, and Charlotte replied that while they were out in the woods, she didn't want to take a chance on losing them. That kind of answer seemed to make sense to Melissa, and she tried the rings on. Incredibly, the rings fit perfectly. There were hugs and handshakes all around, and Charlotte took Melissa off to talk about weddings and society. Overall, the feeling relaxed considerably.

Andre cleared his throat after the ladies left. "I hope you don't mind discussing major company challenges this evening."

"Well, Andre, if, as you say, I need to learn to conduct business within a social context, this would seem a good time to practice."

"I appreciate that. I really do. In scanning the company books, did you pick up on an item about potential adverse legislation?"

"Yes. Actually, Melissa caught it first. There was something about a public audit requirement for closely held companies. What's the background on it?"

"I'm impressed. Yes, that's what we're talking about, and we were barely able to get that little bit of a mention included in the records. Armand didn't want anything to distract from what a perfect deal he'd done in acquiring his father's company. Frankly, it's a pretty good company, and profitable. Still, it raises fears our corporate strategy has changed from simply sampling a few shares of other companies to one of domination. Armand neither considered that aspect of it nor cared about it, particularly. We were never able to get those larger concerns across to him."

"What is the strategy at this point?"

"Jean's counsel has always been to keep our business private. If we lose the legislative battle, it might force us to move the corporation elsewhere. At this point, 'elsewhere' might well be outside the United States. We have significant investments worldwide as you know. Still, we haven't lost yet, and we'd like to stay here if possible. As we see it our best and final chance will be after you two are well and duly wedded. We will acquire an estate capable of dealing with major social gatherings. I have an idea about the specific property, but we'll let it be a wedding present."

"I appreciate that, although it sounds like we'll be living in a banquet facility."

"It won't be as bad as all that, but you'll need to really be on game when the politicians show up."

"I notice you aren't volunteering to live there."

"I was hoping you wouldn't notice that. Well, it's a tough job, but I'm sure you're up for it."

☆ ☆ ☆

They called to let Aunt Millicent know they were coming. Chuck asked Melissa about inviting her family. "My Dad died several years ago. My Mom would not be able to make it." Melissa made the statement in such a flat voice, that Chuck, even though he was not very fast on picking up on things, knew the subject was off limits. Margot was working the wedding non-stop, and made it clear they would have a professional driver as well as having her to keep them straight. So Chuck and Melissa would be passengers on their own coach. Margot had a dress for Melissa and a suit for Chuck. She already studied their taste in clothes, and had their sizes. Melissa sighed as she looked at the dress, not having any input, but had to admit it was a good choice.

The following morning, the coach pulled up to the hotel, and everyone boarded. Everything, including their clothing was already on board, having been loaded overnight. On the way, Margot continued the planning sitting up next to the driver. Chuck and Melissa ended up wandering between the couch and dinette. By the time they were fifty miles out of New Orleans, Margot had contacts in Central Missouri scrambling to get things done. She got the marriage license resolved, using a scanner on board. She pointed out to them that Missouri had a mandatory three-day period between the marriage license and the ceremony.

Melissa did not want a civil wedding, so Margot got a chapel at Lake of the Ozarks. Melissa was showing some signs of stress, but it was more because of not being the one doing the planning. She pointed out even with the British Royals, the bride had significant input, but Margot ignored the protest. Chuck, meanwhile, contented himself with communicating with a vision of Melissa, asking about her family. No information came. He saw it was possible to suppress information, even via vision. It all seemed very strange. He hoped Melissa would someday see fit to include him in her situation.

Arriving in Jefferson City, they went directly to the hotel Margot had booked. Less than first cabin did not exist, and even that would not be good enough. There was a limo standing by as they pulled in. Chuck had little doubt whose that was. They settled in for the night, anticipating an early start since Aunt Millicent invited them for breakfast.

They arrived promptly at 7:30 a.m., Chuck feeling extremely self-conscious as the limo pulled up in front of the modest house, with Margot and the driver in a rental car right behind. If this was low profile, what would high profile look like? Oh, yeah, that would include air cover, motorcycle escort, and secret service. Melissa and Chuck decided their story was that they were both hired by JLG&S, without specifying what the initials meant, fell in love. The trouble was, they couldn't think of any reason why new hires would get chauffeured around in a limo with staff in a chase car. At this point, Chuck would have liked to have gone with the truth, but that would sound more incredible than any tall tale they concocted.

Irv immediately gave his approval of Melissa, who charmed him out of his socks. Aunt Millicent registered a positive initial impression on this new person joining the family.

"Well," Millicent commented after a while, "if I didn't know you were the same person, I certainly wouldn't have thought there could be a connection. You came through here a month ago in a car that we weren't really sure would get you to Tucson. Now, you show up looking very uptown, with a lady on your arm, a big long car at the curb, and another car apparently glued behind it. I'm not going to ask how it happened. It has to be quite a story. Maybe you can come up with a version I could understand. Well, come on in to the table and sit down. Breakfast is ready. Do your parents know you're getting married?"

"I hadn't called them yet. We ... that is, I thought about waiting until we had the actual time we'd be at the chapel, in case they wanted to come. I think, though, that's actually been taken care of, so we'll call this morning."

"We wanted to have a dinner for you after the ceremony, but we need to confirm how many are coming. By the way, your friends outside would be welcome, if that wouldn't break any rules."

"I don't know if it would or not. I'll have to ask them." Chuck went ahead and called after breakfast, and with his father, it was the usual, "Yes sir" kind of exchange. His father didn't mind him getting married, just as long as Chuck wasn't thinking about moving back home. His mother was just leaving, as usual, and it wasn't certain if she even got the message. Neither of them would be coming.

"You know, Chuck, if Jack Edward could see what we're seeing, he might change his mind. Give him some time. He may come around. He only knows how you used to be."

Chuck considered he could do a vision of his father, and see what the situation really was. Almost immediately, however, he recoiled, remembering being with Charles for that long virtual time. He experienced everything Charles did. Yeah, he even experienced the personal details Chuck would just as soon forget. A vision of his parents was suddenly akin to walking into a bathroom they occupied. There was simply no way he'd do it, no matter what he thought he might learn. It wouldn't have made things better, anyway.

With a couple of days to kill, Chuck and Melissa took Aunt Millicent and Irv all around, including out to the old home place, where the limo scraped several times on the country road. As far as Chuck could tell,

Melissa got along with Aunt Millicent and Irv wonderfully. Irv had always loved to indulge in double entendres and word play in general, and Melissa kept right up with him.

The wedding was July 17th. Chuck thought the time seemed to drag before it finally came. Still, everything went precisely according to plan. It had to, since their "wedding planner," social secretary would not tolerate anything else. The minister finally presented the world with Mr. & Mrs. LaGrange. They drove back to Jefferson City and the dinner that was reserved. As expected, Margot and the driver both wished them the best, but thought it wouldn't be proper for them to be at the wedding dinner.

The next morning, they were in the coach, and stopped by Aunt Millicent's house. They promised to send their new address as soon as they had it. Millicent and Irv stared at the coach, unable to imagine how any of it could happen.

On the way back to New Orleans, Margot was on the phone intermittently, making notes. Finally, she came back and advised Chuck and Melissa they had a new address, and asked about his aunt's e-mail address, so she could advise them of the contact information. Chuck declined, telling Margot it would be more appropriate to send a note in his own handwriting. That seemed to satisfy Margot, and she went back to her seat next to the driver. What Chuck didn't mention was that Millicent and Irv never owned a computer, and were most unlikely to ever acquire one. The only way to contact them, other than the mail, was a straight phone call. Chuck wasn't sure Margot, the all competent, could deal with such a situation. In the meantime, they were actually on their way to a place they could call home. If Andre's case wasn't unique, it could even be their permanent home. Still, there was a cabin in Blodgett.

✲ ✲ ✲

It was getting dark as the driver turned off the Interstate before getting into New Orleans, and headed for a destination only he and Margot knew. Finally, they turned into a driveway with a pair of imposing wrought iron gates. The coach was in the process of stopping when the gates opened before them. Since Margot wasn't on the phone, it was evident they were expected. They followed a lane between mature trees, finally arriving at an impressive structure, where a number of people stood to the side of an elegant entryway.

The driver stopped the coach, leaving the engine running and air conditioning on. Margot made sure the cabin door was unlocked, then went forward and stepped outside using the passenger-side cab door. A moment later, she opened the cabin door, and invited Chuck and Melissa to meet the staff. Margot introduced the first person, who was the Estate Manager. Margot then fell back half a step, and stayed on Chuck's left as he proceeded down the line. The introductions included managers of the various household departments. There was Security, Information Technology, Butler (he said there were ten butlers), the Chef, Housekeeper, Maintenance, Grounds, and Events. The Estate Manager said he understood Chuck and Melissa were tired after their trip, and added that all the staff were pleased and eager to be at their service. At the end of the line were three people the Estate Manager did not introduce. Margot switched to Chuck's right, and introduced them. It turned out that Margot had the official title of Senior Personal Assistant to Mr. Charles LaGrange. She then introduced a man who would be in charge of Chuck's private area, including wardrobe. He was described at Chuck's Personal Aide. The second and third were Melissa's Personal Assistant, and Personal Aide.

The Personal Aides then took charge of Chuck and Melissa, escorting them through the front door into the reception hall. Chuck saw how Armand, for all his efforts to impress, wasn't even in the same league as this place. They went up magnificent curving stairways which framed the reception hall, allowing for quite an entrance, should the occasion require it. Upstairs, Chuck and Melissa continued down a wide hallway. Then Melissa was ushered through a doorway.

Chuck's Personal Aide took him through an imposing double door at the end of the hall. A tour of his suite followed. It was a corner room, of course, overlooking the estate's lake. A flood of memories overlay his current reality. His efficiency apartment in Chicago might have fit in this suite's bathroom. Looking at the twenty-foot ceiling, the Blodgett cabin, roof and all, could be placed in the bedroom, with room to walk around it. Another memory came, of Armand's driver finding a place for the sample case in their motel. What would Madeleine's nephew report about this?

His Personal Aide patiently standing there brought Chuck back. Sir's nightclothes were laid out, and the feather bed was turned down.

Did sir require assistance in changing? Chuck specified that 'sir' did not require assistance there, but having appropriate clothing for the schedule Margot had for him might be, which earned an "Of course, sir." Also, do you answer to any particular name? "George, sir."

"George, is there an entrance to my wife's suite, other than down the hall?" "Yes sir, it's that door there, sir." "Thank you, George. I think I can handle it from here." "Very good, sir." George did a half bow (a bow, yet!) and backed himself out the main door. After the door clicked, Chuck headed for the connecting door, only to have it swing open just before he got there, with Melissa's grin following immediately.

"I think that guy, George, is trying to 'sir' me to death. How'd it go for you?"

"Only what I was brought up to expect. Would madam want rose petals in her bath water? What variety of rose petals would madam like?"

They both laughed, and Chuck observed, "You know, we've shared a bed without being married. Now we're married, and they're assigning us separate rooms."

"Well, we can't let the prize stallion just run around with the herd, can we? It might weaken his precious genes. Anyway, who says we're sleeping separately. I'll beat them up, I will!"

"Oh, well, we can't have you getting violent. Wait, I have an idea! You can hide in here. Nobody would look for you in here. If that doesn't work, I could hide in that room," pointing to the connecting door.

"Oh, no, fair sir. The sight and feel of all the satin, silk, and lace in there might do terrible things to your psyche."

"Actually, the sight and feel of satin, silk, and lace do wonderful things to my psyche, but only when they're associated with you."

"Quite the romantic fool, aren't you?"

"I'm only the fool for you, my love."

"I believe you've been hanging around your French ancestors too much. It's rubbing off on you. Maybe I like it."

When they woke up the next morning, George came in and opened the curtains, and advised Chuck his bath would be ready momentarily. Melissa giggled, reflexively pulling the covers up tight to her chin. When he silently exited the room, she grabbed a robe, came around the bed, and gave Chuck a kiss, whispering that she approved of the bed, and maybe he should check out hers sometime. She then went back to her suite, remarking that whatever was happening here was probably happening there, as well. With her gone, Chuck couldn't imagine why he needed to be in bed any longer, although Melissa was quite right. It was a nice bed. In the bath, George came in and inquired what Sir would like for breakfast, and a few minutes later, returned to give him a shave. Chuck considered it was all crazy.

George had laid out casual clothing. That could mean they were just going to hang around their new digs today. He recalled Margot saying she would be in this massive house somewhere, which might mean he had an office of some sort here. Then he chuckled to himself. There had to be any number of offices here. The Estate Manager, if he recalled the title correctly, was probably the equivalent title to a major resort's General Manager. Having an Events Manager said something about what the company did, or planned to do here.

Chuck asked George about what was coming up for the day. "Ah, Sir, after breakfast, Margot thought you would like a tour of your house, and to meet your staff, if you would like, Sir." A cell phone discreetly buzzed, and George glanced at it. "I believe Madam is on her way to breakfast. Did you wish to join her?"

There was a breakfast nook in a bright room overlooking the lake. The breakfast looked like something from a gourmet magazine, and, Chuck discovered, tasted quite good, as well. Chuck laughed, and commented, "I was just remembering having breakfast with Aunt Millicent and Irv. What do you suppose they'd think of this?"

"They sure wouldn't believe you live here. I saw how they stared at the coach when we left. We could say we're just living here."

"Well, we are, actually. The company owns the place, from what Andre said."

"You just wouldn't tell them that you own the company."

"Yeah, well, there is that little detail. Still, we'd be telling the sure enough truth."

After breakfast came further inquiries about whether Sir and Madam would like to tour the place. They hadn't changed their minds during breakfast. Golf carts waited outside, and Chuck and Melissa rode together in one with another following just in case. There were tennis courts, the swimming pool, a stable with horses and riding trails around the one hundred fifty acre property, plus additional trails outside the estate, a putting green and driving range for golf. There was even a helipad, should they need to make a quick getaway. In a separate building, Chuck found the coach, which was being examined critically by the guy who had been his driver. It turned out the driver was considerably more than a refugee from the bus company. He was also a bodyguard, and it turned out he had been most displeased knowing the coach was not armored. "We're going to have that attended to immediately," was the bodyguard driver's comment. On the subject of bodyguards, he offered Chuck an aside. Anyone picking Margot as an easy target would find themselves not having a very good day. Chuck couldn't decide whether he now felt safer or more intimidated.

✡ ✡ ✡

Chuck found his office that afternoon. Finding the place wasn't a huge achievement, since it adjoined his suite. That might make it a super suite, but Chuck did not pursue the thought. Melissa had her own office, across the hall from his office, and adjoining her suite. A short hallway went from his dressing room into his private office. Margot had an office off his, with a reception area in front. There must have been some kind of tell-tale circuit. He just sat down, and Margot was there to let him know about his schedule.

Chuck wondered what kind of scheduling was on his computer, and how it would be synchronized with, for instance, his cell phone. Margot reminded him of what Andre said, when he advised Chuck not to worry about the computer or the cell phone, because she would take care of his schedule. Margot went on to advise Chuck his schedule had no company business the rest of that day, but the following evening, Andre and others from JLG&S would be out to the house, and they would meet in the conference room. Chuck inquired as to the location of the conference room, and found a door on the opposite side of the office from his suite opened directly to the head of the conference table.

That was almost too convenient, and Chuck commented to that effect. Margot replied that since he brought up the subject, his personal health and fitness trainer would be seeing him for an initial consultation presently. Chuck wondered how all this would have been handled had he not wandered into his office, but then considered Margot undoubtedly had it covered. The trainer came in, and seemed pleased and a bit surprised that Chuck was looking trim and reasonably fit. He had Chuck change into workout clothes (George laid them out already, of course), and did some diagnostics in the fitness center of the house, finishing with a couple of sprints and a jog. He said he would have a plan put together for the next day.

After the workout and a shower, Chuck went in search of Melissa, beginning to feel like the focal point for everyone else's activity. Ten steps down the hall, it suddenly occurred to him that Margot would know exactly where Melissa was, and what she was doing. By the time he got to Margot's office, his question had changed. "Margot, I can see, more or less, what you do, and there are job descriptions for everyone around here, with one or two exceptions. What is my function in all of this?"

Margot looked at him. "You're the owner, sir. You are the reason we have jobs. I suppose you could look at it this way: we are the 'how' for things happening here, while you are the 'why.' Without the 'why' there is no purpose for the 'how'."

"That's a most erudite response. Still, I'm accustomed to having a function. Simply being an owner is not how I was raised."

"Well, you already cleansed the company of blood-sucking leeches, if you don't mind me talking about your cousins in such a way."

"That's a good description of them, from what I've been able to determine so far."

"I think your function is to keep tied in to Jean LaGrange, and with his advice, to help the company keep doing what it has been doing. Incidentally, one of the reasons you have a personal trainer on staff is because of the physical toll being in vision puts on you. I must say, however, we don't think the trainer needs to know company business, which includes visions. What you tell him is your call, obviously. By the way, Melissa is with the Executive Chef, planning your dinner this evening."

Margot actually grinned at that point. "Your function, since you want one so badly, is to take a stroll down by the lake."

Chuck thought Margot's directions coming with a grin sure beat her directions coming with a scowl. Okay, yeah, they were directions either way. Strolling by the lake, he brought up a vision of Jean. His purpose was only to vision Jean, not to have two-way communication, and he found that he was able to do it. He already knew he could vision simply by focusing on the individual, and now he also knew he could control the type of vision. Chuck began by asking general questions about conducting business, and found he was getting generalities in return. Then, he thought he would try an extremely precise question, and considered a point made by Charles in working as a store clerk. The answer came back in a form that was so precise Chuck was absolutely certain that what he'd gotten from Charles was an echo from Jean. Charles must have learned his trade quite thoroughly, and from the master. Chuck wondered in passing if the owners of the stores where Charles worked as a clerk knew what an asset they had.

He heard a golf cart, and automatically stepped to the side of the path as he looked to see what was going on. It turned out to be George, coming to get him. There would be exactly the amount of time needed to return to his suite and change for dinner. George then escorted Chuck to the particular dining room, and found Melissa entering by another door at the same moment. The table reminded him eerily of the room in Eugene, and Melissa told him it was supposed to be a reminder, to include his being sent for a walk. The difference being this time, he was where he should be, when he should be there.

The dinner, the company, and the evening were everything Chuck could have ever imagined, and more.

The next evening, standing in Chuck's office, Margot got the cue, and Chuck, flanked by Melissa and Margot, entered the board room. The members of the board were standing and applauding as Chuck covered the couple of steps to his place at the head of the table. After a moment, Chuck gave two taps on a crystal sunburst before him, and after letting the echoes fade, smiled and sat down, followed by the board members.

Margot thoroughly briefed him about all this, and insisted on several dry runs before the members of the board arrived. Chuck was feeling like a make-believe president at a cabinet meeting, or maybe a monarch having council. An organization the size of JLG&S was certainly larger than a number of political states on the planet. It was also vulnerable to political decisions made all over the world. This evening's discussion, however, centered on political decisions being made in their home state.

Andre made the general presentation, which was an expanded version of their conversation when they'd had dinner. Viewing Andre, as well as the others in attendance, Chuck saw little had changed in the interim, and everyone was glad that various tactics aimed at delaying final consideration of the measure had succeeded. There seemed an almost desperate wish for Chuck to be in the game, although there seemed little notion of just what Chuck could do, specifically. Actually, Chuck wished he knew.

When Armand had used JLG&S to acquire his father's company, there was already an undercurrent in the Legislature as well as elsewhere, worrying the company was altogether too cash rich, and too widely dispersed in its investments to continue that strategy much longer. The main speculation was that JLG&S would start acquiring entire segments of the economic base, aiming for constructive control of the state economy, or alternatively, of an industry. Armand's father had a business which serviced several segments of the oil industry. So when JLG&S acquired it, seemingly out of the blue, alarms went off.

Armand's father had a publicly listed firm, but Armand now took it private, eliminating any transparency. The legislation was to require public audits of private firms if those firms acquired the outstanding stock of a publicly traded company. Armand didn't seem to care, even though a public audit would have put his various malfeasances out in the public eye. Chuck's abrupt appearance and nearly immediate disposal of Armand and his friends was taken as divine intervention. It also happened that JLG&S had an option on this very property, which was an excellent match for what they saw had to be done.

With Armand in control, passage of the legislation seemed almost a foregone conclusion. Now that Armand was no longer associated with JLG&S, several legislators already announced they would vote against the measure, since it required taxpayer money to finance the audits. The only hope of recouping the cost rested with the audits finding at least that much due from the company. With new management in addition to all the government agencies already verifying and auditing specific areas of company transactions, that likelihood was suddenly in doubt, at least for those legislators.

There were a number of others who had stopped publicly supporting the bill, but had not come out against it, either. The consensus of the board was that of these unknown quantities, they would need to convince at least six, and if possible, seven, in order to vote it down. Then they got down to cases. Today was July 20. The vote was set for Monday, July 25. Because of that, they wanted to get together with the lawmakers Saturday, July 23. The setting for this 'get-together' would be a social gathering at Chuck's house.

Did Chuck think his staff could handle it? Chuck turned to Margot, who quickly got a message out. The Estate Manager and Events Director had been standing by outside the door, and entered immediately. They both assured the Board it would be done properly and well, adding that they could do it Friday, July 22 if necessary. The Estate Manager also gave assurance that security would be up to the challenge, so it would be absolutely private. The Board was impressed with the offer to move it to Friday, but considered they had a better chance of getting the people they needed on Saturday.

That was the easy part. After the two left, Chuck asked about his part in it, although he already knew quite well, having continued his viewing of the Board during all of it. His part, they hoped, would be to view the various people, especially the really critical ones, to see where they stood, and determine why they were leaning in whatever direction. Chuck assured them he could and would do that. If they could get him a priority list, he would take them from A to Z. The Board was clearly prepared for his response, for Andre immediately handed Chuck a piece of paper.

"Well, then, gentlemen," Chuck said. "It appears I have some work to do. If any of you have ideas on specific questions I can ask while viewing these people please let me know. Remember my questions can't be too long or too complex, because I'll be dealing with viewing them and at the same time appearing to be carrying on a normal conversation. If necessary, and if I get behind in the viewing, we'll have a signal of some kind, so some of you may appear to need to speak with me briefly so I can get caught up."

The meeting ended there, and Chuck and Melissa headed off to their rooms. They both realized their public life was going to be the price for their private life.

✡ ✡ ✡

Chuck and Melissa worked on specific questions. There was the obvious one, of how the individual would vote. There were also questions like why they were voting that way, what would change their vote, what they really wanted, and what they really feared. A good number of the board members gave possible questions. Their submissions were by and large different statements of what they were already planning. That by itself gave them some confidence they were working in the right direction.

A second area of concern for Melissa was getting Chuck as socialized as possible, though there were real limits as to what could be done in the amount of time they had. Finally, Melissa, Margot, and Chuck's personal fitness trainer all worked on ensuring sufficient rest and nutrition for their boy. Chuck was glad that part was only going to be for a few days, even though the personal fitness trainer wanted it to be forever. He was beginning to feel like somebody's prize race horse, Melissa's comment the night they got to the house notwithstanding.

Saturday came, and Chuck had no idea what more he could do to prepare. Once upon a time, the concept of being the center of attention absolutely mesmerized him. Now, with the future of his company at stake, Chuck almost dreaded the very idea. By the time the guests started arriving, Chuck was finding himself alternately longing for that cabin in Blodgett and considering the benefits of being a dishwasher.

The evening of the event, Chuck and Melissa strolled arm in arm into the gathering, with Margot at his shoulder. The reaction from the people there made it apparent that getting to meet and greet the legislators was not going to be difficult. Most of them had come because they wanted to get the measure of this new guy running JLG&S. Their concern was whether he was someone they thought they could work with. Chuck and Melissa ended up working as a sort of tag team, one talking while the other did a vision. Since the individual (or target) had no reason to think the one not speaking was anything less than totally interested in them, they even scored points just from that.

After a first round of meeting and greeting, Chuck, Melissa, and Andre took an opportunity to meet privately and compare notes. Eight of the ten they originally thought were undecided were planning to vote against the audit measure. On the other hand, five of the presumed 'safe' votes were actually going to vote for the measure because of pressures from various quarters. Of interest to Chuck was that one of those quarters featured his beloved cousin, Armand LaGrange. It smelled of "If I can't rape and pillage like I planned, I'll just burn it to the ground and be done with it."

They formulated a plan, based on Jean's advice, and went back out among them. If the audit measure was defeated, JLG&S would divest itself of its wholly owned company. They made it clear that in all honesty, the company was not that good a fit, and was purchased in spite of, and not because of corporate plans and goals. However, if the measure went through, JLG&S not only would keep the acquisition, but would actively begin acquiring other companies, and they would concentrate on companies in those legislators' jurisdictions. Really, however, they would vastly prefer to get back to a pre-Armand mode, and be low of profile, mild of manner, and generous of donations to legislators of great wisdom.

The vote was scheduled on Monday, but ended up actually happening on Tuesday. Chuck and Melissa were at company headquarters, and their legislative liaison let them know the progress of the vote. To their great relief, the legislators they had worked with came through, and the measure was defeated.

After everyone had celebrated a bit, Chuck got up and told everyone about the pressure he'd picked up coming from Armand. "The serpent is still out there. Being frustrated, he's going to redouble his efforts against us. We need to be extremely careful, even while we appear to carry on exactly like everything's normal."

Everyone agreed with that, and the question came up about potential suitors for the company. Several names came up, followed by questions of how they could evaluate the very diverse operations involved. How could they actually determine which one they'd be most comfortable favoring? Chuck smiled, and advised them he was personally acquainted with an M&A firm that could do the analysis. As a matter of fact, he wanted to recommend a specific office of that company to do the work.

11: Settling a Wager

Lee Sherman got a call from a thoroughly mystified operations type in New York. A corporation nobody had heard of before, and about which nothing was known, appeared out of nowhere, wanting to give the company a job without them competing for it. Chicago was being assigned the job at the customer's request ... no, make that insistence. That certainly suited Lee well enough, because it must mean all that stuff about word of mouth advertising actually worked, and he said so. The operations guy said that, no, there was no referral attached to it. There was nothing about old buddies, military comrades, or anything. The instructions were extremely explicit, stating the Chicago office must handle the job, or there would be no contract.

The operations type went on to say the company was called JLG&S. Although this company was headquartered in New Orleans, they had absolutely no interest in going through the more logical placements, which would be the offices in either Houston or Atlanta. It had to be the Chicago office. Lee was to call a certain Andre Moniteau immediately. He had a wholly-owned subsidiary that needed to be spun off post haste. The subsidiary, the source said, was profitable, but it was a bad fit, both for the company's operation and for its relations with the local and state political authorities. There were several potential buyers, but they needed to analyze each deal to see which of them would be best for the company being sold, its employees, and, of course, for JLG&S.

Lee didn't have that much on the schedule, and he got after it, assigning some of his best analysts to get it done right. Somebody somewhere must have had a connection with his office and passed the good word on to this Andre Moniteau. Andre, when Lee talked to him, was pretty impressive. Lee went through his standard questions, and Andre had the answers right then and there, without having to send off to research anything. It was almost as if Mr. Moniteau was being coached by Lee's own people. This promised to be one of the easier deals he had put together in quite some time. It was so easy, in fact, they were able to schedule an initial meeting just based on the first phone call.

The team started immediately getting information about the suitors, what sort of deal each was offering, the likelihood that merging management would result in massive layoffs in the acquired company, the possibility of retirement funds being wiped out, and other details. There had been significant progress by the time Andre Moniteau and members of his management team showed up. Even at that first meeting, Lee's team was able to recommend two of the suitors as not being good candidates.

Full details, as is nearly always the case, came much more slowly than the first approximations, although there weren't very many blind alleys and dead ends. Andre and his group flew up every week in a chartered jet, stayed overnight at a local hotel, had a progress meeting pretty much first thing the next morning, and would afterward depart directly for the airport. Lee knew JLG&S had to be a major player to do it that way, and he would have loved to know more about it. As a closely held corporation, information was hard to come by. Still, Lee could usually find out a fair amount even about a closely held outfit, but in this case, none of his sources could tell him anything. In any case, information about JLG&S was not the object of his analysis. Also, the knowledge that these guys would be there every week kept pressure on Lee to get the thing done.

Lee was ready to present a final recommendation in what had to be considered a very short time. That fulfilled one of the stipulations, namely that getting the subsidiary sold was extremely time-sensitive. He called Andre to let him know. The meeting to present the recommendation would be in three days, and there would be some overtime required to get the presentation and last details done. Lee knew the reward would definitely be worth the cost and effort. The day before the presentation, Lee got a call from JLG&S advising him the corporation's owner, wife, and a personal assistant would be joining the CEO and his team for the presentation. Lee considered such an event extraordinary.

On the morning of the presentation, Lee sat in his office going over his copy of the presentation, while his entire staff was hurrying, trying to ensure there would be no slip-ups. Everything had to be right, because this was pay day. Lee could have set his watch by the time security called to let him know the JLG&S party was in the building. They stipulated the party consisted of the same people as before, plus three additional individuals and they were being escorted to the conference room. Lee got his game face on, and went through his personal pre-game pep talk, repeating, "Okay, they're the customers. I'm the expert. I can go do this! I can go do this with enthusiasm!" He paced back and forth in his office to get the blood flow really moving.

✡ ✡ ✡

The procedure was for a couple of Lee's staff to distribute copies of the analysis and proposal to those attending just before Lee entered, so they would not have to interrupt the presentation later. All of Lee's self-motivation had him standing outside the conference room when his two staff members came out. They started talking the second the door was closed.

"Did you see him?"

"I saw someone that looked like him, but it couldn't have been him. Anyway, this guy's face was thinner, not to mention the fact that he looked intelligent."

"Okay, his face was thinner, but the profile was exact. It had to be him, I tell you."

"They say everyone has a double somewhere. We just happened to see proof of it, because there's just no way that guy we saw could be him."

The two suddenly realized Lee was standing right next to them, and left immediately. Lee knew the same two had distributed updates to the management team previously, so the owner was the only one they could be talking about. The owner evidently bore a strong resemblance to someone they both knew well. That was interesting, and might explain why his office got the commission. Still, Lee couldn't think of anyone at all who could fill the bill. The two appeared surprised – no, make that astonished at who the owner resembled. Call it lack of imagination, maybe, but there were no bells ringing in Lee's mind as he entered the room.

The tables were set up in an inverted 'U' with the lectern at the open end. After the opening comments, Lee tried to take a casual glance at the far end, which was occupied by a man and woman, with a second woman on the other side of the man, and slightly behind him. Oddly, the strip of lights at that end of the room was switched off, leaving the three in comparative shadow. Lee shrugged mentally, set his notes on the podium, and picked up the remote. He was about to open his presentation, but suddenly realized protocol needed to be observed.

"I should direct the presentation to the owner, but I don't have a name."

The owner leaned over toward Andre Moniteau, said something, and went back. Andre then said, "You may direct the presentation to me, since the owner is only observing."

Lee had been looking at the owner while that was going on. The owner didn't appear very large physically, but quite trim, with every hair in place. Also, he had dark hair like Andre. Could the two be related? Lee's research had shown him some French aristocrats had migrated to New Orleans. Perhaps this guy's family was that way. It did seem awfully strange, however, that he was clearly opting for anonymity when, if that were the case, all he had to do was not join the management group for the meeting. There must be some additional agenda going on here.

The presentation went without any questions or confrontations. During it all, Lee got a definite impression about the owner and his wife. Although they appeared to be immersed in the presentation, Lee thought they spent most of their time studying him. It all felt a little bit spooky. Lee proceeded on to the recommendations, and when he was done, Andre Moniteau looked at the owner. Lee thought, "The owner's just observing. It's more like he's running the show from around the corner." The owner waited for a moment, looking thoughtfully at the report, and finally nodded to Andre, following which, he raised a single finger, like telling him to wait a moment, and then motioned him closer, at which point the woman sitting somewhat behind came close as well.

Andre Moniteau nodded, and looked up at Lee. "We accept your recommendations, and want to retain you to prepare the paperwork to complete the transaction. We all appreciate your efficiency, thoroughness, and timeliness in this matter. On another, unrelated matter, the owner would like a word with you privately." With that, Andre arose, walked up to Lee, and shook his hand. Interestingly, the woman sitting slightly behind the owner came to the front of the room with Andre, and then stood to one side. Andre then led the management team out of the conference room.

After the management team left, the woman escorted Lee to the chair vacated by Andre, and seated him. While there was full use of "would like" and "please," Lee had no sense of his going along with the request being optional. After he was seated, the woman pivoted Lee around to face the owner.

"Well, Lee," the owner started, with a slight smile. "It's been more than the two to four weeks we discussed, or should I say, that you gave me. Still, I'm back."

His two staffers were exactly right in their astonishment, and both of them were evidently right. His face and body were slimmer and trimmer. He looked like he was born to great wealth. His voice was even pitched different. It couldn't possibly be Chuck LaGrange. Yet here he was.

☆ ☆ ☆

Lee found himself searching the room for hidden cameras. This had to be some kind of trick. Nobody, but nobody could possibly change so drastically in such a short amount of time. In a minute, after he'd had time to sweat and fume for the benefit of the audience, they'd be telling him what TV show he was now the fall guy for. He only hoped there was enough money to be worth it.

"Okay, so the hidden cameras are going to show up when, exactly?"

"There are no hidden cameras. There's the Chuck LaGrange you knew seventy-five days ago, and there's the person with the same name and more or less the same body sitting here now. I'm still the same person, although I must admit there has been quite a lot of change. At least I hope there's been quite a lot of change. You can ask my wife. Oh, Melissa, meet Lee Sherman, the man who sent me down the road I'm on."

They exchanged greetings, and Chuck also introduced his personal assistant. Lee did not try to shake hands with Margot, having a distinct impression from her planting him in the chair that he wanted as little familiarity with her as possible.

"We had a wager, of sorts, and I'm here to take care of that wager."

Lee snorted. "The money I make from this commission more than makes up for any wager."

"Well, we needed to drop that subsidiary anyway, and it gave me an excuse to get up here. Those two staff members had extremely shocked looks. It was all I could do to keep from laughing, but that would have spoiled the whole thing. Did they say anything before you came in? You were looking my way very carefully."

"They mentioned no names. One thought you must be the person they knew. The other thought there was no way, and that you must be a double. That, combined with the mystery of how Chicago got a job from New Orleans, together with a mystery owner showing up, had my attention."

"Ah, yes. There was that, wasn't there? In any case, our wager was whether the ancestor I was talking about was a pirate. Well, my information is that he was not a pirate. He had quite an interesting life, and did acquire a good deal of gold in a way that was, shall we say, outside the normal channels of commerce. His claiming to be a pirate was a cover story, which you suggested might be the case, as I recall. Actually, there appears to have been an ongoing story about a LaGrange having been a pirate, but I haven't tracked it down yet. It was evidently considerably earlier.

"Now, one condition was that any proof be acceptable to a genealogist, as I recall. While I have amassed a lot of information, none of it could be said to be acceptable. Therefore, I lose on both counts."

Lee considered all of that. "If you know something to be true, then you could go to the locations and dig until you did find documentation."

"You're right. I could do all of that, actually. Perhaps, at some point, I will. But now, I'm going to appear to change the subject. You've been curious about my company."

"You say that as a statement of fact, and not a question."

"Correct. But for what I'm about to tell you to make any sense whatsoever, you should first know what the initials JLG&S stand for: Jean LaGrange & Sons. Jean LaGrange started it in 1870. I am his direct descendant, and the company is his legacy to me personally. We won't go into how that happened, but know that it is a fact. As you surmised back in June, our ancestors did know each other. Jean LaGrange was so named because of the high esteem his father Philippe had for Jean Lafitte. Jean Lafitte evidently had a great deal of trust in Philippe, because he left this with him."

Chuck pulled out a very worn and old-looking ivory pendant on a chain. He released a hidden latch revealing a golden coin about the size of a silver dollar. It was an 8-escudo coin. Lee gasped.

"Do you have any idea what this is worth?"

"Well, actually I do. The coin, just to sell it on the market, would fetch maybe $5,000 to $6,000. I couldn't tell you the value of the ivory case. The provenance, as the antique collectors term it, puts any other possible value to shame. This hung around the neck of Jean Lafitte for many years. It was his 'good luck.' That fact alone makes it incredible. There is, however, something that takes it to the next level. Some of our ancestors called things like this touch stones. By benefit of being in contact with an individual over a long period of time, objects can absorb the experiences of the wearer. A person can then read these experiences, even though the person who wore it is long gone. By sending me on this road, I figured out how to use things like this. I also found dangers.

"It works most easily for those who are descendants of the individual. I did a vision of Jean Lafitte, and found that, as you are quite certain, he is your direct ancestor. The request Jean Lafitte made of Philippe was that this be given to a worthy descendant. I declare you a worthy descendant. To find what information is here, you need to take the coin home, and in a private place, think about Jean Lafitte. Expect a connection. I ended up calling it a vision. Whatever you wish to call it, expect that you'll be basically unconscious while you're in it."

Chuck pulled out a business card, and wrote a phone number on the back. "We're staying in town tonight and tomorrow. Give me a call if you'd like to talk about what you find."

Lee straggled into the office the next morning, rather the worse for wear. Several of the staff looked at him with alarm, wondering if he felt alright. Going into the men's room, he took a longer look at himself in the mirror, and decided their concerns had merit. There weren't any pressing issues, so he signed himself out on sick leave, and called Chuck, who suggested they meet at the restaurant of the hotel where he was staying. It was one of the fanciest hotels around, and suddenly Lee was considering the distinct possibility his bonus from the JLG&S job would go to pay for his lunch.

Chuck looked at Lee, and smiled, but it was far-off and a little sad. "I see you viewed Jean Lafitte. How did it go?"

"It was strange. I guess I thought if there was a vision, the person would just be doing whatever they were doing, but Lafitte just stood there. I finally started asking questions, and succeeded in getting a number of points resolved. I recalled your description of how touch stones absorb experiences, and considered it was something like a data base, that doesn't actually do anything. The user first has to access the file, and then has to formulate ways to query the data within the file, and report it in a way that makes sense to the user. This is, of course, assuming what I saw and experienced was real."

"Your comparing it to a data base is good, and testing it every way I can, it seems to be quite real. Now, I have seen instances where an individual has blocked or repressed memories. Those become an empty space in the data. I've never actually seen a lie in a vision, but I now think it might be possible, although you'd have to be in vision with a sociopath for it to happen. One thing you really need now is substantial nutrition. After that, you need rest." Chuck called a waitress, and ordered a substantial brunch for Lee. Nibbling on some toast, in an evident contradiction to the prescription he had just given for adequate nutrition, Chuck inquired, "Now, you can, of course, see the vision at will, right?"

"That's true. If I think about a particular thing Jean Lafitte did that I saw in the vision, it comes back, and just as real as ever."

"Isn't it strange, how we can forget what we ourselves did, but can count the number of ants crawling by an ancestor over a century ago? In fact, we can perfectly visualize what that ancestor did, even when they probably forgot about it or never noticed it in the first place."

"Yeah, that's strange enough. One thing I'd like to learn is how to turn off the vision. It keeps on kind of spinning, just on the edge of my normal sight."

Lee saw a wave of concern go across Chuck's face. "I mentioned there were dangers," Chuck said quietly. "It sounds like you're already flirting with the main danger, after only a single vision. How much effort does it take to keep the vision to the side? Let me put it another way. If you're relaxed, how much of your personal vision does it take up?"

Juice and coffee started arriving, and Lee sipped the juice, only realizing after drinking some, just how hungry he was. In any case, it gave him a moment to consider Chuck's two-pronged question. As he considered the question, he realized that he couldn't exactly answer it, so he temporized with a return question. "How did you find the Jean Lafitte piece, anyway?"

Chuck almost waved it off, but answered anyway. "When I took over the company, one of the things I received was a box with touch stones in it. One of them was for Philippe, Jean's father. Philippe was born in 1789 in Cap Francais, Saint-Domingue, now known as Cap Haitien, Haiti. His father, Gaston, had a mercantile there, but when the slave revolt got too severe, and it became evident that Napoleon Bonaparte was neither willing nor able to protect his own countrymen in their own land, Gaston sold what he couldn't take, and moved his family to New Orleans. There, he reestablished his mercantile and home.

"It was Jean Lafitte's family who got them out of what became Haiti not long before it became suicide for a Frenchman to be there. It was also thanks to the Lafitte clan that the LaGrange family was able to set up shop in New Orleans. It was only natural for the LaGrange family store to be an outlet for goods brought into New Orleans by the Lafitte family. The relationship continued into the second generation. Jean Lafitte was taking care of business while Philippe was still a child. When Philippe came of age, it was evident his slight build would never allow him to be much account in war. Still, like his father, he had a sharp mind for business, so Jean offered him a position in his operation at Barataria Bay."

Food was being set before Lee, and he started eating without particularly thinking about it, finding himself quite interested in how their two families were connected. From his own personal experience of the previous evening, Lee was seeing truly convincing proof of a Lafitte-LaGrange connection, making him think he probably did owe Chuck a bonus. It was obvious Chuck wasn't interested in any bonus Lee might be able to offer.

Chuck continued. "Philippe went with Jean Lafitte in one of his last sailings from New Orleans. He was on board purely as a passenger, but it was something he told people about ever after, with a great deal of pride, that he had actually sailed with the famous Jean Lafitte. After several years, things got too sticky at Barataria Bay, and Jean moved his operations to the area later known as Galveston. Philippe felt the call of family at that point, more than the call of adventure, so he returned to New Orleans, and took over the family business.

"Jean Lafitte had thought of your piece as 'lucky,' and he had stayed alive, certainly. Still, after being painted as a villain by the Americans, Spanish, English, and others, the question of just how good that luck was began to weigh on him, or at least that is what he told Philippe at a clandestine meeting, where Jean gave it to Philippe for safe keeping. So it stayed in the mercantile safe, and when the mercantile closed, the safe, together with its contents moved to JLG&S. I had to track the safe through both Philippe and Jean to find it."

✲ ✲ ✲

Lee wondered how Chuck and Melissa managed to get their timing down so well, since it was just as Chuck finished his story that Melissa breezed into the restaurant, commenting, as she came up to their table, how she was famished, and dying to hear how Lee had done. Lee looked around, seeing all the tables occupied, with people waiting to get in, and wondered about them homesteading. Chuck just laughed.

"JLG&S put us up here because we own part of it, and so advised management before we checked in. As for using a table for business, they've already told us they're happy to work around us."

Melissa and Chuck stopped for a moment, establishing some notable eye contact, and Lee recalled they were newlyweds, after all. Still, there was suddenly a look of concern on Melissa's face, and her next comment made Lee wonder if there was more to that eye contact than new love.

"Lee, are you married?" Melissa asked. The question sounded like there was more than idle curiosity going on.

"Well, yes I am, actually. Jodi and I have been married, going on five years. Happily married, I might add, at least from my point of view."

"I'm glad to hear that." Melissa fished a card out of her purse, and inspected the information closely. "Could you give her my card, please? Oh, just a second, let me put a note on the back."

Lee glanced at the note, which read, "Jodi, if anything strange happens because of his vision, please call right away, day or night. M." Lee glanced up to meet her steady, serious gaze. "Please give it to her, Lee. I'm serious. You must."

"Does this have anything to do with me continuing to see the vision?" Melissa nodded. "How could you know? I just told Chuck, and ... wait a minute, can you two do visions with each other?"

"We are able to, and we do, along with some other aspects of visions. None of them are aspects of visions we choose to advertise. It has to do with competitive advantage, you know."

"I noticed you two were studying me more than listening to the presentation yesterday. You were doing visions of me?" Chuck and Melissa both nodded.

"So you can do visions of anybody, and, as you said, the visions cannot lie."

Chuck nodded. "It takes personnel review and corporate analysis to new levels. Still, you won't be able to do it just yet. At this point, you have to learn how to control the visions. What you're seeing right now is a symptom of the visions controlling you. You need to know that, but whether you can stop the visions from going to the next level, I can't tell. If the situation does go to the next level, it will be up to Jodi to bring you through it. If all is well between you and Jodi, as you say, she should be able to handle the situation. I don't think we'll say more than that right now."

Lee thought about it a moment, as Melissa's food came, along with some more food for him that he hadn't even been aware of being ordered.

"So, Melissa, I'm seeing that Chuck got into a situation, but you were able to rescue him from it, and it's evidently a woman thing, and intensely personal. I'm also seeing you think I'm headed for the same place, with little alternative to going through whatever it is. Well, I guess that's how it is, although I'm wondering if you two knew this could happen when you gave it to me."

"We thought it might happen, but frankly had no idea that it would. We assumed it could be avoided, but perhaps it's a rite of passage. It has to rank up there with requiring a boy to kill a lion with a sharp stick in order to join the men of his tribe."

Melissa asked Chuck if he'd told Lee about the intertwined lives hypothesis. Chuck allowed as how he'd mentioned it in passing, but hadn't really gotten into it. He said that he'd observed the same family lines turning up time and again. For instance, he and Melissa were distant cousins, which was what led them to meet in Oregon in the first place. She had been searching for what turned out to be their common family line. Even where there had not been intermarriage, there were repeated connections of one sort or another, such as Chuck being associated with Lee under very odd circumstances, and it turning out their separate families had associations going back to at least 1800. Chuck suspected there had been connections prior to that, as well.

"We need to confirm connections, and maybe track ancestry a bit more precisely. So here in a couple of days, we're heading off to do research in Haiti, Saint Malo, France, where many of the French privateers were based, and possibly to Turin, Italy to check on the connection with the mathematician LaGrange, or Lagrangia, as he was known in Italy."

"That sounds like a great trip, but what does it have to do with me?"

"We are certain our family connections go back at least to Haiti, and I suspect we'll also find connections in Saint Malo. We'd like you and your wife to come with us. I'm sure your company will give you a sabbatical, and I can guarantee you no loss in pay. What do you say?"

"Well," Lee considered. "That's an awfully nice offer, and all. But I hope you aren't thinking this 'intertwined lives' hypothesis is anything new. It used to be called inbreeding. It's so common that it has become something of a joke in genealogy that if you trace your family, and there's much lineage in Western Europe, you're almost certainly a relative of Charlemagne. In any case, this is too much, too soon, and I think I need to absorb at least some of all that has happened in the past twenty-four hours."

"I have no problem with that," Chuck replied, smiling. "Still, I had to give you the invitation. You have our cards whenever you're ready for the next step. Finally, I've got to tell you to avoid any further visions until you get some control. Please give Melissa's card to your wife. Try to convince Jodi this is serious."

Lee suddenly realized how tired he was, and said he felt he should go on home. He staggered a little as he got up, and Chuck immediately said they would take him home, and asked for his keys so a second driver could take his car. Lee thought all that food probably overwhelmed his metabolic rate. So Lee rode home in the LaGrange limo, still conscious, but aware the vision was narrowing his field of vision. He knew Melissa and Chuck were talking seriously and quietly to Jodi, but he was far more interested in getting to bed. Sleep would make everything better.

12: Toddlin' Around

Melissa's cell phone rang. Chuck peered at the lit clock in the room, and saw it was a little after two a.m. He knew from the conversation the caller was Jodi Sherman, and she was in a panic. When Chuck and Melissa took Lee home the previous day to his wife, the three had all helped get Lee in bed, and he immediately fell asleep. That was about two in the afternoon. He was apparently sleeping quietly until about ten p.m., when he began to thrash around.

Melissa turned her cell phone's speaker on, so Chuck could follow. Jodi said she was about to go to bed, but his thrashing made her afraid of getting hit, and also afraid for what might be happening to him. She sat up with him, watching as the thrashing continued. Melissa asked if his cheeks were becoming more sunken, and she said that yes, it appeared that way, but she didn't think it was possible, and concluded it must be her imagination. Jodi continued that she thought he must be having a nightmare, but it went on and on, and she wasn't able to wake him.

Then about midnight, he began muttering. It wasn't loud enough for her to understand anything at first, but after a while he was speaking more loudly, and she heard French, Spanish, and English. The English sounded like English from another time. She didn't think Lee spoke like that. Chuck and Melissa had both heard enough, and Melissa turned off the speaker. Chuck immediately began getting dressed. He was dumbfounded that Lee could have gone into a terminal vision so fast. Chuck had fought it off for a week, and that was after a number of visions. What if it had taken him while he was driving all those miles?

Chuck used the suite's dressing room to give Melissa some privacy. When he came out, Melissa had just about shared everything she could with Jodi, and was repeating, once more, that to save Lee, Jodi would have to be his total lover, right then, right there, and that she could hold nothing back. It would be especially painful to do that much giving, because Lee would almost certainly not know what happened. Afterward, hopefully, they'd be able to share their visions, and he would know. As Chuck listened to her, it pained him to once again realize the absolute truth she spoke. Melissa went on to say that they'd be right over, and not to worry about anything other than saving Lee.

While Melissa was getting dressed, Chuck woke the driver, and told him not to worry about taking Margot at this time. When they got to the front door of the hotel, their car was waiting for them, and they headed for the Sherman house. Even though traffic was light, they were still half an hour in transit. Still, Melissa didn't think they'd given Jodi enough time, so they waited in the car another half hour. Chuck told the driver he should wait for the moment. Chuck went on to reassure him that if they were going to be there for very long, he'd be released until they were ready to leave.

They had to ring several times, but at last Jodi Sherman did turn on the porch light and let them in. She was now relaxed, and seemed pleased with everything. Lee was sleeping normally, and Jodi advised Melissa that she should be a doctor. What she prescribed absolutely worked, and it made both the patient and physician much better at the same time.

"I only have one complaint, Melissa. It was the most passionate experience of my life, and you say he won't remember it. How can that be?"

"He was trapped in his vision. That vision was the sum total of everything he could possibly experience. What you did got to him at an emotional level beyond the vision. With the emotional link established and strong, his mind was then able to break free of the vision. His mind would not have been able to comprehend, at least on a conscious level, what it was that freed him."

"You said, though, that we might now be able to share visions."

"Yes, I think you will probably be able to."

"Why couldn't we share visions before he went through all this?"

"I don't really know. I only know what worked for us. I also know it's marvelous when it happens, so why don't you go back in to your husband. Let your focus be on him. We'll be here for you. Don't worry, and don't hurry, at all."

☆ ☆ ☆

Jodi went back in to Lee, leaving Melissa and Chuck in the living room. Chuck seemed preoccupied. His eyes appeared to focus on her for a short while and then move to random spots around the room. Melissa decided she needed coffee, and went into the kitchen to see what might be there. She also called the driver, and told him to take off. They'd call when they wanted to leave. The driver was more than happy with that instruction. However, since he was also their security, she knew he'd have arranged various sorts of protection designed to be both effective and unobtrusive.

She almost had the coffee ready when she turned around and there was Chuck, just staring at her. Actually, he wasn't exactly staring at her, but seemingly alternating between areas beside each ear. Melissa thought it was kind of spooky, but finished getting coffee for the two of them. She found a tray, and took the coffee into the living room, Chuck shambling along behind. She pushed Chuck into a chair, and perched on the edge of a sofa across from the chair.

"Okay, Chuck. Where's your mind this morning. I realize we're short on sleep and all, but this is really crazy. I don't like it at all."

That brought Chuck back to himself. "Listening to what you told Jodi really hit me. It was that bit about connections between our emotions and mentality. I felt like a light went on, and there might be some sort of breakthrough with the visions. But then, it seemed like there was a problem with my eyesight, because there were blurs behind you. Still, when I would look somewhere else, like a wall, there were no blurs. I'm really sorry for acting kind of goofy, but as I began focusing on the blur behind you, after a while I was able to differentiate details, and they are beginning to resolve into translucent lines of people behind you.

"The lines of people are your ancestors, which makes sense from the standpoint of you being your own touch stone. What puzzles me is that I can't get any real focus on your parents, but I can obtain perfect clarity on their parents, going back as far as I care to go. What's fun is that I can look at Sarah Ann Fuller, and pick up all the details I care to obtain, and can see both the line of people coming to you as well as the line of people coming to me. Either there's something off with my visions, or else it must be possible to block people."

Melissa became pale as Chuck was saying that. "I'll tell you about all of it. I'll tell you soon, but just not right now. Okay?"

Chuck nodded, and took a sip of coffee. Jodi came out, her face flushed and radiant. Melissa looked at her, obviously grateful for the interruption, and smiled. "You weren't very long."

"We weren't? It was six kinds of wonderful. The shared vision really, truly works."

"Why don't you go back in and relax. Chuck and I will bring you two some breakfast."

"Are you sure? You don't mind?"

"It will be our pleasure. Now get out of here. Shoo!"

Melissa put breakfast together for Lee and Jodi, remembering her own experience, and happy for them. In their bedroom, Chuck gave Lee a hefty tray of breakfast, and listened as Lee described some of his experiences while trapped in the vision. Chuck was reminded of his experiences, wondering if that was how he was going to die. This was Lee's coming out party, and he deserved every bit of encouragement he could get, as well as all the congratulations possible to Jodi for pulling him out of it.

Then Melissa went and stuck him in center stage with this new little thing he'd done. Chuck sighed, and asked Lee if there were any ancestors he was having trouble finding evidence on. Lee named one, and Chuck looked at Lee's family lines, which seemed to stand out very clearly. He did some checking, and the mystery was easily solved.

"Lee, you were looking for him on census documents in the Vicksburg area in 1890. You couldn't find him, because he had gone to Cleveland for a better-paying job in 1888. He was there through 1892, when he went back to Vicksburg. So you need to check the Cleveland census."

"Cleveland. I'd have been a long time finding that one. Chuck, it looks like you've got a genealogy tool after all. Do you think I'll be able to do that, too?"

"I would guess so. You've followed the same pattern I did, although you've done it a lot faster. You and Jodi already know about real-time visions, so it's just some practice to do the rest of it."

"To what degree do you think your personality has been changed by these visions?"

"That's a good question. The visions have imposed some maturity, perhaps. My personality has probably changed some, much like anyone changes when they are with someone for an extended period of time. I was in Charles LaGrange's body for the equivalent of six months, so there was probably some change there. You and I have both picked up a small ability, certainly. I'll show you."

With that, Chuck switched into French, talking at a normal conversational speed, and Lee answered with equal fluency. Chuck then went to Spanish, and Lee was not quite as fluent, but fully understandable. After a few minutes, Chuck switched back to English, and asked Lee how much foreign language training he'd had. Lee answered that he'd had some high school Spanish, along with a few semesters in college, but that he didn't remember more than a couple of words. Chuck then asked him to consider what languages he had just been using. Lee looked at Jodi, who informed him he had indeed been rolling right along in both French and Spanish, but only he would know if it was understandable.

✲ ✲ ✲

Melissa hadn't said anything during all of this. She had been watching Chuck, and thinking about how he had been progressing in this viewing, doing enough herself to appreciate just how far he had come, and how far ahead of her he'd gone. She could view other people, but she neither went as deeply into other people's stories nor got the apparent visceral pleasure Chuck did from his visions. She wondered if it came from that nearly fatal vision he'd had of his ancestor Charles. Perhaps it was just part and parcel of his psyche. Then again, maybe it was her fear keeping her from reaching further.

The thought of that fear overwhelmed her, and the source of her fear burst through her carefully created mental barricades. She turned and ran from the bedroom as Chuck and Lee were exchanging experiences of their visions, sounding like a couple of soldiers in a bar. Jodi was still halfway in her own vision, and anywhere Lee was, she was happy, at least for the time being. Melissa sank into a chair in the living room, her face in her hands, and sobbed silently. It came to her that her life, up until she met Chuck, had resembled his terminal vision, except hers had been played out in real life.

Chuck came into the living room soon after she got there, and tried to comfort her.

"I just can't do it."

"Can't do what? I don't understand."

"I just can't go through this ... seeing you ... it all happen again," she gasped between sobs.

Chuck started putting things together. "Does this have something to do with your blocking your parents, and with me being able to do new things with visions?"

Melissa nodded, and Chuck gently stood her up, and guided her to the couch, so he could sit beside her, and hold her. Finally, her control kicked in, and she sat up and kissed Chuck firmly. She shook her head to get her hair going the right direction, smoothing it with her hand. Chuck reached around to where he'd seen some tissues, and gave her one.

"Okay," Melissa said firmly, "I promised I would tell you about my parents soon. Now is the time." She took a deep breath. "My father, Reggie Duncan, played football in college. He was the team's star running back, enabling them to win their conference his senior year. He was named All-American. After graduation, he got married and was drafted by a professional football team. By his third year, he was a player everyone was watching, as he continued to improve in nearly all aspects of his play. It seemed like half the cameras at a game would be aimed at him, because of the certainty he would do something spectacular.

"My Mom went to every game she could, and at the advanced age of two, I was there as well. One play, the quarterback muffed a hand-off to him, and as he was trying to retrieve the football, he got hit exactly wrong, and suffered a spinal injury very high up that immobilized him. My Mom turned me away from the field, but with all the video and photographs taken at that moment, the scene ended up being permanently engraved in my mind. That's not to mention all the media attention, asking the usual stupid media questions to my Mom, about how she felt. I even remember microphones being shoved in my face, which terrified me.

"His team, the league, and his fellow players were all very nice, and gave enough money to build a special room onto our house so Daddy could come home. It was quite a deal in 1989, setting up a place for someone with no control more than an inch or two below his chin. There was enough money for some nursing, but Mom ended up with Daddy nearly all the time. It was awful. It seemed like she totally lost her identity, and there was no more Abigail. That was her name, Abigail.

"I felt like I grew up all on my own. That probably wasn't really the case, but that was my impression. Holidays just didn't seem to exist at our house after all of that. What would happen around the holiday season always seemed to feature some genius in the media with the bright idea to do a "Where Are They Now?" piece, and it would be Reggie Duncan's turn in the barrel. They'd come out with their cameras and their lights and their vulture mentalities, and when they left, Mom would cry for weeks. As I grew older, and Mom's grasp on reality became more tenuous, they would try to interview me. After a while, I'd tell them all to get stuffed. Those were my holidays.

"In school, it seemed like I knew more about football than the boys, and I seemed to be smarter than the other girls, so everybody hated me, and stayed away from me. With no social life to speak of, I spent more time studying. That got me good grades, which got me even more alienated. By the time I was in high school, my life was divided between studying and taking care of Mom and doing what I could for Daddy. I got to the point where I didn't care too much about the high school social whirl. So the proms went by without anyone inviting me, or, for that matter, me particularly noticing until they were ancient history.

"Along with money for Daddy, they had set up a scholarship fund for me, which took care of nearly everything, plus, with my grades, I got additional scholarships that got me through college with little financial hardship. I felt a little guilty, though, going off to college with my Mom not really able to take care of herself, much less everything else in her life. Everyone encouraged me to do it, though. My choice in a university was the closest one to home that had the courses I thought I should take.

"Then, during my sophomore year, there was an electrical short in Daddy's room. From what the inspectors said later, the contractors messed up a number of things. There was little we could do about it, seeing as how the contractors had long since gone out of business. Anyway, the electrical short started a fire that destroyed the house. There was no way to get Daddy out. The firemen were barely able to rescue Mom, who was very badly burned in a futile effort to save Daddy.

"Mom was in the burn unit a long time. I remember walking through the charred ruin of the house, trying to find something, anything, that I could save, but there was nothing. There was only ash and fused metal and nightmares. I took care of what things I could, and went back to school even though everyone told me I should take the semester off. Mom barely survived with severe physical impairments, and when the hospital released her, they would only let her go to a specialized care facility. I felt bad about that, but was powerless to do anything else. After all, the only home I had to offer was a college dormitory. Then, I found out they had to keep her separated from everyone else, because she was continually reliving the football game and the fire, and would scream and cry until total exhaustion set in.

"The only thing that would bring her any relief was when I would visit her, and talk about her family. At those times, she would calm down and appeared to be thinking clearly, remembering fairly accurately other discussions we'd had on the subject. That kept me scrambling, trying to find new information, including the fact that she had distant cousins still alive. The problem was if I didn't bring her new information, and we only talked about things that had already been covered, there was little, if any, relief for her. So, when I lost my job, it became an opportunity to obtain a great deal of information, which I planned on rationing out to her, bit at a time. Come to think of it, I should stop by and see her."

Chuck had been listening very carefully, and also doing visions during all of this. "We certainly will go by to see her. I'd like to meet her. Melissa, you are a true heroine, saving me from my vision when you're still suffering from your own real-life vision. I can't do much about your past, but if there's anything I can do to make things better now or the future, just tell me. As for dangers to me, if you see anything that could blind-side me, give me a yell so I can duck."

☆ ☆ ☆

After he had considered the situation some more, Chuck said, "I don't know what could be done for your mother, Abigail. Still, we could move her closer to us. Whatever we do, she can get whatever she needs or wants. Well, I'll take that back, not being able to change history. Let's at least say anything she wants that we can deliver. We can find out if there's anything that can be done for her. If there isn't anything, we can fund the necessary research." Chuck came to a stop, frustrated that with all that he represented now, her mother couldn't be made whole. It occurred to him that the statement that history couldn't be changed ignored the fact that he had arranged with Jean LaGrange to do that very thing.

"I'll invite you to do something, though. Do visions of every part of my mentality. If you find anything that I've blocked, make sure I get it unblocked. It occurs to me that you're quite correct that I'm subject to attack from people and directions unknown. We already know that having these visions is something that people can generally do – that guy running the RV and truck repair shop in Boise, for instance. Who knows who else has what capabilities? We also already know everybody doesn't have good intentions. We have cousin Armand as a case study in that regard. But could you do ongoing visions of me? I know it'll be boring, but maybe we can save ourselves some grief somewhere down the line."

"I don't think studying you will be boring. Maybe I could do a book about the mind of mad man sometime."

They both laughed, and right on cue, Chuck's cell phone rang. Glancing at the caller ID, Chuck saw it was Andre Moniteau. Oof. Back to business.

"Andre, what's up?"

"Armand has filed suit against JLG&S as well as you personally. He evidently started beating the war drums the moment he heard we were getting out from under his daddy's company. He's got process servers out, and has as much media as he could find following the process servers. He's making as big a circus as he can, promising great stories, and secret crimes in high places. I hated calling you this early, but I knew you were planning on leaving on a trip tomorrow, and was wondering if you could move it up to today. They're not going to be long in tracking you there in Chicago, and whatever you do, stay away from New Orleans."

"We were already up, actually. Thanks for letting me know. How long should we be looking at being gone, do you think?"

"Legal says most of the points in the suit are garbage, but it'll take a while to get them thrown out. Also, it will take a while for the media to get distracted by all the other rotten smells in town, although we will certainly be doing our utmost to distract them. Our company plan includes being very boring, as you already know."

"Okay. We'll head for Denver, and visit Melissa's mother. Then, we can do Blodgett, Oregon. There are things out there we can take care of. From there, I think we could head for Tucson, and then take up the quest we mentioned to you earlier."

"That sounds good. Now, I will not call you directly any more. Also, you and Melissa should not use your company phones. As a matter of fact, you should give them to your personal assistants. We have secure means of communication with your personal assistants, although we will not even use that any more than necessary."

"You're talking like they'll be using pretty advanced methods to try to find us."

"I think we can count on Armand. He'll use the funds we gave him to be the ultimate thorn in our side. That will include any techniques suggested to him by all the experts he can buy. For him, buying people is no different than buying chewing gum."

"Could they be listening to us right now?"

"Not likely, but it is possible. Speaking of which, your transportation will have been changed, and we'll support you in any way possible."

"I appreciate your efforts in all this, Andre."

"It's for the company. Your rooms are being closed as we speak, and they'll be by to get you presently."

"So you knew we weren't at the property."

"You'll recall that I apologized for calling early, not for waking you."

The call ended there, and Chuck brought Melissa up to date on the situation. They both went back in and visited with Lee and Jodi, once again inviting them on the adventure, and being refused, as they expected. In about forty-five minutes, their people arrived.

"So, Chuck, you don't even have to pack or check out any more?"

"That's how it seems to be, yeah."

"Nice job if you can get it."

"Getting it wasn't that hard. You just find an ancestor willing to set you up in business back around the Civil War. Putting up with everyone running your life takes some getting used to."

"That part, Chuck, should be really easy. Everyone but you ran your life before all this happened. The difference is that now they're required to at least act like they're listening to you. Not only that, you get creature comforts. Live long and prosper."

13: Hiding & Chasing

When they got to the VIP terminal, there was indeed a different plane from the small work-a-day jet they'd been using. This one was as big as a small passenger jet, and the pilot said it was a Gulfstream G550.As far as he was concerned, it was the absolute top end in executive transportation. Chuck looked at it and whistled. That thing made them about as anonymous as a brass band. Melissa thought it might even be a good ploy. Would someone trying to stay out of sight arrive in Air Force One? Anyway, they could use its long legs going to Europe.

In order to keep their plans as private as possible, Margot only gave the pilot one leg at a time. Melissa's mother was in a facility on the south side of Denver, so they flew into Centennial Airport. Chuck still got a little fidgety about letting others handle the hands-on planning, but it certainly seemed that Margot was getting it done efficiently and effectively. In theory, that left Chuck free to generate overall strategic stuff, although exactly what strategic stuff he should generate was out there somewhere beyond the shrug zone.

Melissa had Chuck stay out in a public area while she went to visit her mother. While she was gone, Chuck asked Margot to verify that Melissa's mother was receiving the best care possible, and also to set up any necessary financial arrangements. Additionally, he asked her to see what would be involved if they moved her to Louisiana. This made an impact on Margot, who hurried off to handle things.

After a while, Melissa came back to the public area, walking beside a woman in a wheelchair. The woman had evidences of skin grafts over a large part of her head and arms. Chuck viewed the woman, who he already knew had to be Melissa's mother, and found a nightmare world of darkness. In that darkness was a single bright spot, which consisted of her daughter and their conversations about family. Her mother, Abigail, was in that bright spot right now. Chuck saw in her a tough and resilient personality, and considered Melissa was truly her mother's daughter in that regard.

Melissa handled the introductions, referring to Chuck as "our cousin, Charles LaGrange." Abigail Duncan regarded Chuck with glittering eyes, and declared that he didn't take after their side of the family. Chuck allowed as how he definitely missed out, in that regard, but he hoped the blood ran true. That seemed to be a satisfactory answer. After a short while, Abigail became tired, and an attendant took her back. Melissa pronounced the visit a success, but Chuck saw that Melissa was drained of vitality for quite a while afterward.

Margot returned, and favored Chuck with the briefest of smiles. He did a brief view of her, and knew she was able to take some positive action for Melissa's mother. Aloud, Margot told Chuck their situation needed addressing right away, and they needed to get moving. Chuck wondered what they'd have to do to get the hounds off their trail.

They flew directly into Corvallis, where the jet needed the entire runway to get stopped. They got rental cars, but left an assistant with secure communications with the plane. Up at Blodgett, Chuck and Melissa got privacy, but they knew well enough that they were anything but alone. Margot was stationed up at the store. If they had any doubts about her proximity, they were erased when Margot showed up to advise them the plane's being at Corvallis was known, and in accordance with a plan of which Chuck had been ignorant, the assistant ordered the plane to San Jose, California. The story given the aircrew was they weren't comfortable flying out of such a small strip on that aircraft. In addition, carrying less weight would simplify their takeoff. The group would get alternate transportation to San Jose and meet them there.

The next morning, Margot arrived with the information their presence in San Jose, California was 'known.' So they knew the tracking was of the aircraft. The Gulfstream was then ordered to San Diego, with further destinations of Port Arthur, Texas; Fargo, North Dakota; Spokane, Washington; Kearney, Nebraska; and Little Rock, Arkansas. At that point, the assistant was to cancel the contract, and rejoin them by whatever means were available. If they believed the ruse was discovered sooner, the remainder of the stops would be cancelled.

Meanwhile, since Margot had determined the problem with their tracking was in the company's purchasing office, she used contacts in another company to get an aircraft to Salem, Oregon in two days. She then pulled back from Blodgett, allowing Chuck and Melissa to just enjoy each other for that period of time. At the end of the two days, she reappeared, seeming almost apologetic to disturb them. They took back roads up to Salem, where they met the new plane, said to be a Cessna Citation X, but which in no way looked like the straight-wing plane Chuck had heard of. This one was big and fast, and Chuck just shrugged and got on board. Evidently, anonymity was where you found it.

The big Cessna got them to Tucson in double-quick time. They went by the old home place, and Chuck wondered about the possibilities of getting the house back to something like it had been in the 1930s. Margot took notes, and Melissa frowned a little, but didn't say anything. Two days after their arrival in Tucson, Margot advised the original aircraft had terminated in Little Rock, Arkansas, and the assistant had rented a car which he drove to Memphis. He turned in that car, went to another car rental, and was on his way to Louisville, Kentucky. Margot had reports of private investigators heading for Little Rock. The aircraft, of course, was on its way back to its home base.

Several days later, Margot reported the leak in the purchasing department was resolved, and that most of the private investigators in Little Rock were now on their way to Nebraska, although some had decided to return to New Orleans, and still others were proceeding to Chicago, to track them that way. Margot estimated the private investigators would need a couple of days in each location, since the assistant (who had now rejoined them) had salted each area with clues, leads, and all manner of totally useless information about which she declined to elaborate further. Chuck was beginning to feel more secure in her keeping even as he was resenting the need for it in the first place.

✲ ✲ ✲

Chuck didn't find much about the family in Tucson. He already knew most of the details, but was able to fill in some detail at the library's genealogy department. There had been so much in such a hurry, that his mind began to rebel against pushing forward very hard. In any case, Tucson's heat was beyond the limits of his tolerance, even though he was only out in it in passing. So when discussion began about trying to get into Haiti, Chuck was receptive to going, even though it was not only hot there, it was hurricane season.

The aircrew informed Chuck by way of Margot, that the Cap Haitien runway was too short for their plane, so they would fly in to Port Au Prince, and get a smaller plane to Cap Haitien. They had been in Tucson a week and a half when they flew out for Haiti, or Saint-Domingue, as Chuck found himself thinking about it. When they got off the plane in Port Au Prince, Chuck's senses were immediately assaulted in totally unexpected ways. There was the tropical heat, so different from the desert heat, and then there were the smells that made him recoil, along with the noises.

While he had inadvertently become fluent in Popular French (as opposed to Standard French) from his contact with Charles, his command of Creole was extremely limited. What came to Chuck was to do a fast vision on several locals, and then, while they were on their way to Cap Haitien, he was in vision with them. The result was that, getting off the plane, he could now communicate, although he was immediately marked as speaking in a dialect from the south of the country. At least he was making progress. By the time they were checked into the hotel, he had chosen a couple other people to vision, and so when they went down to dinner, his speech was such that he fit in as well as a white man could in a black country.

The next day, Chuck and Melissa followed Philippe's vision to where the mercantile and residence had been located. The combination of war, earthquake (they said there'd been a major one around 1848), hurricanes, and time had completely wiped out anything that might have been recognized. Chuck superimposed Philippe's vision, and managed to get some information, but much of it seemed somehow out of whack with the story he already knew. Chuck had carried the family touch stones with him, and thought this would be a good time to actually view Gaston.

In the hotel, Chuck settled back with the chess piece. Melissa sat, facing him, focusing on Chuck. Gaston, like Philippe, had been born in Cap-Francais, and had seen the city become quite large and extremely wealthy. It was a good time to be a merchant in the city, but at the peak of its prosperity, there were slave revolts which were only put down with great difficulty. Then there was the French Revolution. Deposing the king immediately brought Britain and Spain to wage war. The slaves decided they liked the motto of the French revolution, and the British and Spanish were only too willing to support their uprising against the relatively few French.

Gaston had known the Lafitte family all his life, and in 1793, as the sky began falling on his lifestyle, a Lafitte ship happened to be in port. The family along with the crew of Lafitte's ship got out what they could, and had the awful farewell sight of French sailors burning part of the city, and battles between various factions. The change from good times to bad times had been rapid and brutal. They ended up going to New Orleans. There was discussion about going to one of the other islands controlled by France because New Orleans was under Spanish control. It appeared, however, that the Spanish rule was a generally lenient one, so they went.

Chuck attempted to combine the two versions of the story about the departure from Saint-Domingue/Haiti, but seeing as how Philippe wasn't born until 1789, which was the year of the French Revolution, he was all of four years old when they fled to New Orleans. Why was there that kind of discrepancy? It was as though Philippe had built up a manufactured memory because nobody would really care much about his recollections of Saint-Domingue/Haiti at the age of four. So he must have been ten, and they must have somehow stayed until about 1799. So it appeared a memory could be true and false at the same time.

Meanwhile, Melissa was exploring in vision the cracks, crevices, and self-deceits of this man she'd just married. Here they were, on an extended honeymoon, which was nice. On the other hand, they could not return home because of legal entanglements. This place was tropical, but it was also the poorest country in the western hemisphere. On top of that, they weren't even in each other's arms, because they were in separate visions. Melissa didn't think this would have been the sort of honeymoon her mother would have told her stories about, even if her mother had thought about doing such a thing.

So, here she sat, paging through Chuck's mind, looking for blank pages, when she noticed a blur behind him. Her abilities must be improving, as well, if that blur turned out to be what Chuck had been talking about. Ha! It was what he talked about, and what had gotten her so scared. She was seeing family lines. Just for the heck of it, she followed the sharpening outlines to Gaston, and did a vision. She saw an older Gaston consulting his father's touch stone. It appeared Gaston had brought his father, Jean Baptiste, to New Orleans, along with the rest of the family, but Jean Baptiste was now physically gone, and Gaston was trying to get advice from his father, but somehow wasn't able to get it. What puzzled Melissa was that she wasn't able to determine just what advice he was trying to obtain.

☆ ☆ ☆

Margot considered that private investigators from the United States plying their trade in Cap Haitien would have been pretty easy to spot. It appeared the whole country crawled with agents from various countries and causes, and maybe people looking for Chuck might have fit in with them, but Margot and her bunch were quite certain that bad guys of that flavor were not in the neighborhood. One thing she thought helped their cause was Chuck and Melissa both speaking the local Creole dialect fluently, which Margot knew impressed the locals mightily. She was certain they'd cut Chuck a break a long time before some outsider. Her people in Port Au Prince hadn't seen anything suspicious, either.

Still, a week had given Chuck everything he was likely to find, so they headed on to France, to Saint Malo. Even in a plane the pilots described as being the fastest civilian aircraft currently in the air, it was a long trip. Still, all the wiggles and jiggles in even the largest airliners at 30,000 feet were noticeable by their absence at 50,000 feet. The pilots said they would have usually refueled somewhere in the United States, but Margot advised them to avoid Stateside landings where possible, on the off chance that some private investigator could get FAA information. Because of that, they kept away from American air space, off the eastern seaboard, and far above all but military traffic. Their refuel point was in the Canadian Maritimes.

The relatively cool, crisp air was a great change after Haiti. Actually, when they opened the cabin door, the outside temperature was hardly different than the inside air conditioning. They spent the rest of the day there, exploring the area, and enjoying the food. A highlight for Chuck and Melissa was doing visions of the locals. Then, after a leisurely dinner, they departed, arriving at Saint Malo the next morning. Chuck had prepared, using the touch stone from Jean Baptiste to find out where he'd been and what he'd done.

Chuck joined Jean Baptiste as he walked toward the gates of the walled city of Saint Malo. He considered those who told him it was a long way from Turin, had lied. The fact was that it had been an extremely long way. The only redeeming consideration of walking all the way across France was that nobody was comparing him unfavorably to his much older brother Joseph Louis, the genius, who was already a full professor at the university, and whose services were being requested by the Kaiser of Prussia. Before Jean Baptiste left, all the chatter was about how Joseph Louis had turned down an offer to go to Berlin, because somebody he respected was still there.

Thirteen years younger than his brother, Jean Baptiste couldn't remember his brother as anything but famous. About the only notable thing about Jean Baptiste was that after Joseph Louis, he alone survived infancy, out of eleven siblings. In what should have been a large family, there was the first brother and the last brother. That seemed to be his fate, to always be the last brother. So, when he got old enough to be on his own, he had also reached the utter end of tolerance for being perpetually compared in an unfavorable way to his brother.

Jean Baptiste had a plan. He would follow the family story about an ancestor who had been a privateer and a pirate, and whose gold, won on the high seas, founded the family fortune. His father lost the family fortune, and Jean Baptiste would win it back. Yes, indeed, the time had come in the cycle of life for him to renew things, and Saint Malo was the place to do it. It was where his ancestor had been based as a privateer. So Jean Baptiste stood as tall as he could, and looked as fierce as possible, and strolled into town through the open gate.

He finally found his way to the port. His idea was to get to know the captains, and get on a crew. The way to do that, Jean Baptiste thought, was to work as a stevedore. He tried to engage the sailors, but they were a clannish bunch, and not inclined to talk. What stevedores were there hauled massive loads, and mostly laughed at Jean Baptiste's puny build. One of them finally pointed to the next bag, and said if he could get it onto the ship, he could work. Instead of him taking the bag to the boat, the bag took him to the ground. Everyone around thought it hilarious, and Jean Baptiste slunk off in defeat.

A shopkeeper who watched the whole thing, called him over. "You must really want to work, to be willing to be a stevedore," he said.

"I need a job, yes, that's true. I can work at anything, well, except for being a stevedore, maybe. What I really want is to go to sea with a privateer, like my ancestor did."

"You seem bright enough. I'll make you a proposition. If you work for me, you can learn about being a merchant. I'll give you a place to sleep and food to eat. If you're smart, you'll make some money, as well."

Jean Baptiste went to work for him, even though it seemed like he was going in the wrong direction. Almost in spite of himself, he learned how to keep stock, and how to negotiate sales. At least the shop overlooked the port, and he could keep thinking about what to do. There was also the fact that sailors came into the shop, and he learned how to talk to them, slowly learning how to be in their society. He also figured out how to make some money as he learned with the merchant, and came to have, at first, a little, and later, quite a lot of stock of his own that he sold along with that of the merchant.

As months went by, and he had some money, he'd sit in the tavern and listen to the sailors. One evening a ship captain came in and after a time began talking about his ancestor, who'd had a puny kid on board and had found good fortune. Later, the kid decided to go back to being a land-lubber, and left the ship. The kid took his ancestor's good fortune with him when he jumped ship in Genoa. One of the men with him asked if he thought good fortune would run in the puny kid's family, and the captain answered in the affirmative.

Jean Baptiste never knew where the urge came from, but he got up and walked over to the large man, who appeared to be in his cups. "Captain, this puny kid of good fortune – did your family preserve his name?"

The man looked up somewhat blearily. "As a matter of fact, we did keep the name, though no one really knows why. It was LaGrange, The Barn. He was a puny barn on a boat. That's a good joke, yes?"

"That is a most rare joke indeed, sir. Your good luck, I think, may have been my ancestor, for I am Jean Baptiste LaGrange."

The effects of the drink seemed to evaporate, and the man stood up to examine this person. "Does your family run to men who are slight of stature?"

"It has been the case, yes sir."

"You dress like a shop clerk. Do you work for one of 'These gentlemen of Saint Malo?'"

"I have never heard anyone refer to the merchants here in that fashion, but yes, I work for one of them, and sell some of my own stock besides."

"You have learned the trade from the sharpest traders in Europe, and have become one of them. You may be my good fortune, indeed, and you might perhaps make a fortune of your own, as well. I have my own ship, but I could do much better if I had someone on Saint Domingue to buy my merchandise. Oh, I am Captain Lafitte."

So Jean Baptiste gathered his stock and the best wishes of the merchant, and sailed with the trader and occasional privateer, Captain Lafitte.

☆ ☆ ☆

Chuck and Melissa wandered the waterfront that had been largely destroyed in the course of World War II. The locals restored the area in the years after the war. Still, comparing Jean Baptiste's view of the area in 1765 and 1766 with the present, everything seemed quite different. It occurred to Chuck that he had somehow visualized the area as totally unchanged in all that time. Acknowledging that reality and long-buried history might not look exactly the same, they proceeded on to tourist things. Just up the coast was Normandy Beach as well as other items of interest in the region. Finally, proceeding by car, they reversed Jean Baptiste's trek across France, and headed to Paris for several days, which Melissa absolutely enjoyed, and pronounced as being nothing like New Orleans.

They then were driven on to Turin, where the plane had already flown. From all reports, the flight crew decided this job was almost a vacation. One of the flight crew was single, and was having the time of his life. LaGrange research in Turin was very simple, since the birthplace of Joseph Louis LaGrange was a museum. Margot got them private tours of the house, and Chuck came to discover Joseph Louis LaGrange was Jean Baptiste's "big" brother physically, as well as in notoriety. The older brother was regarded as being of medium height and a pale complexion, where Jean Baptiste was of less than medium height, and possessing a darker complexion.

Chuck found some notable family ties on the Italian side of the family, including a Pope. His major focus, however, continued to be on the LaGrange/Lagrangia line. Tracking the visions, it seemed as though Jean Baptiste favored his paternal line, Chuck finding strong physical similarities in that direction. Those ancestors' slight build had an advantage as cavalry. The horse was really the weapon, designed to sow panic and confusion among opposing infantry. Less weight on the horse equaled more force available to be applied against the enemy.

Melissa noted that Chuck was a bit moody, staring at visions, or maybe just having an internal dialogue. Whatever was going on, he was blocking her from his current thoughts. She had promised to bring up any blocking she found in him. Still, she thought he should have some privacy. The worst part of this was how it seriously got in the way of their having good times together. So she set out to jar him out of it. Neither a terminal vision nor this moody stuff was going to get in the way of their life together. As far as she could tell, this moody thing didn't stand a chance. After all, they were in Italy, and they were going to have a good time, la dolce vita.

The first step was to get Chuck to use his visioning to bring his Italian language skills up to date. He spoke Italian, sure enough, courtesy of Jean Baptiste, but it was the Italian of the late 1700's, and tended to draw stares when he used it. A few visions and maybe a day and a half later, Chuck was keeping up with the best of them. It seemed that all the good places to eat were on a street with a familiar name: LaGrange. That area became their center of operations, as they started roaming the area, which included the Italian Alps.

There still wasn't any word from New Orleans, and since Margot was continually confirming nobody seemed to be looking for them, Melissa got them moving to Tuscany, which was a place she'd always fancied, and after that, Rome. Naples and Pompeii followed. Melissa finally checked whether Chuck had indeed gotten everything he needed by way of information in Turin, knowing the question might cause a problem, but, better now than later. Chuck thought about it a little bit, and considered there really wasn't anything more in Italy he needed to find.

They had gotten to the point of talking about a cruise in the Aegean, when Margot got word from New Orleans. The lawyers had gotten most of the trash points dismissed, and all the legal verbiage had finally beaten the media into submission. More to the point, it was no longer of interest to their audience, so it was no longer news. The private investigators were all off investigating other cases, so the plan was for them to fly in to a private airfield, and a helicopter would bring them to the house.

Their aircrew brought the plane to a field near where they were at the time, and not long after, they were headed back to the west, and to challenges as yet undefined. Chuck was quite certain, though, that Andre had a briefing ready that would totally update them on the situation.

14: Legal Matters

Chuck entered the courtroom flanked by Melissa and Margot. He suddenly realized being out in public this way now felt normal. When court was called to order, the judge introduced himself, and began by announcing the judge originally assigned to the case had a health problem. It was of such a nature he had to withdraw from the case. This was now his case, and he would conduct it according to the law. He would only accept as evidence items that were accepted by law and normal practice. There had been talk about supernatural things nobody could prove. Such extraneous testimony would not be accepted in his court, effective immediately.

Margot whispered to Chuck information about the distinguished-looking judge. He was very strait-laced and enforced absolute decorum in court. He frequently used contempt of court to enforce both civility and a smooth-running docket. Anyone making the judge's life more difficult got contempt citations routinely. Near the top of the list were people failing to appear in court. She suspected this could be a difficult day.

Chuck originally had one goal which had now become two goals. The new first goal was to stay out of jail. The original objective was to get the case moved out of open court and into chambers. The idea was to keep himself and the company out of the media. As he listened to the judge, Chuck was also in vision, getting his own information about the judge, along with the judge's family.

He came up with a plan, but the next step would depend on factors out of his control. As it happened, human nature was on his side. Word of his arrival got passed down to Armand's legal team, one of whom turned and looked at Chuck. Armand also turned, and looked at him with an evil smile. One of Armand's team immediately got permission to approach the bench. After a moment, the judge cleared his throat.

"Is Charles Louis LaGrange present in the courtroom?" Chuck stood up. "Yes, your honor."

"Kindly approach the bench." When Chuck got there, the judge continued, "This court has desired your presence for some time. A subpoena was issued, but the servers could not locate you."

"I was out of town. When I learned my presence was desired in court, I returned to New Orleans voluntarily, to save the court's time and taxpayer money."

"May I ask where you were?"

"I went to Chicago, to complete a transaction divesting JLG&S of a wholly owned subsidiary. The sale was to meet a state legislative requirement."

"That transaction took two months?"

"No, it didn't your honor. My wife and I both have a passion for genealogy. We had leads on an unexplored family line. Having leased an aircraft, we utilized that time and flew to Oregon." Chuck knew from his vision the judge was into genealogy, so it seemed like a good way to go, and was true, besides.

"Did you find anything in Oregon?"

"Well, yes, actually we did, and it led us to Tucson, Arizona. We were able to establish a number of things there. With paid-for time on the plane still available, we flew on to a place known as Cap Francais, Saint-Domingue when my ancestors lived there."

"Can't say I'm familiar with that place," the judge said, checking his notes.

"It's now called Cap Haitien, Haiti. In any case, we were able to verify some things, and to expand our knowledge, which led us to Saint Malo, France, and subsequently to Italy. Word reached us there about this situation. We, of course, returned promptly."

"Okay, your story matches what information I was already given, so I'll not hold you in contempt at this time. Now, can you tell me anything about this touch stone vision stuff that has standing before the law?"

Chuck favored the judge with a sad smile. "I can show you it works, but frankly, the entire concept flies in the face of everything the law holds dear."

The judge frowned. "You can show me it works? So far, the record only shows a few people have taken old objects, stared at them a while, and claimed to have gotten certain information. Most of it cannot be proven, and the part that can be proven, could have come from any number of sources. What can you show me?"

Chuck came alongside the judge, and whispered in his ear, "There is a story your mother liked to tell when you were quite young, and threatened to bring up periodically, but never did. When you were about three and a half years old, your mother and father had a number of guests at your house in the evening. You woke up, and went from the nursery into the library, where you found a bottle of ink. You took off your diaper, potty training not having been a strong suite in your development, and painted your privates, using your fingers and palms. You then headed down the hall, evidently with the intent of showing everybody what a pretty job you had done. Your mother, fortunately, happened to be coming to check on you, and managed to intercept you before you went public. Oh, it was permanent blue-black ink, and took a long time to wear off, in spite of constant diligent scrubbings."

The judge flushed red as Chuck started to tell the story, but had gone white by the time he finished. "My mother died three years ago. She hadn't told anyone that in over forty years. Only a few people knew I was being assigned to this case. The idea that your company not only knew I would be assigned this case, but also managed to come up with that story, and coached you to tell it exactly as my mother told it is even more preposterous than the idea that memories remain in objects. What do you want?"

"I would like you to move the case into chambers. I believe we can settle most of the points more agreeably there."

In chambers, Chuck was given the floor. "Armand's main contention, as I understand it, claims he is the appropriate and proper head of JLG&S, and that I deprived him of this position improperly. The by-laws of JLG&S specify the chief officer of the company, under whatever title, must run it in accordance with Jean LaGrange's wishes. It may be considered superstition, perhaps, but obtaining a vision of Jean LaGrange using what is termed a touch stone is a requirement, and one with which Armand claims to have complied."

Armand nodded his head. Chuck tried to visualize the scene when Madeleine found out about Armand doing visions, and the nature of the ensuing conversation. He thought he'd do a vision of that sometime. The bottom line seemed to be that Madeleine was more interested in money than in superstition.

"I viewed Jean last night, and obtained from him a certain citation that should still exist in this court's records. If the citation exists, the name of Jean LaGrange should appear in the middle of that paragraph. If Armand is the rightful head of JLG&S, he will be able to obtain the citation, as well. However, before proceeding, your honor, perhaps you could have a clerk verify this information." With that, Chuck took a folded piece of paper out of his jacket, and handed it to the judge.

While they waited, a coffee service was brought, and Armand's nervousness was evident in the constant clinking of the china. The clerk came in a bit later, with a photocopy of the citation, and the judge noted Jean's name was exactly where specified. "I'm beyond shocked," the judge commented, "but after your earlier demonstration, I'm not sure how to describe myself. It's your show. Carry on."

Chuck had Margot give Jean's touch stone to the clerk so no one could think he might be connected to it. Chuck instructed the clerk to simply hold the object so Armand could see it comfortably without moving his head. This way, whatever happened would not be due to anything in the touch stone interacting with Armand any way other than mentally. Then Chuck looked at Armand, "You don't have to do this. You can walk away from the whole thing now, and be no more the worse for wear. Madeleine doesn't really want you to do it. Still, if you want to play for all the marbles, you're going to have to ask Jean about the time he was included by name in a legal citation."

Armand looked at Chuck, and Chuck saw the fear in his eyes. "Are you seeing prior visions in your peripheral vision? If so, you'd better not do it, because the vision can take you, and you'll never get back out on your own."

Armand hesitated, and Madeleine gave him a sharp kick. He looked at her, and she mouthed, "Do it. Now!" He sighed, settled back, and looked at the touch stone. Armand was in vision almost immediately.

He began to flail around, and the fullness left his cheeks. Armand started saying things, mostly in French, sometimes in Spanish, and once in a while in English. The judge was appalled. Chuck and Melissa both studied him carefully, and neither of them liked what they saw. Melissa flashed Chuck a message that she needed to speak with Madeleine right now. Chuck nodded.

"Your honor, a problem with visions when you first start using them, is that they will use you, and will, in fact, suck the life from you. It happened to me, and it was only because Melissa helped me through it that

I'm alive today. After getting through that, and learning to control the visions, much progress can be made. You'll have to take my word for it, but Armand has just proven that he does not know how to use the visions, because they are using him, and you are seeing the results with your own eyes. I would suggest you postpone the hearing for several days. Armand's wife, Madeleine, can help him, but she will have to want to, or else the vision will destroy him.

"Should we call for medical support?"

"That would be prudent. There's nothing they can do, but it will at least be evident that you have taken what steps are available to you."

✲ ✲ ✲

As they waited for the EMTs to arrive, Melissa had Madeleine over in the corner of the Judge's office. Melissa was making her case as forcefully as possible, but Madeleine was getting increasingly defensive, and what little logic existed in her position was becoming more tenuous. Melissa knew her chances of getting anywhere were decreasing to near nothing, and she tried one last gambit.

"You do believe in God, don't you?" Melissa asked.

"Well, of course I believe in God. I'm very religious."

"Do you believe God is Love?"

"Well, certainly. It's in the Bible."

"You're convinced that Armand is under some kind of curse. A curse like that would be from the Devil, wouldn't you say?"

Madeleine stared at Melissa. "That ... that's what I said, sure. Of course it's from the Devil."

"So if you give Armand love, which the Bible says is of God, and that breaks the spell, what's wrong with that?"

"You're just trying to confuse me." Madeleine slumped into a chair, and cried, obviously marking the end of the exchange. Melissa looked at Chuck and shrugged.

Across the room, Chuck had moved his chair over alongside the Judge's desk as they listened to the exchange. The judge considered the situation. "Your wife missed her calling. She should have been a lawyer." After a moment's pause, he added, "Am I understanding this correctly, that a session of wild sex could snap Armand out of this terminal vision thing?"

Chuck considered the question a bit before answering. "It's more than that, actually. There's an emotional involvement – make that a massive emotional involvement. I suspect the prospect of this intense emotional involvement is what is troubling Madeleine. It appears to me she fears an emotional involvement very much, and she either can't or won't do it."

"I don't understand where you're coming from. You and your wife both seem to be fighting for your opponent here. I'd think you'd be celebrating. After all, that happens to be the individual who's trying to put you out on the street. If he cannot be brought out of this condition, I'll be forced to entertain a motion for dismissal. In fact, I'd guess your attorneys are doing that very thing as we speak."

"Your honor, I've been in Armand's situation, and no matter how he's attacked me and mine, I cannot let him go that way. I keep hoping we can find a better solution than simply calling it off. One question: If this is dismissed, since this is a civil case, the same questions and challenges could be posed in the future, is that right?"

"Naturally, double jeopardy doesn't apply in civil law. People can sue for any reason at all. Sometimes they sue simply to be a nuisance. Your legal team is very adept at dealing with that sort of thing. They're some of the best in the business, if you don't mind me saying so."

"Could we do about a three-day postponement, to see if the doctors can improve his condition sufficiently to continue?"

"That would seem appropriate." Armand's legal team was apprised of the postponement, and Chuck was gathering his people together as the EMTs came in, having been routed through the back to avoid undue publicity. Margot had already updated Chuck's calendar, and the company's attorneys were coming up to Chuck.

"We would have preferred you had let us in on the postponement. We were about to hand the judge a move to dismiss."

"The judge figured you were doing that very thing. I'll ask you what I asked the judge: Will dismissing this case make the underlying issues go away?"

"Well, not really. But if this is a terminal vision, then Armand will never be back to pursue it. Oh, by the way, getting him to do that vision was sheer genius, sir!"

"If getting him into the vision was genius, then allow me the consideration on the other hand that I'm not an idiot. As it looks now, Armand cannot come after us. On the other hand, his heirs and assigns can come after us, and they can come after us forever. I don't see that our corporate mission statement says anything about perpetual lawsuits. More specifically, what does that do to our bottom line?"

"Well, that is your call, sir. Still, we can best serve your interests if you keep us in the loop. If you don't think I'm too far out of line for saying it."

"No, you're absolutely right for saying that, and I appreciate how you guys have been keeping the legal issues down to a dull roar."

The judge suggested they follow the EMTs out the back. By using the secure garage, they could avoid having to talk to the press. That seemed advisable, and as they walked, Margot was busy, ensuring their transportation would be on hand when they arrived at the secure portal. At the dock, the garage full of vehicles, they could hear the EMTs telling Madeleine that she could ride with Armand, and her attorneys telling her that's what she should do. Madeleine was half-hysterical, and saying she couldn't. She just couldn't. She had to go home. She just had to go home.

Chuck glanced at his attorneys, and saw the junior attorney, with a grim face, holding his cell phone, pointed at the scene. The whole thing was recorded. Madeleine was now the star of her own little melodrama. There was little doubt that it would be a featured piece of evidence if the case went forward. Chuck considered he'd better be able to come up with a solution that would stop all this insanity. He and Melissa looked at each other, recognizing there would certainly be some rough weather ahead, and quite possibly a major storm.

✲ ✲ ✲

The next morning, Chuck went down to the lake, and found a shady place to sit. Getting in two-way communication with Jean took less effort than dialing a telephone. Finding an answer to the legal problem was another matter. Chuck considered Jean a genius, but he was still human. Further, the complications imposed by the contemporary legal system left Jean absolutely dumbfounded. After considerable discussion, they decided they both needed to think about it some more.

Coming out of the vision, Chuck discovered he'd been so involved with Jean he hadn't seen the golf cart roll up. It turned out he had a phone call.

"Hey, neighbor!" A cheery voice on the phone was a welcome change of pace.

Chuck knew the voice, but it was out of context. "Lee?"

"That's the one. Say, do you recall giving me some off-the-cuff advice, about establishing two-way communication with an ancestor back around the Civil War, and getting that ancestor to set me up in business?"

Chuck puzzled over that one. "Well, it sounds like something I could have said. It seems like a long time ago."

"Well, you did say it, and it was damn fine advice. I managed to contact a direct ancestor in the Civil War while he was wondering if he'd ever live to have a family. He was gratified to get proof of life after all that carnage. He listened when I suggested he set up a business, but protested he was no businessman. I recommended he ally himself with Jean LaGrange down in New Orleans. He should figure out what Jean was doing, and follow it as closely as he could manage.

"He told me his unit had been decimated, and he was trying to decide what to do next. Finally, instead of looking for another unit, he slipped away from the war and into New Orleans. We have talked every few days, by my reckoning, while I watched my world change around me. He worked for Jean LaGrange for a while, and found he was pretty good at some stuff that would support the LaGrange enterprise. By the time the mercantile had been superseded by JLG&S, he had a growing business of his own, and enough capital to mirror at least some of the JLG&S strategies.

"Pretty soon, I found myself supplied with a corporate smart phone along with other implements of destruction. Not long after that, I had to tender my resignation up in Chicago, with all my time and attention dedicated to this project. Turns out, much of my staff came from JLG&S, and when I lose staff, it's usually to your outfit. I called you neighbor, because Jodi and I have moved into the mansion up the road. I called earlier, but they said you guys were out of town, being really vague about it."

"That's pretty funny, Lee. I take the scenic route home, and by the time I get here, discover you've become a multi-millionaire or billionaire yourself. Not only that, you moved in before I got back. I take it everyone's treated your sudden arrival in the land of the rich and famous as perfectly normal?"

"Yes, indeed. Actually, my ancestor made several missteps he corrected when I told him how it changed things at this end. One time, he was looking at doing a thing one way, and I ended up seeing the result here. He changed his intention, and when the result looked good, I let him know. So we sort of helped each other."

"Now that is fascinating. Kind of like those old stories about fine tuning a TV antenna on the roof. Actually Lee, you've just helped me solve a situation I'm working on. Say, you and Jodi should come by for a visit. I'll let my staff know to let you guys in whenever you'd like to come."

The call over, Chuck thought about Lee's ancestor, as well as Jean LaGrange, and considered neither he nor Jean could see any alternative to having the judge dismiss the case. The question was the effect on future generations. Just that fast, Chuck found himself in two-way vision with a descendant. The individual he saw looked neither futuristic nor prosperous. "How far in my future are you?"

"I'm 140 years downstream from you. I'm somewhat astonished we're actually communicating, and not just me reading you. I've always been curious why things took the turn they did just at your time."

"You know, I've been having two-way conversations with Jean LaGrange. Maybe I can get him in on this, as well."

"You're talking about THE Jean LaGrange?"

"If founding JLG&S makes him "THE," yes, indeed. He established it as a favor to me. What kind of a turn did things take at my time?"

"There was the infamous court case of Armand LaGrange vs. JLG&S, Charles LaGrange, et al. The case was dismissed, and Armand died in a coma. His widow managed to gather up all manner of strange people who either sued JLG&S directly or supported the cases. Many experts cite it as the causal or pivotal moment when reactionary forces took over the United States. Science and technology died, space travel was outlawed. Every interest group turned into a militia, and they commenced perpetual internecine armed fights with every group unlike themselves, and even with those too much like themselves. The company went bankrupt, and the LaGrange family stands accused and convicted of being devil worshippers and sometimes the devil himself."

Chuck had been contacting Jean, even as he was listening to his descendant. Chuck brought Jean up to date, and made introductions. "So, since you've been studying the situation, what needs to happen to avoid this outcome?"

"That has been the subject of more than a little debate. About the only thing that could avoid it is if the court case never happened at all."

15: Rewriting History

Chuck felt his old nightmares of being a dishwasher rolling back over him as he asked, "Would it change the situation if I had never claimed ownership?"

"You know, it just might. Just a second. ... Everything seemed to change for the better when you asked that. But how would you do it? The company can't own itself."

Jean broke in. "We could have a holding company that would own the stock in the company. But where the holding company controls the company, we could instead have the holding company set up so it cannot use the shares to control the company. Um, maybe it would be the trustee, holding the shares in benefit for ... what was your name, there, so far in the future?"

"Robert. Robert LaGrange."

"Okay, Robert LaGrange, this holding company will protect the shares of JLG&S until such time as Robert LaGrange shall come to recreate the holding company in a form satisfactory to the laws of the time. Meanwhile, the holding company may not dispose or devaluate the shares in any way. The holding company may not vote the shares, or otherwise intrude on the operations of JLG&S. In turn, JLG&S must defend the holding company. By the way, Robert, I'll need your LaGrange lineage for you to use to prove yourself."

"So now I must be on the sideline," Chuck commented. "Well, it is a sacrifice I volunteered to do."

"Not at all, Chuck. You are the pivotal person that Robert and I revolve around. Without you, none of this could happen."

"Well, I'll see what tomorrow looks like when it gets here, I guess. By the way, do you work with a guy who had fought in the war, who was related to Lafitte?"

"Of course I know him. He's got his own company and is doing splendidly."

"Well, it seems that he and his descendant, a Lee Sherman, also do two-way visions. I hope what we do doesn't wipe them out."

"We'll just have to see about that," Jean replied. Then, "Robert, what do you see, there?"

"It's an incredible amount of change going on, and it all feels good, somehow."

Chuck considered that, and remembered what Lee told him. "This seems like a good first approximation, at least. Jean, let's go ahead with what you were saying there. I'd offer to try it here, but I'm not sure the situation would allow it at this point. In any case, our goal is to avoid the legal situation altogether, and in my time, that's already been under way for several months."

"By the way," Robert came in. "When you change things, I get the impression that only the people making the change have any memory of what it was before the change."

"That seems to be the case," Chuck said. "Although, in the cases I've been involved in to this point, or know anything about, the people forming the pivot of the change were either years before, or many miles away from the scene of the change. So I really don't know what your experience will be. I don't know what my experience is going to be, either. For all I know, I'll wake up in the morning, and go someplace to wash some dirty dishes."

Robert suddenly gasped. "You don't think these changes would make me no longer exist, do you?"

"I wouldn't think so. You have become a pivot for events. Events will invent a place for you appearing to make sense, considering the situation."

Chuck suddenly realized just what this doubling of the two-way communication was costing him in terms of energy, because he felt weak, and it was becoming a physical strain to maintain the two connections. "We must end it here," he said. "But as soon as things stabilize, we must reconnect."

With that, Chuck broke the two connections, and slumped off the bench onto the ground as if all his bones had melted. There were people out to him in a couple of minutes, who took him into the house. Melissa saw him as they got him into bed, and was very frightened, remembering how he looked when she broke into the RV. Doing a fast vision on him, she saw he was not trapped in a vision, but had been drained by attempting too much. Then she saw what Chuck, Jean, and Robert had done, and worried what might happen.

A moment later, however, the vision disappeared along with the knowledge she had ever done a vision. Then, she was simply horrified at his gaunt appearance, when he looked just fine at breakfast, and worried about what she could tell the children. At the same time, she knew she didn't have any children, but even that knowledge was evaporating. Outside, parts of the landscape were altering, and everyone, everywhere, was changing, some in a small way, while others were gone altogether.

Personal histories of the past 140 years were being rewritten, and even the national history was changing, bit at a time. There was only one person who knew how things were in the previous time line, or even that things had been different. That person, Chuck, was in an exhausted sleep. Medical staff woke him every two hours to take some food and drink.

Chuck gradually became aware of the passage of time and the return of his strength. He knew he was in his bedroom, but many of the details of the room seemed different. Margot came in, and he knew it was Margot, but she seemed different, somehow. He did a vision on her, and found she was different in a number of ways. One change was the fact she had been his Personal Assistant for eight years. Chuck asked what was on the schedule, and Margot said his schedule included getting better, and only getting better.

In vision, he knew he was the object of many other people's schedules, but that it was as she said. They were all working on getting him back to health after a particularly draining vision. Chuck had to admit that was indeed the proper diagnosis. Further examining the vision, there was no mention, none at all, of court appearances, past, present, or future. Well, then, what about Armand LaGrange? That took a bit to find. There was never an Armand LaGrange running the company, so there was no lawsuit about his being deprived of it. In this new order of things, Andre Moniteau was the CEO, and had been for quite some time.

Sorting through this Margot's memories, Chuck finally found Armand was a lower-level executive. As a family member, he had a particular set of perks. Based on this, he and his wife, Madeleine, (Chuck thought it was interesting they were married in this time line) requested the company to send them and their children (Chuck couldn't recall children mentioned in the previous time line) on a sailboat cruise. Specifically, they wanted a "primitive" cruise in order to relive past glories of the age of sail. The boat had no radar, only a single radio and an emergency beacon. A hurricane was tracked in the same general area where they were sailing, and calls were made, but got no response. Then the signal from the distress beacon was picked up, and aircraft scrambled. Armand and a couple others barely survived, but Madeleine and his kids all perished. So, Chuck reflected, in this time line, the tragedy of Madeleine repeated itself. Armand went into seclusion, and was not heard from very much.

Medical people came in at that point, and after looking at him, thought he should start moving. Other than feeling weak, Chuck was able to walk around the room to their satisfaction. He ended up in a chair, and ordered some food. Doing visions on the staff, Chuck found his position now was that of corporate visionary, which made him something like the shaman of a tribe. He also discovered Melissa was his wife, and they had three children, two boys and a girl. This was a totally new world, indeed, and it suddenly occurred to Chuck that Melissa might be different in some ways. Actually, make that must be different.

George was still taking care of him, he saw, and Chuck requested some casual clothing that wouldn't look too ridiculous with his current situation. George was, of course, prepared for the request, and Chuck did a vision on George to see where Melissa was at the moment (she was with the children), and where that might be (they were all in the children's suite at the far end of the floor). While he was obtaining this information, he also got George's angle on himself, which was holding him in some awe and a little fear, perhaps, thinking him a sort of magician or wizard. Well, it wasn't washing dishes in a greasy spoon. In passing, he got a vision of the floor plan of the house. It was indeed a bit different, and would come in handy, he was sure.

Chuck wandered around to his office, using the back way. His office was, like everything else, a bit different. The huge desk and chair did not appear to have been used very much. There was, however, a new addition to the place. It was a form-fitting chaise longue (a lot of people he knew would have called it a chaise lounge, but now, having learned four flavors of French, both new and old, he automatically considered it in its French form) that actually showed some fair amount of use. After the walk, he found it was calling to him. He wasn't surprised when Margot brought him a cup of broth almost immediately after he was in the chair.

Now that Chuck was fairly certain any changes for him were apparently benign, he thought about his descendant, Robert. Chuck was somewhere in the middle of this crack-the-whip thing Jean had done back about 1870 (actually, it must be after 1870, since he had already founded JLG&S in their last conversations). Robert was the popper at the end of the whip, and he needed to know if they had done something worthwhile. When Chuck established communication, all of the communication was coming from Robert.

"I was telling you that even while we were just talking about what could be done, things were already changing. When we last talked, or communicated in vision, JLG&S no longer existed, there was nothing in space, and Earth had become a wasteland. I blanked out, and when I came to, I was in a really pretty meadow. I felt very weak, but there were people there to assist me back to a JLG&S spaceship. They gave me some special food. They said it would replenish the items depleted from being in vision. Then, they asked if I'd had a profitable vision. I looked at a sort of view screen, and found we were already very high up, and soon achieved orbit.

"We docked at a private space habitat. The crew made it clear this was my house. JLG&S is one of the premier corporations in the human sphere. We have colonies around the solar system as well as in other star systems. Using vision, we communicate instantaneously with those colonies. The LaGrange families, together with allied families are now accepted as a "First Family." By demonstrating that we could improve our own history in a positive way, we passed the entrance exam.

"The other first families have a restriction on us, however. They say we are not to attempt changing our history any further back in our time line. If we attempt anything like that, they will know, and will wipe us out."

"How can these other families wipe us out without wiping themselves out?"

"That part's simple. They aren't human. They allowed us a certain domain, which should be adequate for quite a long time. There will have to be adjustments eventually, as our galaxy will be colliding with another one, but we should find the space allotted to be more than ample for our needs."

"So when did these other First Families fence us off?"

"About fifty years ago, as we began seriously going extra-Solar."

"Think about it, Robert. How did we change our history? Jean took actions which increased in scope and volume over time. The only way these so-called First Families could make a realistic threat is if they had already been messing with human history. Of course, I've been doing visions for something less than a year at this point, so who knows where my trail might lead next? In any case, the main point is that you, Robert, now have a situation you can live with."

☆ ☆ ☆

Margot appeared soon after he came out of the vision, inquiring whether he wanted to eat in the office or downstairs. Chuck thought eating downstairs would be a good thing, but he wanted to look in on Melissa and the children. Just imagine. He had three children, and Melissa was their mother. It was obvious the way the time line had now gone, the changes in Chuck happened earlier in life. Speaking of which, he should look up Lee, as well, and see how Jean's changes had affected his bunch.

Melissa was in the hall when he approached. She ran up to give him a kiss, with Chuck doing visions the whole way. Her life was different, indeed. Now, her father had recovered from his injury, but no longer felt he was competitive, so he went into coaching, and was doing extremely well. Her mother was just fine, as well. It seemed that he and Melissa had met while in an accelerated program at college that saw them graduate in two and a half years, and married soon after their graduation. Chuck's ability to vision was seen early on, and he was designated as the company's next visionary. Melissa, meanwhile, managed to complete her MBA while also being a socialite wife and mother.

It was fortunate that Melissa met him outside the children's' rooms, because it gave Chuck an opportunity to vision the three, Stephen, the oldest at four years, Francoise (Franky) at two years, and Cherisse, who was six months old. It also gave him a chance to figure out how he was expected to act around them. He thought they might give him a break on account of being in the early stages of healing. He also saw Melissa did not vision, and had absolutely no intention of doing so.

In that regard, she was quite different from "his" Melissa, and he was suddenly struck by the fact that this change in things, while generally okay, had cost him dearly in a number of important ways. It was quite unfair to this Melissa, who occupied the same body, and was so much like her, but did not have the same strength of character and tragic history. As a second blow, he reflected that he wanted to make Melissa's life better any way he could. Now, suddenly, her life had become much better, and she would be able to know her parents as everyone moved down the track of life. Still, he missed "his" Melissa.

Chuck asked if she would like to have lunch with him, and she declined, saying she was about to breast-feed Cherisse, and had some lunch coming up. She told him to go ahead, but to not try to prove anything by taking the stairs, but to please use the elevator. After all, that's why it was installed in the first place. He was getting a bit weary, actually, and didn't mind when George showed up to make sure he got there without any problems. Lunch was in the same physical area as where he and Melissa had breakfast their first morning in the house. He did notice changes in the windows. The view of the lake was also different, somehow, but he elected not to concern himself about it.

Andre showed up while he was eating, expressing how glad he was Chuck was up and around. The company hadn't found another visionary, and needed this one. Chuck promised to be careful, and kept the chatter going while he did visions of Andre. Chuck's father, Jack Edward, was a department head within the company. Kenneth Otto had stayed in academia his entire life, and so had stayed largely true to his life's story, only ending in a different university. Otto S. had the same experience in Louisiana he'd had in Oregon, and finished World War I as an artillery instructor, but was advised to head to the desert because of asthma contracted from contact with mustard gas.

Kenneth and Millicent both grew up in Tucson, although in this reality, there was always help from the company, both directly and indirectly. The company opened a branch office in Tucson that Otto managed the rest of his life. Skipping around a bit, in this reality, Charles did contact the family after he married Minerva, and finally brought Minerva and the two children, together with the gold back to New Orleans. Minerva didn't like New Orleans. She especially didn't like the social role expected of her. After a year, she went back to Oregon, taking her daughter, but leaving her son, Andrew Tyra, who seemed always sickly.

Charles, on finding a company was founded and funded for the benefit of his descendants, was more than happy to add his gold to the company's coffers, with the effect that the company, which had achieved its second multiple, was suddenly boosted, resulting in a current net worth of close to four hundred billion dollars, four times the amount of the previous reality that Chuck thought was pretty incredible. Along with Chuck's working title of visionary, he was also the designated protector of the holding company and the shares it represented. Jean had built well.

Chuck knew he needed to contact Jean, in order to bring him up to date. But first, as long as Andre was there, Chuck asked if he knew of a Lee Sherman. Andre was somewhat taken aback by the question, but allowed as how he did know Lee. Andre wondered how Chuck had heard of him, and rather than get into any long drawn-out explanation, Chuck just remarked that he picked up on it through a vision, and it was his impression that Lee was descended from Jean Lafitte. Andre agreed that was true, and Chuck was then able to get some impression of how Lee was getting along. It seemed Lee was doing just fine, and so Chuck put in the back of his mind that he needed to get together with Lee as soon as possible.

✲ ✲ ✲

When Chuck connected with Jean after lunch, he saw Jean had aged noticeably, and commented on it.

"Chuck, I took what you said about looking at a person, and being able to see their past, and wondered why that person would be the last word in the line. In other words, I wondered if the same principle could be used to look at the future. As it happens, it does work, and I have done quite a lot of it. I already knew you had not come up with this application of the vision. Also, I know how Robert is doing, and I know some other things as well that are about to have an impact on all of us. So I will ask if you were ever able to find LaGrange the pirate."

"As you said, I hadn't pursued using the shadows to look forward in time. It sounds quite productive. I'm glad you already know how Robert is doing, and frankly, I'm a bit puzzled about the question on the pirate. Surely you already know."

"Humor me. I want to hear it from you."

"Okay. Let's see, it was the second great-grandfather of Jean Baptiste. He went to sea with a privateer who also happened to be an ancestor of Jean Lafitte. They came upon a ship flying the Spanish flag, and boarded it, only to find it was already the prize of a French privateer. On top of that, the privateer with the prize was a favorite of the Crown. He was returning home from a successful voyage, having captured the Spanish ship, among other things. The prize crew was trying to sneak out of Spanish waters by flying the local flag. They hadn't counted on another French privateer targeting them.

"Lafitte's crew decided the other privateer needed to reimburse them for their trouble. The other crew took exception, but with only a skeleton crew on the prize vessel, and the privateer itself over the horizon, there wasn't much they could do. Later, when they did a port call in Saint-Domingue, word arrived their letter of marque had been revoked, and they were declared pirates. They attempted to get another letter of marque there in Saint-Domingue, and were not only refused, but were advised to leave immediately if they didn't want to be hung.

"They sailed back to an area near Gibraltar, where they took a Dutch galleon. Two British men-of-war attempted to come to the Dutchman's aid, but they got away before that could happen. The British men-of-war gave chase, but were neither as fast, nor as skillful in their sailing as Lafitte. Lafitte and company were finally able to lose the British off Sardinia. The ship landed at Genoa, and LaGrange decided he didn't like the life of a privateer, especially if it could get him hung as a pirate. He took his share and left the ship. He walked back to France, and found along the way that he quite liked the country between Genoa and Turin.

"He later married, had a son, and told him about his adventures, or maybe misadventures. His son took the stories to heart, stayed ashore, and became a cavalry officer. Later, when he had the chance to go train the military forces of the Kingdom of Sardinia, he jumped at the chance, and, as they say, went native. He married a local girl from a good family with lots of connections, and homesteaded. So the story went on down through the years, changing a bit as each generation saw fit. When I think about how the family pirate story ended up, the reality seemed closer to a bad joke."

"You saw this vision while you were in Italy, right?"

"That's right. Melissa wondered about my mood at the time. I wanted to have a noteworthy ancestor, even if he was a pirate. I blocked her so she couldn't get a vision of it. That mood of mine created another problem, since she was trying to make that trip a substitute for the honeymoon we never got to take. Now, of course, she doesn't know anything about it.

None of that trip is part of the experience of the current Melissa. Also, she doesn't do visions."

"All of your ancestors are people. None of them were more than that, nor were they less. That includes me. It also includes the pirate. Now, take another look at your vision of the pirate. Do it right now. Just split your focus and do it."

Chuck did as Jean ordered, and brought up the vision while he kept the connection to Jean. The vision was following the path, and then abruptly got completely confused. Chuck let it continue while going back to Jean. "What just happened?"

"You had a question for me back when I first offered to start JLG&S. My only thought at the time was to reward you for letting me know about Charles. Your question then was whether we were changing history. I didn't think anything about it, believing it my duty to take care of my family any way I could. There was no way to imagine how many lives would be rewritten by that act. Then, when we redesigned the thing, even though it appeared a fairly minor piece, adding the dummy holding company changed many, many more lives.

"I now believe the stream of life might be compared to a bell. Any action taken that has an impact on the future, also has an impact on the past. Larger actions will have larger reactions. The clangor of a bell hits only one spot, but causes the entire bell to reverberate. There is no way to know what our family line will look like when this is done. All we can do is hang on, and hope for the best. I am old, and can no longer bear the physical abuse these communications cause me. God bless you, my son, and walk in peace, as best you can."

The communication with Jean stopped there, and the confusion continued to increase in what had been the split vision. Chuck finally cut it off, and just lay back in the chaise with his eyes closed, considering how Jean had it right. He wondered how long it would take for the reverberation to reach him, and how large a change he would see. He suddenly felt extraordinarily sad, realizing he had never been able to physically meet his children in this time line. It didn't seem long at all, until confusion reigned, and he felt himself being first sucked dry, and then blown away.

✲ ✲ ✲

Chuck just lay there with his eyes closed, waiting for the reverberations to die away. After a while, they did, but one rather annoying aspect kept on, getting louder, if anything. It finally came to him what he was hearing. It was an alarm clock. He thought that was very odd, since he hadn't used one since he lived in Chicago, working for the M&A firm. He carefully opened his eyes and found he was looking at what appeared to be that very alarm clock, and it was buzzing away. After turning it off, he peered around to see a place he remembered all too well. This was his efficiency apartment in Chicago.

There were some changes. The chest of drawers was there, but the television set which had previously been both at the center of the apartment atop the chest of drawers, not to mention its place at the center of his life, was missing. Looking further, the old laptop computer that always took up half the table was gone as well. It was evident the place lacked even the few personal effects he'd had. It seemed like this was a place he was momentarily staying, rather than someplace he was living.

He carefully got up, feeling quite weak. He made the couple of steps to the bathroom, where he found an unpleasant surprise looking back at him from the mirror. His cheeks were sunken to the point of appearing cadaverous, and his sunken eyes glittered back at him, suddenly looking disproportionately large for his face. His whiskers showed several days' growth. Chuck splashed some water on his face, and thought about shaving. He looked at the safety razor, seeing the blade had been there long enough to rust, and considered that was going to be a painful experience, particularly considering the lack of shave cream.

After considering the possibilities, Chuck concluded his highest current priority was his body's need to be fed. So he turned around and went to the refrigerator. Opening the door, he wondered why the thing was even plugged in, since there was nothing in it. In the cupboard was a single can of French-cut green beans. It didn't qualify as breakfast, but was going to have to do. He found a semi-clean pan, opened the can and dumped it in, trying not to waste a single bean. While it heated, he poked around, and confirmed the Chuck in this time line was not in the least domestic.

After consuming the can of beans, Chuck found that eating simply shifted his appetite into high gear, and he was ravenous. Still, there were matters of greater import. How was he here? Maybe he could use his vision to find out more about this edition of Chuck LaGrange. He saw some fairly nasty looking clothes thrown over the back of a chair. They smelled like the greasy nether end of a kitchen. He did a fast vision on the clothes, and found out what he did for a living, and where he did it. That part seemed a summary of his worst nightmares. Then he saw a vision of his boss, and laughed.

Chuck managed to walk to the greasy spoon that was apparently his current place of employment, as well as his only hope of getting fed, since his wallet and pockets were completely void of anything resembling money. Fortunately, it was not that far from where he was staying. Oddly, he didn't remember the diner being here before. The place was a couple steps lower than the sidewalk, with booths set against windows that appeared waist-high inside, but just above the sidewalk on the outside, so passersby saw both the patrons and their meals. A counter with the usual stools ran the length of the place. It was empty except for a large man behind the counter and now Chuck, as he entered.

"Well, you've managed to break free of your visions long enough to come to work. Bully for you," came the familiar voice of Lee Sherman. Then Lee looked at him closer and shook his head. "Those visions are worse than drugs, I swear. You look absolutely awful. I don't think you could start a shift, much less finish one. Here, I'll make you up some breakfast. You can even eat it out front, and make it seem like this place gets customers now and then."

Eating as calmly and slowly as he could, in order to help the feeling of fullness, Chuck did a vision of Lee, and found in this "here and now," Lee knew about people doing visions, but was generally against Chuck doing them. Neither Lee nor Chuck had worked for the M&A firm in this line, and Lee tolerated Chuck's irregular working habits since the diner barely attracted enough business to pay the bills. Lee had a night job to support himself, seeing this diner barely broke even. For whatever reason, Lee made sure Chuck had something to eat and a place to stay.

Lee leaned against the counter with a cup of coffee in front of him. "I was hoping beyond hope you'd have remembered we were going to try having this place open for breakfast. Frankly, you didn't miss much this morning. Do you think you could at least try to make it in tomorrow?"

"That's not a problem. I'll be here."

"Did you at least have a vision of a better life?"

"One vision of a life was better than what I'm seeing here. There was a second vision of life that was very nice, actually. Then there were a couple of visions of life that were absolutely astonishing."

"Were you considerate enough to take me along?"

"You bet. You were prospering mightily until I woke in this time line a little while ago. For that matter, you weren't doing too badly in the first vision."

"Well, having you eat out front might have been a decent idea. A lady just slowed down to check us out."

Just then Chuck became aware of a shadow on his table, and looked up to see Melissa looking at the diner, a puzzled look on her face. At the moment he looked at her, she glanced down at him, and her look of puzzlement became one of recognition and fright. A second later, she was walking purposefully down the sidewalk. He just stared as she disappeared from sight a moment later.

"Well, then. It seems you're attracting girls from your visions, I'd recommend you clean yourself up before tomorrow," Lee advised. "Take a bath, and get your clothes washed. By the way, it's gratifying to know you consider the Mergers & Acquisitions world at least a little bit better than this."

Chuck just gaped at Lee, not knowing whether to be more astonished at the undeniable fact of Melissa walking by, or at Lee knowing about the previous time lines. After a minute, he finished off his plate of food, and went in the back to start doing the clean-up. By the time the lunch rush came, he had pretty well figured out how to run the equipment.

✲ ✲ ✲

Chuck was making a real effort to look better, and had his meal in the same booth after the breakfast rush was over. Every day, about the same time, Melissa would walk by, slow down, and look at Chuck, as though he might be someone she knew. Chuck usually just kept eating, but then the third morning, she stopped. Chuck turned his head, smiled, and nodded. Doing a vision, Chuck knew this Melissa was very much like the first Melissa, although he was quite certain there had to be differences.

She seemed to decide on a course of action, and came into the diner. She was fairly well-dressed, Chuck thought, though at the lower end of what might be considered fashionable. His vision established she was not married, and they had never met in this time line.

She got a cup of coffee, and stirred in an amount of cream Chuck knew would take her coffee to a precise shade of caramel brown, and studied Lee's face.

"You look familiar," she informed him.

"Okay."

"No, really, I've seen you before. I know I have. Except there's no way. How long have you been here?"

Lee shrugged his shoulders massively. "I've had this place something over six months."

"What was it before you got it?"

"This other guy had it for, I don't know, ten or eleven years. At least, that's what he said. Finally, he got sick and couldn't do it anymore, so I got what I thought was a good deal on it. His sickness was most likely lack of bucks, in turn caused by no business."

"Well, that certainly matches the look of the place. There's only one problem. None of this was here last week. I walk that sidewalk between my apartment and my office twice a day, and until this week, the entire block was a blank wall, the back of a warehouse."

"I'm sure you're right, but I know I've been trying to make a go of this place during the day, along with working a second job a night. It's kind of hard to invent ten years of history over a weekend, don't you think? Anyway, most of the blocks in this area look the same. Though if nobody could see the place like you say, it could certainly account for our lack of business. Don't you think so, Chuck?"

It was fortunate that she had the cup of coffee firmly on the counter at that point, since it was extremely likely she'd have dropped it at the mention of his name. She got a firm grasp on the coffee and walked over to his booth. After setting the coffee down, she leaned on the table, supporting herself on clinched fists, staring into his face.

"I don't know you, but I know you extremely well. When you smiled at me, it set off alarms in my very soul. I'd swear on a stack of Bibles that I've never met you, but I know your name like I know my own. Why is that, Chuck?"

"There's an explanation for it, but I don't think you could accept it right this minute. Consider for the moment that where we are now is out of context to where you know me."

"So tell me. In what context would I know you?"

"Try the context of a small cabin set in tall pines, in the coastal range of Oregon."

She became pale and whispered, "I've never been to Oregon, but I see you there next to a cabin, in front of a small motor home, and we're about three blocks from a general store. I see something else. I see myself remembering I saved your life."

Her eyes widened and her face turned crimson as she thought about it. "Ohmigod! I saved your life like that?"

She slid into the booth, facing him and studying him intensely. "Are you psychic?" she asked.

"No, but I do visions."

"Have we met?"

"I don't believe so, not in this time line."

She took a deep breath. "What was my name in this other time line?"

"You were Melissa Ann Duncan there. That's your name here, as well."

"Is there more than one time line besides this one?"

"There are several, of which I'm personally aware. I'd guess it's likely there are lots more I don't know about."

"Have we met in many other ... um, time lines?"

Chuck slowly chewed on a piece of toast. "If we had, would it matter?"

She took a sip of the coffee, trying to relax. This line of conversation was becoming very uncomfortable. "I guess not," she shrugged.

"It sure seemed to matter when you were thinking of the cabin in Oregon. That was one other time line. Then, there were a couple of time lines where we were in New Orleans with JLG&S"

Melissa got a faraway look. "I remember New Orleans. There were hot and cold running servants. You had a Personal Assistant ... Margot was her name. That was funny. She insisted on always marching in formation with you when we went anywhere."

Chuck looked back at Lee. "This doesn't make any sense. How can Melissa remember previous time lines? I thought it was only the people involved in a change who would be able to recall how it was before the change. For that matter, how is it that you know about things before the change?"

"You talked about this with Jean and Robert. I think the term used was 'pivotal person.' In any case, where there is a strong emotional bond with the pivotal person, the ability to recall previous time lines can occur. As for my ability to recall, I think it's that I am a First Family member. Anyone who is First Family is automatically a 'pivotal person,' as you call it. Being First Family is more a matter of realization than of blood ancestry, by the way."

"How do you know about my communications with Jean and Robert?"

"When you showed up, even before you got something to eat, you did visions on me. I did visions on you. It's as simple as that."

"You don't approve of me doing visions."

"That's the story for this time line. Still, there's what we both know."

Melissa had been sitting there, still fully focused, but finally broke in. "I remember doing visions on you, Chuck. In fact, you told me to monitor you. Then, there was that day we were in court, and I tried to talk Madeleine into getting Armand out of his vision. Not long after that, I remember what seemed to be a kind of dream state where I had three children. Even more suddenly, it seemed like that dream state shattered into a million pieces, and here I was. I figured out where I was working, and went there, only to get a pink slip."

"Can you do visions on me, Melissa?"

"For the past several minutes, I have. There's a question neither of you gentlemen have brought up as yet: Does JLG&S exist in this time line?"

"If it does exist here, it's evidently not answering to me, so that wouldn't appear to be an issue. For that matter, I have no idea what situation Robert is in, although, as a pivotal person, he's got to be out there."

"Don't try to change the subject. JLG&S is very much an issue. As far as you were concerned, it was only a matter of a few days from when Jean promised to give you a business until you became one of the richest people on the planet. Meanwhile, for the people involved in the business, and there were a bunch, it was a century and a half. As for Robert, I only know about him through doing visions on you, but his fate and that of JLG&S are inseparable."

"You're right, of course. The first iteration of JLG&S was okay for us in the present, but resulted in a dystopia. When we attempted to tweak it, we succeeded in creating a better situation both for the family and for humanity in general, but it pushed too far, evidently, since we got pushed back to this."

Melissa considered the situation, and wasn't coming up with a solution, so she changed the subject. "Lee, what's your situation with Jodi in this time line?"

"In this time line, she left me several years ago. Why?"

"I was just thinking that whatever we did, it would be nice if we did it together. That's all. By the way, how did both of you end up in Denver?"

Both men chorused, "Denver?" Lee laughed. "No wonder you never saw the diner on your way to work. This is Chicago."

Chuck was working on a thought. "Melissa, do you have your pink slip with you?"

"Um, yes, I think I do." She pulled it out of her purse and handed it to him.

"You say you walk to work."

"Yes."

"What did you wear to work when they gave you this?"

Melissa did a quick survey of herself. "Oh my. This is what I was wearing. That was three, no four days ago. That can't be."

Chuck looked at Lee for support. Lee nodded, and took a deep breath. "My guess is that you haven't seen much by way of support or security in your life."

Melissa's face hardened, and she nodded.

"So when your employer sent you packing, you felt you were out of alternatives. Still, in the back of your mind was the information there was a person who cared about you, namely Chuck. So you changed your own time line to ensure finding him. What you didn't know was where that would take you. You probably haven't been anywhere at all between the times you walked by here. In fact, the three days that passed for us may have been almost nothing for you."

Chuck looked at Lee. Then he looked at Melissa for a while. Finally he looked back at Lee. "What I'm hearing is that we can design our own time line. We have to really want it, or maybe really need it. Then the universe sort of rearranges itself so that we are both where we need to be, and when we need to be, in order to obtain it. That sounds like some motivation books I've read."

Lee nodded. "That's about it. The motivation authors would be astonished to know how much further that idea could be taken. Like the man said, though, be careful what you ask for. For instance, you never thought of yourself as anything but a dishwasher in a diner, so here you are."

Chuck extended his arms across the table, and Melissa took his hands. "Where do we really want and need to be?" he whispered.

"Like you said that time in New Orleans, a cabin in the Oregon woods sounds exactly right to me."

They shared the vision of the pine-scented breeze, and presently both Lee and the diner simply ceased to exist. Instead, they were sitting across from each other at a picnic table beside the cabin in Blodgett.

Lee watched the couple as they disappeared, and smiled. "Well, if you two had bothered to ask what I really want, and where I really need to be, I'd have told you the answer to both questions must be Jodi. So, Lee closed the diner. As he walked away down the sidewalk, the front of the diner began to lose definition. By the time he had turned the corner, only a vague shimmer remained on a blank brick wall. A torn piece of paper slowly slid down the vacated sidewalk. It was a fragment of a receiving report belonging to the JLG&S Corporation.

16: Dedications, Alibis

This book is dedicated to my Mom, Millicent Jacqueline LaGrange Schindler, the last living person in our family line to be born a LaGrange. It is also dedicated to my wife, Vesta, who encouraged me to write a historical novel about LaGrange the Pirate, and put up with my mumbling. It is based on family stories, and is my fictional reconstruction of a possible way the family stories might fit into historical reality.

First, I must apologize to the real people in the story. I'm sure they are neither portrayed as they really are, nor as they would want to be portrayed. The main characters are completely fictional. Kenneth Otto LaGrange, my uncle, really existed, but never married. His sister, Millicent is real, as was her husband Irvin. Melissa, and her family line is wholly fictitious, back to Elizabeth Fuller, who was a real person, but died young, and had no children. Sarah Ann Fuller was real, and is a direct ancestor of our line.

LaGrange Family Members, both real and imagined:

Charles Louis "Chuck": Fictitious

Jack Edward (Chuck's father): Fictitious

Kenneth Otto: Real, however he was never married and never had children. He was a member of Merrill's Marauders in World War II, and had a PhD from UCLA.

"Aunt" Millicent: Real, married to Irvin, and my parents. In the story, Irvin is still alive. Sadly, Dad died in 2007.

Otto S.: Real. He told me (and others) that he spent the last of the gold. He also claimed our LaGrange line was descended from a brother of Joseph Louis LaGrange, the mathematician.

Andrew Tyra: Real, with a great deal of fictitious embroidery. His son, Otto, was born in 1898. He married Otto's mother, Tryphosa Belle James in 1900. He died after 1920, but before 1925.

Charles L. F.: married Minerva Lillard, and had two children. Minerva subsequently sued for divorce on grounds of abandonment. He claimed to have been a privateer and pirate, as related in the family story. Place and date of birth is not known, but possibly Louisiana or France. Place and date of death are not known.

All ancestors of Charles L.F., including members of the LaGrange family listed (Jean, Philippe, Gaston, Jean Baptiste) are entirely fictitious. I have found some biographies of Joseph Louis LaGrange which state he was one of two siblings who lived beyond infancy, out of eleven children. I have yet to locate any information on the sibling. There are, actually, other biographies stating Joseph Louis was the only one of his generation to attain adulthood. The LaGrange, or Lagrangia family did date back several generations to a French cavalry officer, who came to Turin to instruct the king on modern cavalry warfare, and ended up staying. The history of the family is entirely unknown, and is inserted mainly to make sense of the family story including galleons and men-of-war.

Lee Grant Sherman, his wife, and family lineage are all fictitious. Jean Lafitte himself is, of course, quite real.

The Laubscher family (from the Tucson chapter): Oliver was in fact Otto's lawyer. The individual in the story is fictitious.

The Fuller family is real. They came to Oregon in 1845 in a wagon train with the King family with whom they intermarried. Both of the Kings and Fullers are direct family lines. The Fuller-James-LaGrange links really did happen.

The Lillards and Mulkeys are real. There are still a large number of Mulkeys in the area. The Mulkeys, along with the Lillards, were among the first settlers in Harlan, Oregon. They had lived in Missouri for several years, having come from Kentucky and Tennessee. The details surrounding how Charles married Minerva are wholly fictitious, as are the characterizations of the families.

The Bullion Bend robbery did occur, and Captain Ingram, as he styled himself, was one of the leaders of the gang. Newspapers reported about $3,000 in gold on board the two stages, while other reports would indicate considerably more was actually there. Whatever the actual amount, it doesn't appear that much of it was ever recovered. The LaGrange involvement is, of course, wholly fictitious.

The Steamship Golden Gate did go down when and as described, on an isolated beach north of Manzanillo, Mexico. Nowhere near the amount of treasure on board was ever accounted for, and was in fact the subject of law suits between the insurance company and the people contracted to do the salvage. Gold coins still show up on Playa del Oro (Gold Beach) periodically.

While Charles L.F. being in New Orleans is fictitious, the hurricane that wiped out the hotel on Last Island was very real, and did unfortunately kill most of the people there. Attitudes of the French inhabitants of New Orleans given in the story are fictitious. There were a great many French who escaped to New Orleans from the turmoil on Saint-Domingue, later Haiti. Saint Malo, France, was a major privateer base. The connections in the story with these places are wholly fictitious.